OTHERWORLDLY ONBOARDING

JANELLE SEEGMILLER

This book is a work of fiction. Names, characters, incidents, and places are the products of the author's imagination or are used fictitiously. Any resemblance to actual people or events is coincidental.

OTHERWORLDLY ONBOARDING

ISBN 979-8-9914035-0-4 (paperback)
ISBN 979-8-9914035-1-1 (ebook)

First Edition: 2024

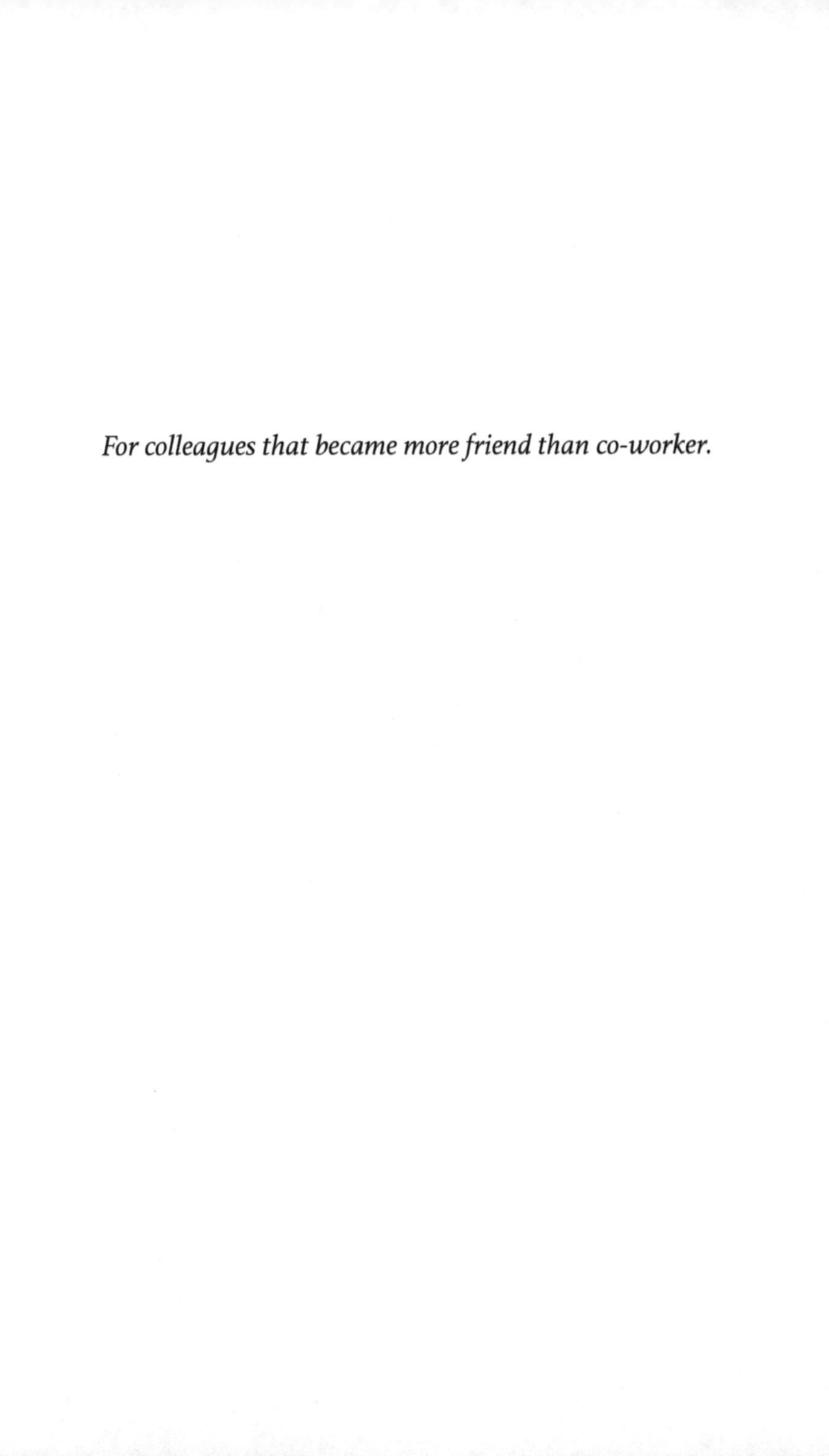

For colleagues that became more friend than co-worker.

1

———————

I had an anxious stomach all morning thinking about how the call would go. The rumor mill around the office had been talking for the past several weeks about how the numbers were down and the partners had been in a lot of closed-door meetings. The general vibe at the legal office of Hurst and Gramble was off. I'd been working there as an executive administrator for several members of the executive team for just over two years, and it had never felt like this before. I joined the video conference call with a lump already sitting squarely in my stomach.

The call was filling up with familiar faces and names on black boxes, but I kept glancing at my own box on the screen. My full name, *Linda Moss*, was in the bottom corner. Though many at the company went by their first name, like some kind of pop star, another Linda started working here before me and we wouldn't want anyone to confuse us even though we looked nothing alike and had very different jobs.

I tried to focus on other people's faces. It didn't work. I kept watching my own face. I don't think I'm an overly vain person, but it's just too easy to analyze myself and wonder what other people saw when they looked at me. My dark brown hair was flat as usual—no amount of scrunching would bring it back to life. I needed to wash my hair, something I tended to dread. Not for the washing, but for the blow drying I'd need to do so that my hair wasn't unmanageable from being slept on wet.

I scrunched my nose and watched as the lines webbed out from my eyes. Those lines reminded me of my mom. She always said that each line on her face corresponded with a happy memory. I'm not sure mine did. Along with the similar lines on my face, I had her eyes, light brown with flecks of gold. My angular face and tall, slender build likely came from my dad. Having never met him, it was hard to say for sure.

The HR rep and one of the partners had finally joined the call. I bet they waited on the other side until everyone else had joined. Only half of the folks had their cameras on, and no one looked happy to be here. We all knew what was coming. It had been playing out in my dreams on loop for the last week.

"As some of you may have heard, this last year was challenging for the firm," the partner started off. "Our projections for the year were higher than what we were able to achieve. We had hired staff to match the growth of those projections."

Everyone who was still on the screen clearly knew what was coming next. I'm sure the faces behind the blank screens had the same expressions. I started to pay more attention to who was on the call and who wasn't, not sure which side it was better to be on. If you got let go, the severance wouldn't last long. Staying would mean more work for the same pay, but at least there would be pay.

The partner was wrapping up sharing some numbers. Numbers that they had committed to and that we had not been able to achieve. More cameras had turned off, filling the screen with more black boxes or smiling avatars replacing the bleak faces. I watched the stricken faces blink out. My best work friend had tears starting to fall before her box on the screen changed to an image of her holding her dog and smiling. My camera stayed on, my face blank.

"We unfortunately need to reduce our team size. If you are on this call, you are in the group that we need to part ways with," he concluded and then immediately muted his mic.

The HR rep took over the call. "Each of you will receive an email to the personal address you have on file with the HR team." Their tone was noticeably different from the partner's, who wasn't cold but clearly resigned to the already-processed changes coming. He just sounded ready to move forward. The HR guy sounded more like a hostage reading from a script. "The email will include information about your severance package. That will be based on the tenure you had with the firm." He slightly stumbled over his words and looked away from the camera so we just saw the side of his face. "There is also a link in the email to schedule a time with someone on the HR team if you have questions. Please don't hesitate to set up a call."

There was more information about access to email and work tools. They had all been shut off at the start of the meeting. Any company equipment we had would be returned. Instructions to do that would be in the email. I'm sure there was other important information, but my brain couldn't process it and there would be an email with the information. He kept repeating that. So I let the details he was sharing drift in and out of my head.

I snapped back to the call when I saw the individual boxes disappearing quickly. *And that's the end of that,* I thought as I clicked the *Leave Meeting* button for the last time.

Opening up my inbox, I saw that the promised email was already waiting for me. A brief read let me know that I would be getting eight weeks of severance, four weeks for each year. Fairly generous compared to what I'd heard from other layoffs. The news and social media posts had been full of them in the past several months.

Eight weeks of pay and some savings that I had would give me some time to figure things out. Even though I had felt prepared for this—all the signs were there—the weight of it still settled heavily on my shoulders. There wasn't anything I could do right this moment, so I let myself dissociate and daydream about what the future could hold. Nothing could prepare me for what that future turned out to be.

· · ·

I NEVER THOUGHT I would miss video calls and meetings. Six months into not working, I would give anything to see another human on a small screen and talk about something semi-intellectual or even a mundane office problem to solve. I'd be happy to find, highlight, and email someone the specific paragraph in the travel policy about how you can book business class for a flight over six hours. I'd be excited to track down four back-channel references for a candidate and then not even complain when the hiring manager didn't call any of them. I'd be overjoyed to make a phone call to a hotel that an executive was staying at and ask for them to remove any plastic cups from the room before his arrival. True story. I never did figure out why he had such an aversion to plastic cups or what they ever did to him.

My days were now filled with an hour or two of forcing myself to work on the job hunt and then hours of trashy TV and jigsaw puzzles. I had tried to read both work books for education and fantasy novels for fun. Neither type would hold my interest. That was not a good sign for my mental health as we headed into Seattle's gray season.

It was also hard to come to terms with how much I had let all my friendships go. After my mom died two years ago, it had gotten harder to feel up to going out with friends. Everyone was young and happy. They wanted to talk about new relationships and jobs, not how it felt to be an orphan in your mid-twenties. They slowly drifted away. I didn't really blame them. I had been the one to decline offer after offer to go out. I still had work friends and went to happy hours every now and then. But with no work, there were no work friends to Band-Aid over the missing friendships.

I had tried to go for walks to get out and get some sunshine during the brief Seattle summer. Half the city was out walking or hiking. I at least walked to the grocery store, but that was all the activation energy I could work up. I had managed to keep myself and Ilka—my mom's cat that was now my responsibility—fed. That felt like enough for now.

The thought of uploading my résumé again and then needing to input that same information into a form made me want to run away to an off-grid cabin that didn't have internet. I could raise chickens and have a roadside stand. I joked with myself that the research on that would start in earnest if I got another rejection.

I applied to dozens of jobs and had several screening interviews. But that had only resulted in three full-loop interviews, and each had decided to go in another direc-tion. Posts on social media and groups I had signed up to follow reassured me that this wasn't just my experience. The job market was bleak, with more people being laid off every week.

The spreadsheet I had started at the beginning of my job search confirmed that. My mood was as bleak as the market. Emails had slowed down, and it felt like more of my applications were just being ghosted. I reminded myself that I was determined to stay dutiful in the search.

If nothing came through soon, I'd need to start looking for anything, not just executive admin roles. Anything to put off needing to sell the house. Other than Ilka, it was all

I had left from my mom. I also really needed to have something to get me out of the house.

Sitting at the computer that morning, I wasn't expecting to hear back from anyone, so I could easily check off clearing my inbox from my to-do list. Among the typical spam emails, there was only one that hinted at a real possibility of a job: *Executive Administrator at the OPT Agency*. The title sounded like it had real potential, not just spam. I read the email quickly to decide if it needed my full attention or if I could call it good for the day and go finish the reality TV dating show I was watching. It was near the end and I was pretty sure that at least one of the couples was heading toward a messy breakup.

The email was from the CEO of the company, Helen Pendleton. They were looking for an EA to support them and they wanted to do a phone screen with me. The company was a small legal and private investigation agency. My previous EA role was with a legal firm, but the private investigation side would be new for me. The tasks in the job description attached seemed in line with what I had been doing in previous roles: handle schedules, organize documents, book and manage travel, and take on other assignments as needed.

Unlike many job descriptions, this one included the compensation. It was high. Had I received this email in the first month of my job hunt, I probably would have deleted it as a scam. There was no way that they would be paying an EA that much. It was well over what I had been making previously and also higher than what my internet searches of expected compensation revealed. But it was month six, I currently had no other leads, I didn't have to say yes, and I wasn't sure what they thought they'd get out of scamming the unemployed.

Checking my job-tracking spreadsheet, I couldn't find this company or any indication that I'd applied for something like this. I wasn't likely to have missed recording something I'd applied for. However, I had asked several former colleagues to let me know if they saw anything available that may be a fit for me or give a good word to a hiring manager. Maybe that's where this had come from—although no one had given me a heads up.

I typed the agency's name into the search bar. The results were full of different uses of that acronym. Even going to the second and third page of results, I couldn't find anything that seemed to match this agency. They weren't on LinkedIn or Glassdoor. The email hadn't included a website address, only a phone number. I tried the ending of the email address it had been sent from to see if I could get to a website, but I just got a "Page not found." My brain said this was feeling more like a scam, but my gut felt like it was something I should pursue.

My mom had always said that I should trust my instincts. It could have been the cabin fever that had clearly set in and the dwindling bank account, but something inside pushed me to respond. While I had been pondering what to do, Ilka had wandered into the office. That in itself was strange; she mostly avoided me until it was time to eat. Her big eyes stared at me and she let out a meow that I decided to take as a nudge to go for it. Also, I figured a phone call couldn't hurt.

· · ·

LOOKING BACK, the call was painful and painfully short. I let it ring three times before I picked up so that I didn't seem too eager or as if I'd been staring at the phone waiting for it to ring for the ten minutes leading up to the call time.

"Hello, this is Linda," I said as I picked up, trying to sound warm and professional at the same time. I was normally good on phone calls. Being an executive admin, I often had to make calls and I'd gotten over that fear years ago. But today felt different. Today I felt a bit desperate.

"Hi, Linda. This is Helen Pendleton with the OPT Agency," a calm and firm woman's voice on the other end of the line responded. She did not sound desperate.

"Hi, Helen, I'm excited to talk with you today," I said, trying to match her tone and pace a bit better but still coming off a bit fast. I held the phone away from my face as I took some steadying breaths, hoping that she couldn't hear that through the phone.

"As am I," Helen responded. "For the call today, I'd just have a few questions. We'll make sure we have time for any questions you have, and then we'll decide if we'd like to continue with an in-person interview."

"That sounds great." I clicked my pen and readied myself to take notes.

"First, tell me a little bit about your last job."

This was an easy question and one that I'd perfected over the seven phone screens that I'd had in the past six months. "I was an executive admin for two teams: the HR team and the Finance team," I started off, trying to keep a steady, even pace. "I supported those two executives with their schedules, travel, and special projects as needed. I also supported the team members of those orgs as needed with travel and project support."

"That's great," Helen offered after I paused for a second. "Tell me more about the special projects you did."

"I organized three team off-sites, including location, food, agenda, and travel for the teams. I worked with a small team in HR to complete a research project on leveling and compensation planning company wide. And I organized the meetings for and summarized outputs from performance reviews for both years."

The practiced words were starting to roll more easily off my tongue, and my heart had finally slowed down to a normal rate—although I could still feel the sweat gathering in my armpits and under my bra.

"Thank you. That all sounds great. Do you have any questions for me?" Helen asked.

"Oh, um, yes," I said quickly. I was shocked that she hadn't asked me any more questions or wanted more details. That was usually a sign that they weren't interested. I raced through my thoughts to see what insightful questions I could ask to get things back on track. I had read enough blogs and articles on this that I should have had something. "What would a successful person in this role look like?" I finally said after a too-long pause.

"That's a good question," she said, but I couldn't tell if she was being sincere or just playing the role of a good interviewer. "They would be a quick learner with an open mind. They would be willing to pick up reasonable tasks that may be outside of the formal job description. They work well with a team."

Nothing about that answer felt strange. It was the typical corporate language used by managers everywhere. Code words for you are going to get thrown into the middle of things, we don't have enough staff to cover all the roles that we have, and the team may be full of jerks but you'll need to get along with them anyways.

"I know that sounds vague and it's probably what you've heard from any job you've applied for," she said, and I worried for a minute that I had said those thoughts out loud or maybe she was just reading my mind. "We are a small team and pretty close. Most of us have been working together for a long time. There are a lot of opportunities to get involved with the cases and projects we tackle as a team. You'll probably find it a lot different than work environments at bigger corporate offices."

It's like she said the magic words. Both of the jobs I'd had since graduating were in bigger companies. I was one of thousands. I had made friends with the people I worked closest with, but it always felt a bit impersonal. The smaller team size was interesting, and it would be fun to try that out to see if it would be a better fit for me. If it didn't work out, I could always keep applying to bigger companies and go back to being more of a number than a name.

"That sounds good," I replied as calmly as I could. "I'd be interested in learning more."

"That's great," she replied with genuine enthusiasm. "I'd

love to have you come in for an in-person interview if you are interested. Would this Friday at three work for you?"

"Let me check my schedule." I fibbed a little bit. I knew I had absolutely nothing on my schedule but didn't want this prospective employer to know that. I counted to five in my head. "Yes. I can do that." My heart rate had ticked up again. I tried to not get too excited. I'd had in-person interviews before that hadn't worked out. But I told myself it was always a good sign that they wanted to keep talking. Getting past this first step, any hesitation I had in wanting this job was gone, and my self-esteem could really use the booster shot of getting an actual job offer.

"Great. I'll email you the details. I look forward to meeting you in person," she said. I could hear the smile behind her voice. I smiled on my end in return and wondered what I should wear to the interview.

2

"The first floor is for client meetings. That's the waiting room with the reception desk." Helen, the smartly dressed CEO of the OPT Agency, led me through the office spaces that filled an old house in an even older neighborhood. She'd insisted that we do a quick tour of the office before starting the in-person interview.

I followed behind her swishing, sleek, dark ponytail as she walked ahead. I hustled to keep up, adjusting my black work bag repeatedly on my shoulder like a nervous tick. We passed by three progressively smaller rooms that looked like fancy and cozy conference rooms, making our way toward the back of the house—mansion would be a more appropriate term to use, but that sounded too pretentious to use for a space that was so comfortable and inviting. At the back of the house was a beautiful and large kitchen with an eating area.

"We use this space for clients as well. Some of them

feel more comfortable sitting at a kitchen table and having a chat over tea. And of course, meals are served here during working hours," she continued, as if everyone worked in a mansion with a magical kitchen that smelled like your grandma's house and looked like it could be in a magazine. To the side of the kitchen was a small hallway. "The restroom for the clients is down that hallway, as well as a bedroom suite that clients can use if needed."

Out the back door, I could see a lovely garden. It was beautiful in the gray light of this very typical fall Seattle afternoon. Several raised garden beds formed around a series of gravel paths. A table with chairs for eating in the sun and a couple of benches were strategically placed to enjoy what would grow there. There were some green plants, but nothing currently in bloom. I couldn't imagine what it would be like in the summer when it was full of color.

Beyond the patio and garden beds was a small building. Probably a guesthouse—it was too big to be a shed. I didn't have time to figure it out. We were already heading back toward the front of the house. We then made our way up a very grand-looking staircase.

"Upstairs we have the offices for the staff. Clients don't usually come to the second floor." She continued with the tour as we climbed the stairs.

Walking up the stairs was like changing buildings. Ultramodern and sleek, but still comfortable, not sterile like modern decor can become. A lighting designer had definitely been here. It felt like soft afternoon sunlight was filling the space, although looking at the large picture window at the front of the house showed it was still a gray day beyond these walls.

Straight off the stairs we walked into one large room with a conference table surrounded with chairs. Whiteboards and stylish sideboards lined the walls that led to the front of the house in between six closed doors. Off the stairs and through the conference room were a set of double doors flung open. Beyond was a good-sized room with a waiting area and a desk.

"This would be your desk." She pointed out as we made our way through to that room. Past that desk was another set of double doors that we walked through next, leading into what could only be her office.

This office was a perfect, cozy blend of antique-looking furniture and modern amenities. I spotted a pair of small, stocked refrigerators set into a sideboard. A standing desk with a monitor sat to the right side of the larger, L-shaped, antique desk. And I'm pretty sure there was a walking pad tucked under the standing desk.

One wall to the side of the desk was filled with books. There were leather-bound law books that could be found in every law office. However, filling up even more space was a rainbow of book spines. I wasn't close enough to make out specific titles, but I was itching to explore what was on that shelf. I'm a firm believer that the books on someone's shelf can tell you a lot about that person.

Everything in this office seemed to play together and felt like a collection amassed over time. Not like it came from an office furniture display floor like so many executive offices I've been in. Or an office that was clearly decorated by a well-meaning spouse or assistant but didn't fit the personality of the person using it daily. The office was a collection of items that reflected the tenant of this room, and I was intrigued.

She walked behind the old and stately desk and motioned to a pair of wingback chairs in front of it. I sank quickly into the one on the right. Without missing a beat, she sat down in her chair and continued, "The third floor has four suites. Three for staff if they need them, and my suite. I often stay overnight. However, Linda, please don't think that means you need to stay overnight here as well. You are welcome to use the suites if needed, but overnights are not a job requirement.

"There is also a basement. We mostly have storage and files down there. No need for us to tour that space." She seemed quick to dismiss the basement. Basements can be dull, I supposed, and I was fine not exploring a dark, dingy basement.

"We just finished up a big case, so most of the staff are on a well-deserved long weekend. As a rule, we also don't have client meetings on Fridays. So things are quiet around here, which gives us a great chance to talk," Helen said and then shifted topics. "So, Linda, let's talk a bit more about the responsibilities of the role, and then I'll answer any questions you have."

I nodded my agreement to her suggestion, not wanting to speak just yet because I was trying to hide the fact that I was still recovering my breath from the quick tour through the office and march up the stairs.

"As we talked about on the phone, this role is for my

executive administrator. Your primary responsibility will be to manage my schedule, help coordinate logistics for the staff, complete research projects as needed, and ensure that the home office runs smoothly," Helen said gracefully. As the woman who could become my new boss, I tried to think of her as Helen and not Ms. Pendleton as she had very firmly requested.

I pulled a notepad from my bag and jotted down what she had shared. This was already familiar to me as it was like the other two EA roles I'd had. Not many surprises in a role as an EA, at least in the types of tasks. The surprises came later as you learned about the people you'd be supporting and working for. There were always surprises. A good EA learned how to roll with them. And I was a good EA.

She nodded approvingly at my note-taking and kept going. "The home team, as staff often refers to them, comprises my EA; Annie, our receptionist, whom you already met when you came in this morning; and Mrs. Clark, whom you'll meet later. Annie keeps this office stocked and organized. She also greets clients and ensures that they are comfortable, and helps with other tasks as needed.

"Mrs. Clark is the housekeeper and cook for the office," Helen continued. "Although she does a lot more, that is the easiest way to describe her role on the team. She lives full time on the property in the guesthouse."

That confirmed it was a guesthouse I'd seen at the end of the garden. Also, there seemed to be a lot of extra, unspoken tasks done by employees here. I guessed it was a small team, many hats and all that, as a former boss of mine used to say. For him that had meant doing more with no extra pay so we didn't have to hire more staff. The compensation for this job was enough that I wouldn't shy away from doing extra work. Also, I tend to get bored easily, so having a lot of things to jump between keeps me going.

"If you join the team, you'll work closely with both Annie and Mrs. Clark. You'll be taking over some tasks from them," she continued. "There would be ramp-up time, of course. Most importantly, if I am on the road with the team, you would be responsible for the home office."

That sounded more ominous than it had in the written job description, and she hadn't mentioned it when we spoke over the phone, but I guessed she just liked to have a proper chain of command. I could work with that.

"In addition to me, Annie, and Mrs. Clark, we have four other full-time employees," she said, and I readied to write down names and roles, but she didn't expand on the other employees. "I should also let you know that we start all of our employees off with a thirty-day probation period."

I tried not to react to that and instead wrote it down in the notebook with a question mark next to it. I think Helen sensed my unease anyway.

She softened her tone. "It's nothing to stress about, it just gives us both time to make sure this is a fit for everyone."

"That seems reasonable," I managed to say and even smiled. It would be a stressful month knowing that I had to pass a probation period, despite what she said, but I could make it through a month.

She nodded at my response and continued, "We typically have only a few clients at a time with active cases, although we have many clients on retainer and try to see to their projects promptly regardless of how many active cases we have."

I added that to my notes.

"As I mentioned, we serve clients across North America, and our clients' projects often require travel. Travel isn't a part of your primary job requirements, although you'll help with travel arrangements for me and for members of the team as needed."

That was fine with me. I didn't mind booking travel for other people, but I was really a homebody and didn't do too great on planes.

The interview felt like it was wrapping up and things were sounding good so far. Small team. Manageable client load. Job responsibilities that I felt confident I could do. And clients with money if the office and the salary offered to me was any indication.

"We talked about the agency and the role expectations over the phone. Do you have any additional questions about either? Or are there any areas that you'd like to discuss more?" Helen asked me politely.

I cleared my throat as I hadn't said more than a polite *hmm* or *okay* in the last twenty minutes. "The role and responsibilities seem clear. From what I understand, the agency handles legal cases, mediation, and private investigations for your clients. I hope this doesn't offend you, but it sounds a bit like you and your team are fixers."

I held my breath as soon as the words came out. Although that's what I'd been thinking this whole time, I was never planning on saying it out loud. My mind had connected what she was saying to the common fixer trope in TV shows and books. It seemed like a crude way to put things in front of this commanding, elegant, and—let's be honest—intimidating woman. What was probably only thirty seconds felt like an hour.

Helen's straight face broke into a sly grin. "That is exactly what we are, Linda. How do you feel about that?"

"Um, I like helping people." Elegant answer, right?

"Any other questions?" she prompted gently.

"I wasn't able to find a website for the company," I stated more than asked, but I was hoping she'd be able to explain.

"Correct," she replied without any hesitation. "We only take on select clients, and they find us through word of mouth. We do not advertise our agency."

I did not realize that there were companies in existence today that weren't obsessed with their digital presence, SEO, and marketing campaigns, always pushing for the lines on the revenue graph to go up and to the right no matter how much they were already making. It was a bit refreshing to hear that that was not a concern here. And again, this agency didn't seem like they were hurting for money.

She inclined her head and waited for me to ask another question. The compensation that was listed in the email seemed like a typo, and I needed to know if that was the case. I had no idea how to ask questions about money. Despite the articles and videos that were supposed to teach me how to negotiate for salary, I still felt awkward even talking about it.

Taking a deep breath, I went for it. "I noticed that the compensation was listed in the job description," I started off, trying not to talk too fast and breathe like a normal human person. "Is that the amount I should expect if you offer me this job?"

She furrowed her brow a bit. "Let me check."

My heart sank a little as she turned toward her laptop and clicked some buttons. It had to be a typo, but as long as the number was within spitting distance of what I was getting from my previous job, I'd take it.

"Oh, yes. That is correct," she said and turned back to me.

"Okay," I responded, trying to remain calm and not give away that I would have taken less. "That would work for me."

"Great. Any other questions?"

"No questions that haven't been answered already," I said, trying to sound confident.

Helen leaned back in her chair. Her dark eyes slightly narrowed, and she seemed to see directly into my soul. I tried not to stare back and tried harder not to be intimidated. I sang "Happy Birthday" in my head to keep myself calm and focused on the noises I could hear. There was a hum of warm air coming in from the vents, the crows outside talking to each other like normal, and Helen's foot softly tapping against the desk.

The tapping paused for a moment and then one loud tap drummed against the side of the desk. This was followed by a shuffle behind me and a soft knock at the door. Someone had been summoned.

"I've invited Steve to join us for the next part of the interview," Helen said, inclining her head to the door where a man now stood.

I know it's cliché, but there is no other way to describe him. A tall, dark, and handsome man walked through the double doors and sat down in the empty chair to the left of me. He was older, maybe late forties, and gave off a serious vibe with his arms folded solidly in front of him.

"Linda, we would love to have you join our team," Helen said, getting my attention back to her. Her smile matched the words, but her tone did not. There was a hint of hesitation even though her statement was straightforward. I didn't have time to get excited about the offer before she continued, "However, there is one part of the job that we haven't shared with you yet."

She paused as if to let the words sink in. She looked slightly flustered for the first time I had seen in thirty minutes of knowing her in person.

"I'm going to share something with you about the agency that I haven't yet. It's nothing illegal or that would get you into trouble with any governments." She held my gaze. "Once you've heard this information, I'll need you to make a decision about joining the team before you leave this office today."

Not for the first time did I wonder if I shouldn't have followed my gut and applied to a job from a person and company that I had never heard of. One that I couldn't find anything about on the internet. I had soothed my concerns by telling myself I didn't have to take the job if I didn't want to. I had followed my gut and my curiosity won out, and now here I was, being told that I wouldn't have to do anything illegal. I snapped my concentration back to the conversation as Helen was still talking.

"I will answer any questions you have for ten minutes. After ten minutes, if you decide you don't want to join the agency, you'll need to take a pill that Steve will offer you." She inclined her head to Steve. He just continued to stare at me, at the edge of his seat as if waiting for me to bolt. Which was starting to become a real possibility. "This pill will remove the last hour from your memories. If you don't want to continue or potentially have to take the pill, we can end the interview now." Helen sounded like she meant business.

I was still trying to process the fact that they thought they had a pill that could erase an hour of my memories. How would that even work? Was this actually the CIA? I was still a bit confused by all of this. Based on how she looked at me, I think Helen knew I was confused too.

"Let's take a small break," Helen proclaimed before I could utter a response.

As if right on cue, the doors opened again and the receptionist, Annie, rolled in a cart with tea and treats. Floral smells laced with hints of honey wafted over to me and made my mouth start to water. The cookies were topped with candied lemon and were generously sprinkled with sugar crystals.

Annie took her time to pour the tea for the three of us. I studied her to try to figure out how this normal-looking woman could be in league with the two maybe-CIA agents sitting around this desk.

Annie was about the same height as me, and with her light brown hair and hazel eyes we could have been sisters. The one key difference was Annie obviously had good taste in clothes and the money to spend on them. I'd like to think I have good taste but neither the time nor the money to express it properly. I started to daydream about a shopping trip with her to have her help me pick out some new clothes to spend my new salary on. The new gray trench coat I pictured was especially cool.

I shook my head slightly to get my mind back in the present. The information and decision I was being asked to make was sinking in. Something so secret that I'd have to take a memory pill. What the hell was a memory pill—was that even a thing? I was still stuck on it.

Annie passed around small plates filled with the lemon sugar cookies. She placed a delicate teacup with a saucer on the side table next to my chair. Annie held up a sugar cube and waited for me to look up. We made eye contact, she smiled warmly, and I nodded my head. After dropping in the sugar, she held up another. I nodded again and the sugar dropped into my cup—this was for sure a two-sugar-lump kind of day. I shook my head at the cream offered.

The three of us settled in with our cookies and tea. I followed Helen's lead and sipped my tea, letting the soft, sugared, herbal drink calm me down a little bit. Annie placed the cart off to the side and made her way softly out of the room, but not before catching my eye one more time. With barely hidden glee painted all over her face, she nodded her head as if urging me to take the offer to continue.

I was still skeptical, but the tea and delicious treats were helping to soothe my nerves. Maybe they put some magic pills in the food too. So, as I understood things, I could leave now and give up this job. Or I could risk having to take a random pill that supposedly would wipe my memory so that I could hear what could only be something truly batshit bizarre, but, according to this woman I barely know, not "illegal." Oh, and it wouldn't get me in trouble with the government, whatever that meant. Obviously, my curiosity could not resist finding out what the secret was. I was never good at risk-reward trade-offs when it came to my own life choices.

"I'd like to continue the conversation." There was no turning back now.

3

———

Helen and Steve exchanged glances and then both turned back to look at me. Helen took a deep breath and plunged right in, "As we've already discussed, we are, as you put it, fixers."

She said that last word with a bit of humor in her voice while she glanced at Steve, sharing a look. I wasn't able to tell if they liked thinking of themselves as fixers or if they were going to accept that for now in order to move the conversation along to other topics.

"We help our clients however they need us," she continued. "Like you summarized, usually legal advice, mediation between parties, and private investigations. However, our clientele are not politicians or billionaires."

She paused as if for dramatic effect. It worked, and I leaned forward, urging her to continue.

"We very discreetly provide services to the supernatural, magical, and otherworldly community."

The teacup that was making its way to my open mouth

froze in midair. I don't think I was blinking anymore. No words were coming out and I was trying hard to keep a blank face, worried that it was reflecting my merry-go-round of a thought process and giving away too much.

I quickly went through the emotions of surprise, thinking it was a joke, stunned with disbelief, and back through that loop a few times. I stand by all of my responses. They all feel like legitimate reactions I'd assume people would have if they had just heard a well-dressed, seemingly normal woman who could be their future boss tell them that their clients are supernatural, magical, and otherworldly.

What shook me the most was how casually she had stated it and that she sounded so sincere. I'm usually a very good detector of lying. While I don't like calling people out on it, I can easily sort truth from fiction or embellishment in my head, plucking out what is real from the stories people like to tell. Either Helen really believed what she was saying was true, or it was in fact true. The idea of it being true turned over and over in my head until, like a stone in a river, all the rough edges of it were smoothed off.

Like many people, I had felt there was more going on in the world than what most people saw or talked about or wanted to admit to. It also helped that I had a pretty open mind to untraditional ways of thinking. My mom had been what many would have called a hippie. She had taught me about moon phases, herbal medicine, and pagan holidays, among other not-so-everyday, average mom stuff. But all of that didn't mean supernatural beings and magic existed and that they needed lawyers and private investigators.

A clearing throat to my left snapped me back to the moment. My focus went to the woman in front of me backdropped by a huge picture window overlooking treetops. Helen was looking at me over the cup of tea that she was sipping, seemingly not affected by this conversation or the time that had ticked by while I sat there with a dazed expression, making sense between what I thought reality was and what it could be.

"Not to rush you, but we have about nine minutes to talk before we need a decision from you. Questions?" she asked simply, as if she were asking me if I had any questions about the office decor.

Although my mind was racing, no questions were coming to me. All the articles about interviews said that you should ask good questions. I'd poured over example questions and had a file on my laptop listing the top ten questions I'd want to ask a future employer. None of those applied here.

What's a good question to ask about finding out that supernatural people are real? Or at least that the people interviewing you thought that supernatural people are real. Those questions were not on my prepared list. I thought I may need to see it to really believe it. *Should I ask for proof?* The clock was ticking, so I blurted the first thing I could think of that seemed reasonable and not rude.

"So you mean like witches, vampires, and werewolves are real?" Silly question for a job interview but it seemed like a pertinent one in this case. And these were the first supernatural beings that came to mind as they filled the fantasy books that I usually loved to read. However, I don't think that was what the job interview articles meant by good questions. Maybe I could write a new article for the job board blogs.

"Yes," Helen said flatly, as if I had asked her if the sky is blue or if the grass is green. "Among other things." Back to the tea sipping and the staring.

The man sitting to my left remained stoic and still, although I could hear him breathing loudly next to me. I kept staring ahead, not wanting to make eye contact with him.

"And they need lawyers and private investigators?" Another brilliant question. I was on a roll.

"Yes," she responded with a touch of amusement now.

More questions. Think of more questions. My mind was blank. I stalled for another minute and reminded myself to blink. No other questions were coming to mind. So of course I blurted out my go-to question that I had prepared to use at the end of an interview if I was made an offer: "When would you need me to start?"

Helen's smile was back and she settled her teacup firmly in its saucer. "We would love for you to start right away. But if you need some time, we can accommodate you starting within a few weeks."

"I can start on Monday." I wasn't currently employed, and the days at home were starting to get weird. I needed something to do, and I needed to start making money again.

"Great. Any other questions?" Helen asked. "We still have seven minutes."

"Um, not right now. I'm sure I'll have more as I get

started on the job." Another canned response from interviewing prep. I was on autopilot. Was it too late to ask for proof? Would waiting for my first day on the job be a better time to ask? Or maybe not until after my first paycheck.

Helen looked at the man sitting next to me, and then she gracefully stood up. "Welcome to the team. Steve will walk you through the paperwork and details to get you started. I'll see you at nine o'clock Monday morning."

Steve—I'd forgotten his name during the last five minutes so I was glad Helen had said it again—stood up and gently took my teacup from me. I had not realized I was still gripping it in midair. He set it back on the side table in its saucer and gestured to the doors. I stood up and struggled to put my notepad back in my bag. That accomplished after a few tries, I hoisted the bag onto my shoulder and froze, feeling like I should have had more information but not knowing how to ask.

Steve made a small cough, getting my attention. Then he guided me out of the room. Any questions I had would have to wait for Monday. Annie was sitting at what would be my desk trying to hide a sly smile, but the glee was still painted on her face. We locked eyes and I couldn't help but smile back.

THE MISTY WALK from the bus stop to my front door gave me time to calm down, clear my head, and start to make sense of what I'd gotten myself into. On the one hand, maybe supernaturals were real and this would make my life really interesting. On the other hand, maybe these people were just delusional.

I could put up with that for a while, get a good paycheck or two, and then make a soft exit to another gig, or maybe give up EA work and go back to working in a coffee shop or learn how to code. Either way, I had the weekend to not worry about the job hunt that had been a constant weight on my shoulders for the past six months.

The paperwork I had filled out with Steve had all been pretty standard. I filled in the personal information and signed an NDA that I had skimmed. It hadn't seemed any longer or different from the other legal documents I'd signed before. He was going to email a copy of the scanned documents so I could read through it more later. Let's be honest: I probably wouldn't though.

ILKA WAS in a mood the minute I walked in the door. She sulked toward me, sniffed the air, looked up with a scowl, and then strutted toward the kitchen. Of course I followed like the dutiful roommate with thumbs that I am. I opened up the expensive cat food that my mom had gotten her hooked on and placed it into her dish to the side of the counter.

Dinner for Her Highness secured, I sank into the couch in the living room to go over every detail of the day. I'm really good at recalling events, replaying them over and over in my mind. It helped me in my job a lot but often led to overthinking about interactions.

The lamps had already turned on, their timers set to

come on at dusk. The cozy glow illuminating the artwork on the walls and books lining the shelf added to the sound of rain now picking up outside. The atmosphere was calming and began to relax me so that I could focus. Usually I was grateful for my ability to replay past events in my head like a movie. Right now I wasn't so sure.

Anybody would have been nervous in a job interview, and I thought I had handled my nerves well. I didn't blabber on. I didn't think I had said anything really dumb. I controlled most of my stray thoughts and didn't make too many reaction faces. That was a weakness of mine that I'd been working on for years.

Maybe I was too quick to jump to say yes to the job offer. Maybe they thought I was desperate because I had accepted what they had shared with me without a lot of questions. They said I had ten minutes—did most people take ten minutes?

The money was great, better than any other job I've had and far better than what I could make at a coffee shop. There also weren't any other options on the horizon. And I did need the money.

The layoff six months ago had been a huge weight and was impacting my personal and social life. I had cocooned myself in the house and lost touch with friends. The job I lost wasn't my dream job, so it wasn't a loss in that sense. I had tried hard not to be resentful or have it impact my confidence, but it still did. Anyone who says not to take layoffs personally has probably never been laid off. On the money side of things, what savings I had were starting to grow thin and I needed to get into something that paid soon.

My mom had been okay with money. It always felt like we had just what we needed. She had paid for my college tuition and I worked part time to cover living costs. That made it so I didn't have to take out loans and graduate with debt. I'd moved back in with her after graduation, mostly because we both wanted me to. Saving money was a bonus. We lived simply and didn't really travel a lot. Everything was how we wanted it.

But then she died two years ago from a heart attack. It turned out that we were living just barely within our means. She had saved money but not a lot, and I had been saving up slowly to eventually buy a house or condo. For some reason, Mom didn't believe in life insurance, so covering medical bills and funeral costs had taken most of what we had.

I had been surprised to find that the small craftsman we had shared in Queen Anne was paid off. Without a job soon, I'd have to start to seriously consider selling the house. I had considered getting a roommate, but living with a stranger made my stomach ache. But the thought of selling the house made my stomach ache worse. I should have been grateful that I had options, but those options sucked.

Money aside, this job sounded interesting. A legal and investigation agency would have interesting cases that I could learn about, and a small team to support would be a nice change from the larger corporate teams I'd had at my previous two jobs.

It would be nice to work for a woman as well. All my bosses and their bosses to this point had been men. Helen seemed nice enough. The job was basic executive admin stuff. I was good at that and could do it in my sleep.

Surprisingly, I was also excited to be back working in an office full time. I had loved the hybrid work from home and in office two days a week setup I had with my previous company. But these last six months of having nowhere I needed to be had taken its toll. I may regret having a regular office job again someday, but for right now I was looking forward to having a reason to put on pants and go outside my house.

And then there were the otherworldly supernaturals and magic. Witches, werewolves, vampires, and such. Replaying that part of the exchange made me cringe, realizing that we spent all of maybe three minutes on that small detail of the job.

Sitting alone now in my living room, I had so many questions I wanted to ask. However, at some point earlier in the evening I'd decided to just settle into believing that it was true, at least for now. Fairy tales and stories that my mom told me growing up came flooding back to me. Almost all of her stories had a character that could be grouped into the supernatural category. Choosing to believe it for now made it easier to move on to thinking about the other new job-related stuff.

Aside from the shock of that revelation from Helen and the way she had delivered the news, I was surprisingly not surprised. I always thought there had to be more to what we saw around us. However, my money would have been on aliens.

THE REST of the evening passed as usual. I pulled out the air fryer to make some cheese fries for dinner. I toyed with the idea of making a salad as well, but when I pulled out the bag of lettuce, it was clearly past its edible stage. I watered my plants, washed Ilka's dinner bowl, and cleaned the kitchen a bit frantically. Basic care-taking tasks done, there was still a few hours before I could easily go to sleep. I settled in to relax for the rest of the evening.

However, I couldn't relax or concentrate on the book I was trying to read. I had read the same paragraph at least five times. The words wouldn't stick. My mind kept turning over the day and the single phone interview I had with Helen earlier in the week. It also didn't help that Ilka had decided to sit on the chair across from me and stare at me for the past twenty minutes. She really was a strange cat.

Going over the day and the job interview for the hundredth time, another anomaly stuck out to me. Other than some basic questions about my last role, Helen hadn't really asked me anything about myself—not today or when we had done a phone screen earlier in the week. There wasn't the usual behavioral *tell me about the time* types of questions. I wasn't asked how I dealt with conflict or how I communicated to leadership. I wasn't asked to talk about a time that I failed at a job and what I learned from it. I wasn't even asked to talk about a time I collaborated with my peers on a project and what exactly had my role been.

During the past six months I'd perfected answers to all of those and more. I think I was more annoyed than confused that I hadn't been asked to recite my practiced responses.

THE WEEKEND PASSED TOO SLOWLY. I cleaned the house top to bottom, twice. All the laundry was done and I'd even rearranged the linen closet. Nothing could hold my attention for long. I kept daydreaming about the office, my new coworkers, and what the cases would be like.

The daydreams swung wildly from boring estate planning for an aging vampire, to the whole team on the tail of a serial killer where all the victims were werewolves, to preparing a prenup for two fey royalty who were joining kingdoms through their marriage. Anything seemed possible. Still choosing to believe that this world existed, I was more excited than nervous by the end of the weekend.

At last it was my first day of work. *We can do this Linda,* I said to myself over and over in the mirror. A pep talk, a glass of orange juice, and a few deep breaths got me moving. I had picked out five different outfit options the day before. It was good to be prepared and have options.

Deciding that morning to go with a classic—black pants and white button-up—I was feeling good and professional. Ready for all the first-day things like getting my laptop, new office supplies, and key card. Learning where the bathroom was. Meeting and trying to make small talk with as many new coworkers as I could.

I'd practiced my new-person professional greeting in the mirror Sunday night. I was ready for all the good first-day-of-work things. I wasn't sure what might be different at a supernatural fixer agency. That I would have to just wing. Unless that was just a joke for the newbie—not sure if I hoped it was or not.

THE BUS DROPPED me off three blocks from the house-slash-office. I had taken a Lyft to the interview, so I was happy to learn that I could easily take the bus to work every day and that the bus schedule would fit my work schedule nicely. I walked up the steps and froze. *Do I knock? Do I just walk in?* Luckily the decision was not left up to me.

The clip of a pair of heels was marching up the walk behind me. Turning, I watched a tall blonde woman in stylish jeans and a plain black T-shirt quickly closing the distance to the front door. She glanced up from the phone she had been reading from and stopped in her tracks, a bit startled. "Oh, hi. Are you Linda?"

"Yes," I responded quickly.

Switching her phone to her left hand, she put out her right hand and reached past me to open the door. "I'm Jordan," she said. "Come on in, I'll walk you up to Helen. I'm sure she is already here and ready for you."

4

———

I hustled to enter in after her, closing the heavy wooden door behind me. Following Jordan through the house, it was much the same as Friday. Quiet, comfortable, well-decorated, and empty rooms. The smell of coffee and fresh-baked pastry wafted from the back of the house. Walking up the stairs to the second floor, I noticed things were very different than last week.

A group of loud and animated people were scattered throughout the conference room. A man I think was Steve was standing next to the table, a woman with dark hair was sitting casually in a chair, another man with lighter hair and fair features was perched leaning on a sideboard. Everyone seemed comfortable and in their element. The man who wasn't Steve gave me a bad case of déjà vu. A small shiver shook me when he made eye contact and then quickly glanced away.

Looking around, four of the six doors lining the halls that were closed during the tour were now flung open.

From what I could see, each room had a unique vibe that I guessed reflected heavily on the occupant.

One was painted in a deep green. Another could have been lifted from a chic office in the 1950s. The first on the other side of the hall was all glass and metal, clean lines and a bit sterile. Through the last open door was a room that looked like a cozy den you'd find a dad from a TV show reading the newspaper in. The quick glances left me wanting to explore all the interiors more.

Jordan was booking it across the room, not giving a glance at the other people, so I had to hurry to keep up. I was very conscious of their eyes on me as we passed through.

While the unknown man had me apprehensive, the other women radiated good vibes. They chatted easily with each other but gave me a warm smile and nod when they noticed me with Jordan.

Steve stood off to the side with his arms folded, watching everyone like a dad watching his kids at the play-ground. I skipped a bit to catch up with Jordan as she headed toward the set of double doors. Helen came flying gracefully through the doors before we made it the last several feet, flinging them open and startling everyone.

"We have a new case," she announced with more than a hint of excitement. The room quieted as if someone had pushed a mute button on the small chatter that had been going on. All eyes were on Helen. Due to proximity, all eyes seemed to still be on me as well. I shrank next to Jordan, uncomfortable with the continued attention.

Jordan cleared her throat to catch Helen's attention.

Helen turned toward us, taking me in with a quick scan. I panicked slightly, my mind going to the worst possibility and wondering if she had either forgotten I was starting today or had decided I shouldn't be here.

"We also have a new member of the team," she said excitedly. A quick nod in my direction and she was back to business. "Grab your laptops and be back at the table in five."

The group of people didn't ask any questions and dispersed to offices and down the stairs. Jordan squeezed my elbow. "Welcome, and good luck," she said. And then she was off, disappearing into the office that looked like a cozy room painted a dark green that I could now see was filled with books, glowing lamps, an overabundance of plants, and plush seating.

Helen faced me with a smile. She looked much the same as on Friday: Long, dark brown hair slicked back in a ponytail. Bright brown eyes topped with full eyebrows. Not a lot of makeup, or if she was wearing it, she tended toward the natural look. Soft laugh lines flanked her mouth and spidered out from her eyes, clearly a face that was used to joy and sunscreen. I guessed she was probably in her mid forties. Her outfit was simple, as most of the people in the office had been dressed, but stylish and looked like it was tailored specifically for her. I was feeling a bit overdressed in my pressed trousers and button-down shirt.

Even in all the hustle that was happening around us, I felt like all of her attention was on me now. Not in a creepy way, but in the way that makes you feel special. It still made me feel uncomfortable and unsure of what to do.

This was the most people I'd been around and was expected to interact with in almost six months. I hitched my work bag back to my shoulder even though it had never left.

"Sorry this is going to be such a fast start. I was hoping that we'd have a few weeks to get you settled in before we got a new case. But here we are." Helen gestured toward our offices for me to follow her. I walked into the space with her close behind.

"Cam has your computer all set up. There are also pens, notebooks, and such on your desk. Feel free to rummage through the drawers and cabinets in your office —they should be stocked. If there is anything you need that you can't find, just ask Annie. You met her on Friday and I'll reintroduce you today." Helen spoke at the same quick pace that she had on Friday during the tour. I was amazed that she could talk so fast without stumbling over the words or running out of breath.

Having rushed through this room on Friday's tour, I now had a bit more time to check out the space. The walls were a calm gray, almost green-looking where the light hit it differently. No big overhead lights—I realized that was actually a common theme, how the normal buzz of office fluorescent lighting didn't fill any of the spaces. Instead there were sconces on walls, lights used for artwork illuminating whiteboards as well as paintings, lamps strategically placed, and even some under-cabinet lighting that gave the room a soft glow around the edges.

The room that would be my office was divided into two spaces. To the left as you entered the door, a modern gray couch was flanked by two orange chairs that looked like they would swivel. A wood-and-glass coffee table sat in the middle. A tasteful rug defined that area. Behind one of the chairs was a sideboard that contained a mini fridge and had glassware arranged tastefully on top.

Slightly in front of the doors and to the right was a large walnut-topped desk with metal legs. At my new desk now, I could see that it was neatly organized, everything evenly spaced in parallel and perpendicular lines. A shiny new MacBook sat in the middle. Likely I'd get along with whomever had set this up. They clearly appreciated order as much as I did. New office supplies still gave me the warm-fuzzy feelings that they had when my mom let me restock my backpack with freshly sharpened pencils and colorful notebooks for a new year of school.

Another sideboard matching the style of the desk was against the wall flanked by two gray chairs. Tasteful artwork depicting mountains and evergreen forests in muted shades were on the two side walls. No windows in this room, but the lighting made up for it. I could see that sitting at the desk I'd be able to watch out the double doors but my back would be to the other set of double doors that led to Helen's office.

"Don't worry about setting up the laptop for now," Helen said, already pivoting to make her way back out to the conference room. "Cam, our in-house tech expert, can walk you through that and help you set up passwords later today. For now, just come, listen, and take notes on the meeting of any questions that you have. There will be a lot to learn."

"Sounds great." I resisted the urge to open all the drawers in the desk and two sideboards to explore everything. Instead, I grabbed a legal pad and a pen that had been set out on top of the desk. A quick double-take confirmed a shiny new blue ORCA bus card to the left of the laptop—not a perk we had talked about in the interviews, but gratefully accepted as I counted on the bus for transportation.

THE TEAM HAD ALREADY ORGANIZED around the table, claiming most of the chairs. I recognized Annie. She had joined the group and was walking around to finish laying out coffee and pastries. There were three chairs left open. One at the top and one to either side. I figured that the head of the table was for Helen. Not sure where I was supposed to sit, I stood waiting to see where everyone ended up.

"Have a seat right there," Annie said, helpfully pointing to a seat on the right side of the chair that Helen was settling into. Jordan, from the front door, was sitting next to me. Steve was toward the end on the opposite side of the table. I watched the rest of the team as they chatted and ate their pastries, unable to stop myself from making predictions and daydreaming in my head about what their stories were.

Helen sat patiently and waited for everyone to get settled. Annie brought her over a cup and a donut. She then brought one for me too. I hadn't made a move to get my own—the nerves of meeting new coworkers started to really settle in and had frozen me in place. I watched as Annie scanned the table as if checking to see if anyone needed anything else and then sat down opposite me. Now that everyone had a drink and food, Helen started the meeting.

"We do have a new case, and we'll get to that, but first and more importantly, we have a new team member."

All eyes shifted from Helen to me. Normally not a shy person, I tried not to shrink again or grimace at the attention, but this was one intimidating group.

"This is Linda, she will be our new executive administrator. I'll have Linda introduce herself, and then we'll go around the table and do a quick round of introductions," Helen finished and turned to me. I was a bit surprised that they all seemed to know who I was. My interview was just last Friday and it was first thing Monday morning now. Maybe this group was just really on top of their emails.

Even knowing this moment was coming, I had not really prepared anything to say to the larger group. I kicked myself for only practicing the individual greetings and interactions. Those were always easier for me as opposed to bigger group interactions. "I'm Linda. I grew up here in Seattle. I was most recently working at Hurst and Gramble. I've been an EA for seven years for two different companies."

Not exactly going to win the introduction of the year, but I saw some heads nod and nobody booed, so I took it as a win. I ended with a glance back at Helen, begging her a bit with my eyes to let me be done and to not ask me for a fun fact. Thankfully, it looked like we'd move on.

Helen smiled and inclined her head slightly. "And you know who I am, so we'll skip my introduction. Annie, let's start with you and then continue around the table."

"Welcome, Linda. I'm Annie," the approachable woman next to Helen said. "We met briefly last Friday. I'm the receptionist, among other things. I meet with the clients and handle their needs when they are in the office. I'm also available if you need office supplies or anything house related if Mrs. Clark isn't available. My desk is downstairs, but if we don't have clients coming in, I'm often up here working at the conference table."

Already I could tell that Annie and I would get along. She was clearly someone people automatically felt comfortable around and had a face that pulled people into telling her their stories. She probably also knew about everything that went on in the office. And I bet that she was the one to meticulously set up my desk. I made some notes on my pad about Annie and then looked up to see the next person watching me, waiting politely for me to finish up.

"Hey, Linda, I'm Harrison. Most everyone calls me Hank, but I'll answer to either." Harrison, or Hank as he liked to be called, was an average-looking guy, someone you wouldn't think twice about. Not to be rude, but he just seemed forgettable. He had lighter hair and average features. The weird vibes I had gotten from him earlier weren't as strong now. It was probably just my first-day nerves. The feeling of déjà vu I had at first seeing him was still there, but I couldn't put my finger on why.

I tried to push that to the back of my head and keep

polite eye contact as he continued, "I mostly handle logistics, operations, and away missions. My office is the first door by the stairs on the left."

I couldn't see into his office from here, but I had a feeling it would be one of the plainest ones. Jotting his name and role down on my notepad, I made a small question mark next to *away missions*. Sounded a bit military. Helen said they had private investigation cases, so maybe that was what he was referring to. I wasn't sure if that was just Hank's personality or if it was how the team really thought about what they do.

"Linda, so happy you are here. I'm Cam." With a quick peek up from my notes, I confirmed that Cam was not some typical IT dude as I had thought when Helen had shared the name with me as the person to go to for help with my computer. I silently chastised myself for having such stereotypical thoughts. Cam was a lovely, girl-next-door type. Dark, bobbed hair and an easy smile. Hard to judge her age. She could easily have been early twenties or in her forties depending on her facial expression, which seemed to dance across her face as she spoke.

"I handle all things computers and gadgets," she continued as I found myself staring a bit trying to figure her out. "If you need any help with your computer, just let me know. I'll come help you set things up with your laptop and new phone as soon as we are done here. My office is next to Hank's, but I'm mostly in the basement with the servers or in the lab."

Did she say lab? I almost, but luckily didn't, say that out loud. Another line in my notebook with a question mark. I wasn't sure what the lab was for and I definitely didn't see a lab during the tour of the office on Friday. Maybe it was just what Cam called her space. I made sure to give Cam a friendly smile. I'd have to grab lunch with her—it's always a good idea to be friends with the computer people.

"Linda. Steve. We also met last Friday." No way I would have forgotten Steve—well, unless he gave me one of those little memory pills he supposedly had. Although he still fit the tall, dark, and handsome category, I could see now that he had some edges I didn't pick up on as we handled paperwork on Friday. His tone was clipped and short, like he had other things to be doing and needed to get to them right away. He reminded me a bit of the stern, mysterious dads that my friends had growing up. "I head up security for the team. I also handle HR stuff. We'll need to meet later today to finish up some paperwork. My office is the first door to the right of the stairs."

Adding that to my notes, I made a reminder to talk with him today. The paperwork was what would ensure I would be getting that much-needed paycheck. I mentally checked my work bag to remember if I'd brought my two forms of ID required; I had. Also, a quick glance at the doors luckily showed that there were names posted on each. I had already forgotten to write down some office locations. Steve had finished up quickly and looked to his side for the next person to go.

"Linda, I'm Jordan. We met at the door. I'm the medical expert on the team. I also deal a lot with research and often go on away missions. My office is just to the right of Steve's. I'm also often down in the lab." Jordan smiled at me and then dropped a bit of a bombshell: "We'll meet later this week to get your physical done and put together your health plan."

Mid sip, Helen choked a bit on her coffee. "Oh, we hadn't covered that yet. Sorry to spring this on you." She gave Jordan a small look of disappointment. Jordan just shrugged and then glanced my way with a *what are you going to do* type of look. Helen turned back to me and switched to a smile. "No worries, normal checkup like you'd do on your yearly physical. And if you aren't going on any away missions, you aren't required to do any of the plans. Though knowing Jordan, she'll encourage you to try regardless."

Probably good that Jordan went last in that circle of sharing. I wasn't sure if I'd be able to pay as much attention through the rest of it after that announcement. The checkup part I wasn't too worried about, although I'm not keen on needles. But a health plan did not sound super great. I was fit—well, fit-ish—mostly thanks to good genetics. But I was also lazy, and I really didn't like the idea of employment-required health or exercise. I'd always managed to get out of any employee wellness competitions that companies seemed to like doing.

"Thanks, team," Helen said to the group and then addressed me directly. "We also have Mrs. Clark, whom I'll introduce you to later. She doesn't normally attend the daily staff meetings. That comprises our full-time team. We do have some contract and part-time folks who assist as needed, and we'll introduce you to them as they come in. Also, we'll be happy to remind you of names and roles or answer any questions. So no worries if you didn't get it all from this quick run-through.

"Now, our new case," Helen said with a single clap of her hands. "The Northwest vampire family has asked us to find a missing family member."

The room went silent. No one was talking before, but it somehow got even quieter with this proclamation. I looked around to see if anyone's faces would give away a clue as to what was going on. Everyone just looked grim.

"As you all know—well, most all know"—Helen glanced at me with a kind half-grin, indicating that I was the only one who didn't know—"the vampire families are notoriously closed off. We haven't had them as an active client at the agency in over fifty years, although we do keep tabs on all of the families to stay as up to date as we can."

Nodding heads around the room confirmed that everyone indeed knew this, or at least pretended to.

"I'll get a written brief out to everyone by the end of the day with the information that the family has compiled for us. But with the urgency of this case, I thought it best to brief everyone now with the basics, so feel free to take notes and please ask questions."

This suggestion by Helen seemed to shake everyone out of their stupor and open laptops started to fill the table. I felt a little redundant with my sad little notepad. I thought wistfully about the shiny new MacBook waiting for me at my desk.

"About five months ago, the family adopted a new member, Jane Davidson, thirty-seven years old at time of adoption." Everyone typed what Helen had shared, while I wrote on my sad little notepad. "Approximately two days ago, Jane was discovered to no longer be in residence at the family estate. Newly adopted family members are not allowed to leave the estate for at least a year. Her disappearance seems to be accounted for within a two-hour window.

"Steve, we'll want to identify a more precise timing if we can. The family provided a timeline, but I want you to double-check it. And, Hank, the normal proximity checks for canvassing and closed-circuit video. It's unlikely we'll find any additional video footage this close to the estate, but it's worth checking."

Both of them gave one sharp up-and-down nod almost in unison without a break in typing.

"The family did their own search and preliminary investigation but they have hit a major complication. That's where we come in," Helen said confidently.

Kidnapping had not been in the list of daydreams I had had over the weekend. Was there not supernatural law enforcement that the vampires should be working with? There was a lot for me to learn about this other world, and I was beginning to think that the hours of listening to true crime podcasts would not help me as much as I had hoped.

Everyone nodded again to Helen's proclamation. There was a lot of nodding going on, and I felt my head bobbing along with them even though I wasn't sure what I was agreeing to. The main difference was that everyone was typing furiously and I had nothing to write, so I started to draw in the margin to look and feel busy.

Helen let the typing go on for about a minute, then continued, "While we'll want to do our investigation from the beginning, the family did have one theory that they feel is promising and I assured them we would look into it. However, before we get to their theory, I want to hear initial thoughts and impressions."

I followed Helen's eyes as she looked around the room, waiting to see who would speak up first. Everyone looked deep in thought but it took a minute or two before anyone spoke up.

Jordan was the first to throw out a thought. "Are we confident that the adoption process wasn't hitting complications? Could there be a medical reason Jane isn't around or hasn't turned up?"

Helen nodded approvingly at Jordan and then indicated to Hank.

Hank stood and walked over to a whiteboard. He wrote down *Jane* in a circle and then drew a line to a new circle. In that he wrote *dead*. Seemed a harsh summary of Jordan's question, but I made the same drawings on my paper to copy what he had on the board.

"Next thought?" Helen prompted. I guessed she didn't want to push into the first idea too much yet.

Annie offered up, "Well, we know that a roving, newly adopted vampire can lead to close contacts with humans, risk exposure, and maybe even killings. That'd be something to look into." Hank wrote that in a new circle and drew a line connecting to the Jane circle.

"She could be on the property but injured severely,"

Steve suggested. Hank added a new circle on the board. I added the same circle on my notepad.

"Do we have in the file why she was adopted?" Jordan asked.

"Yes," Helen answered, "and, Annie, let's make sure we include a copy of that in the case files. It seems pretty standard though. Jane is an unmarried orphan and only child who inherited quite a bit of money after her parents died in a plane crash ten years ago."

"Could she have left and gotten lost? Or are there any other human family members who would have been looking for her?" Cam asked, throwing out more ideas. More circles went up on the board and new matching circles were added to my paper.

The team went quiet after that, but you could see everyone's minds turning over the questions. Helen's eyes continued to look around the table, waiting patiently for any other suggestions. None came. At this point no one was making eye contact with her, but the subtle glances and faces around the table seemed to be the team members daring each other to say something. I watched in fascination at the nonverbal communication happening among many of the group.

Not angry or frustrated, but firmly, Helen broke the silence. "No one wants to say the obvious motive." Faces around the table reflected the truth in that statement. "Well, it turns out that is exactly what the family thinks is going on."

5

There were more winces around the table than I was comfortable with. I hadn't connected the dots that they all obviously had. Although something was tickling the back of my brain, I pushed back the urge to daydream about the possibilities.

"The prevailing theory by the family is that a rival family has taken the newly adopted vampire." Helen let the words sink in over the group. No one was typing but everyone started to come around to the idea on their own time. "Hence, we were asked to get involved. Jordan, can you share more details about the adoption process so we all have the same context?"

"Adopting vampires is dangerous, both for the adoptee and for the adopter." Glancing my direction, Jordan explained further, "During the adoption process, the adoptee loses about ninety-three percent of their blood volume. It is replaced with a significantly smaller, although more potent, portion of the adopter's blood."

That seemed familiar to me, at least the swapping blood part. I was sure that I'd read that in a novel at some point. However, I tried not to think about it too much. Similar to needles, I don't do well with blood. There is a strong reason I didn't go into the medical field.

"If the adoptee's body accepts that donation and is able to start replicating the new blood's properties, then they survive. If their body doesn't start replicating the new blood cells quickly, they don't survive." Jordan's tone was getting more serious. "The new adoptee also needs regular blood from the adopter in the first year. If Jane isn't getting that, I would expect her to already be declining, and it would be fatal within a few weeks depending on several factors."

Everyone around the table seemed to already know this, and now I understood the urgency of the situation. I was surprised that the family didn't ask for help sooner. We were already two days into a relatively small timeline.

Jordan continued, "If the adopter gives more blood volume than their body can afford, then they don't survive. The stats on survival rates aren't great for adoptee or adopter. And those statistics have become more dire, resulting in family size declining for the past two centuries. No one is sure why the survival rate continues to drop."

"And size is vital to a family's standing within the global vampire and otherworldly communities," Helen concluded. "Please include a summary of the adoption process and the statistics around the decline in survival rate in the shared case summary file."

Jordan nodded at the request.

"So," Helen continued, "we know that adoption is risky for both parties involved and family membership is declining. Usually all the families celebrate new adoptions, at least publicly. But we've been hearing some rumors that a few of the families want to update the vampire laws governing adoption in an effort to address the decline. These families appear to also be the ones that are less successful with their adoption efforts. The Council has been worried for a while now that the situation may escalate."

Hank hadn't written this motive on the board yet. For some reason it seemed like no one wanted to acknowledge the fact that the adoptee, Jane, was likely missing due to a rival vampire family. Also, Helen had made mention of a Council; I added that to my notepad as something for me to follow up on.

"We also know that there are severe penalties for interference between families. Both from the families and from the Council. The consequences of even accusing another family of breaking a law and then being wrong are dire," Helen said. That explained why we were being asked to take on this case for the family and also why no one wanted to write it down yet, kind of—I was honestly still a bit lost. But it did seem like the families and the Council were different things; I noted that for myself.

"The Northwest family may be basing their theory on bad blood—no pun intended—between the families. But at least they don't want to accuse another family without strong evidence to back it up. So we will investigate, discreetly," she emphasized, "and then advise our clients on the likelihood of this scenario so that they may make a decision on how to proceed. But our primary goal is to find Jane quickly and return her to the family."

Keyboards clicked and faces pinched in concentration. Hank, still at the whiteboard, hesitantly wrote *rival family* and *declining family size* in circles, connecting them to the web he had created. My notepad had a mirror of the board framed by random doodles on the lower half. Hank returned to his seat and started typing at his laptop like the others. You could feel the tension in the room; I supposed that was to be expected with a missing new vampire and rival families at play.

After a few moments, Helen took in a loud, deep breath and all eyes looked up at her. Keyboards went silent. "I know this feels like a very serious case, and it is. But we will work it like any other case that comes to us. The family knows who we are and they believe that we can handle this. I believe that we can handle this. You all have the tools and skills needed. So let's talk through how we are going to tackle this."

Jordan started things off again: "I'll compile the known background information on the family, the adoption process, and the biological implications that there may be for separating an adoptee from the family this early in the process. I'll also help review the timeline of events provided by the family and see if there is anything we'd want to know more about."

"I'll review the security measures of the estate," Steve added without missing a beat. "And, with Jordan, review the timeline of events that the family sent over and look for gaps or anomalies. We'll want to interview them once I have a gap analysis to see if they are willing to provide any other information. Helen, I assume you'll want to be in that interview?"

"Yes," Helen confirmed. "And we'll want to have that as soon as possible. I'll arrange for a general meeting tonight with them. This will be a good chance to fill in any gaps that we want to know from the family. If anyone else has anything, please pass them along to Steve and Jordan."

Cam spoke up next. "I can help Steve with the security and timeline review. I'll also start pulling notes on the other families."

"I'll also need your help to set up a model to identify potential travel paths and locations where they may be most likely to go to ground. After you help Steve or before?" Hank asked Cam.

"Before," she answered quickly. "Then I can be the third pair of eyes on the timeline review." A quick nod from Steve confirmed that would work for him. I jotted all that down, although I bet everyone had already captured it in their own notes.

"Have Jordan review the model and add in any biological factors that may influence that," Helen added. "Annie, can you help Cam pull the files that we already have on the families? Let's start marking them with any questions or points of interest we'll want to confirm or get updated information on. Linda can help you with that."

I nodded at the mention of my name, eager to help wherever I could.

"Please get Linda access to the general brief we have on vampires. We also need a new file started for Jane and the case. Her adoption file should have been submitted to the Council already. You can use that to get our own file started with the basics. Then hand off to Hank and Jordan to add more specifics we may need to consider.

"Steve, let's run Jane through the normal background checks. Hand off anything you get to Annie to add to Jane's file. Let's also see if we can pull any financial records that are still in Jane's name." Helen was smoothly connecting the right people with the right tasks.

The team continued to throw out assignments and tasks either for themselves or for another team member to tackle. They had clearly all worked together for a while and everything seemed to flow. Other than my task to help Annie and get up to speed on the fact that vampires exist, I didn't get anything thrown my way. Made sense for my first day.

"Our main needs for this evening's meeting with the family will be the security and timeline gap assessment and then any questions we want to try to get answered about Jane," Helen concluded. Almost as an afterthought, she added, "I'll also want a surveillance plan for vampires in the area who do not belong to the Northwest family laid out. Steve and Hank please coordinate on that, but do not start any surveillance yet."

The tone on the last part made it sound like this may have been an issue in the past. Based on this meeting alone, I couldn't imagine anyone going counter to what Helen directed.

"Any last thoughts, opinions, or feedback?" Helen asked the group. Everyone sat still and looked thoughtful. No one spoke up. Helen waited as if she knew someone would say something.

The pause was making me uncomfortable, and I sang "Happy Birthday" in my head three times to try to control my mouth. It didn't feel like my place to speak up, but I couldn't help myself. "Shouldn't we be looking in the woods for Jane?" I blurted out.

Everyone turned their eyes on me. Helen looked interested and asked, "Why do you think that?"

I didn't have an answer. Had we been talking about the woods? Did I just make that up? I had tried hard not to drift off into a daydream during the meeting. Maybe I just wanted to feel like I was adding something to the conversation. "It just seems like something you'd do within the first forty-eight hours of someone missing," I said quietly. Oh no, I sounded so dumb. I swear I heard someone scoff but I wasn't sure who it came from. Probably Hank, he seemed the type.

"Interesting," Helen said in a tone I couldn't read. "Well, in this case, Jane has already been missing for more than forty-eight hours and the family did conduct a search of the area. But, Steve, let's add to the interview questions to ask for more details about the search they conducted."

The meeting ended with a few more questions, but I barely heard them. Even though Helen's reaction to my out-of-the-blue question was nice, I could still feel my ears burning red with embarrassment. The first-day nerves were overshadowing the lingering doubt I had about the clients this team helped. I kept my head down and jotted some final notes as the meeting wrapped up.

EVERYONE WAS DISMISSED to tackle their assignments. I made my way back to my desk to make a list of what else I needed to get done for my first day. Cam was going to come by to help me set up my computer, and Annie had let me know that she would stop by in a while so we could work on the case file together. Organizing case files would be one of my tasks once I got my feet under me. I was excited to learn how they did it here so I could help in future cases.

"Linda, do you have some time now to chat?" Helen called softly as she walked up to my desk. I wasn't sure what else she thought I'd be doing that would keep me busy on my first day.

"Of course," I responded and grabbed my notebook to follow her to her office.

Sitting down in the chair in front of her desk, I took in the space again. The gray morning light filtered in through the big picture window. The shelves seemed to hold even more interesting treasures as I took more time to look around.

"I want to apologize again for the busy start to your time here," Helen said calmly, pulling my attention away from the decor on the shelves and back to her.

"That's alright," I said as reassuringly as I could. "I'm happy to jump right in."

"Great," she said and leaned over her laptop. Clicking

through, she scanned the screen as if she was looking at a checklist. "Looks like you've got all the paperwork done with Steve that we needed." Helen looked up to see me nod my agreement. "You've got your laptop and now you've met Cam if you have any questions about that." Another glance up and another nod from me. "There is one thing that we haven't had a chance to talk about in detail," she said somewhat cryptically.

I wasn't sure what else there could be, unless she was going to confirm that in addition to vampires and were-wolves being real, aliens were visiting earth.

"Like I mentioned in the interview, with the nature of our work, it's hard to fully gauge how someone will adapt and perform in an interview. That's why we have everyone do a thirty-day probation period." Helen spoke as if it was no big deal, but I felt like the rug had been pulled out from under me.

Probation periods were not uncommon in the corporate world. It often just meant that it was easier to fire someone during that time period. Even though it was common, it didn't mean it wasn't stressful. And thirty days seemed short. I thought the normal was usually ninety days. What could I accomplish in thirty days to prove that I should be here?

"Okay," I responded as calmly as I could, even though I could hear my heartbeat in my ears. It wasn't like there was any other way to respond.

"For the probation period, we'll just want to see that you are engaging with the team, picking up your responsibilities appropriately, and generally meeting expectations," Helen continued.

I wrote those down on a fresh page in the notebook that I had brought with me out of habit. For that last item, I put a big question mark next to *expectations*. It would be important that I understood what those were.

Again it was like Helen was reading my mind, or maybe she just saw the notes on my paper. "We'll go over the expectations in more detail tomorrow," she said. "For today, I just want you to settle in and get a feel for the office."

"Alright, that sounds good," I said and made a mental note so that we really did follow up on the expectations.

The conversation was naturally wrapping up. I scooted to the edge of the seat, ready to get up, and then Helen offhandedly but sincerely asked, "Why did you ask specifically if we should be searching the woods?"

I tried to sound nonchalant about it. "It's just something that popped into my head. Probably something I'd seen on a TV show."

"Okay. I'm glad you spoke up," Helen said. She glanced back and looked down at my notepad that was filled with notes from the meeting but also doodles of trees filling the margins. A small smile leaked through her face. Surprisingly, that smile didn't make me feel any shame. Rather, for some reason, it made me feel better about my question. "Let me know if you have any other questions today," she said to close out our meeting.

I left the office quickly with a grin growing on my face. I could do this. I needed to just keep telling myself that.

· · ·

CAM WAS at my desk when I walked out. She quickly helped me set up my computer and work phone. She also showed me a few tools that the team used and where to find the shared drive full of documents. The interaction was quick and down to business, but Cam was nice and reassured me multiple times that I could reach out if I had any questions.

Annie came around a bit after Cam had left. We worked on setting up the file in the shared drive with folders for the things the team would be adding in as they were collected. She also showed me the general briefing folder that contained the documents I could read to get up to speed on vampires. Still not sure if these people were all part of a shared delusion or not, I was excited to read through what they thought otherworldly supernaturals were.

There were dozens of folders, and if they were anything like the vampire folder, there would be dozens of folders within those folders all containing several documents. The knowledge base system was well organized, better than any I'd seen at other companies. I was looking forward to diving into these as soon as possible.

Jordan found me after lunch and asked if I'd be okay to do a quick checkup right now before things got too busy. Hesitant, but not feeling like I could decline, I followed her to her office.

"I'll just be asking a few questions and taking some measurements today. We'll do the whole assessment when we have some more time," Jordan said as she gestured for me to sit in a chair in front of her desk.

I nodded in understanding and sat down.

"How would you describe your level of fitness?" she started off.

"I'm fit-ish," I replied, not sure what she meant and feeling like it would be better to be honest.

"Do you participate in any regular physical exercise?" she asked.

"Nothing formal," I admitted, "but I do walk most places."

She made some notes on her computer and continued, "Do you have any history of playing sports, gymnastics, or martial arts?"

These questions seemed weird to be asking someone who would be an executive admin, but I was curious to see where this was going, so I answered, "I didn't play sports in school. But I did take self-defense classes for a couple years in college."

She looked up at that and looked pleased. She nodded and then wrote some more notes on her computer. Jordan seemed to have forced nonchalance. "How would you rate your capabilities in self-defense?"

"Medium," I offered with a shrug. She made a face for me to continue, so I did. "I can break most holds and throw a punch, although I'm more of a kicker," I said with a joking smile. Jordan smiled back, so at least my joke landed.

"Good," she said and made a few more notes.

The self-defense classes had been my mom's idea. I

had finally given in and signed up after months of her badgering me about how important it is for women to know how to defend themselves if needed. The classes had actually been really fun and the instructor had said I was a bit of a natural. She, like my mom, encouraged me to trust my instincts. But unlike my mom, she taught me how to punch without breaking my thumb and where to kick someone to incapacitate them quickly so I could run away.

"Anything else about your health that you think we should know? Like allergies, medications, illnesses, and such," Jordan asked and then tilted her head, waiting for my response.

The question was also strange and it probably violated some employment laws. I wondered what exactly she was trying to get at. I wasn't allergic to anything and didn't have any chronic conditions. I had been on antidepressants for a little over a year after my mom had died, but my therapist and I decided to wean me off them. Good thing too—without health insurance for the last six months, I wasn't sure I could have afforded them.

"No," I answered, not really wanting to reveal my mental health history to this woman I barely knew.

"Alright," she said and finished typing some notes on her computer. "So we typically do measurements like height and weight for the fitness plan. As Helen mentioned, it's not required unless you'll be going on away missions or if you want to do it."

I nodded along, still unsure if I would want to follow a wellness plan. On the one hand, it was free and maybe it was a perk of this job. I probably could have benefited from some attention to my physical health. Whether I did it or not depended on how serious of a plan it was.

"We also take measurements for clothing and shoe sizes. Or if you know what those are, you can just tell me."

I waited to respond to see if Jordan would explain more about why they needed my clothing and shoe sizes. She didn't, and I let it go, assuming that it would be for company swag in the future. My closet was full of fleeces, button-ups, and T-shirts with logos that I was determined to pick out or patch over so I could wear the clothes without promoting companies I no longer worked for.

Jordan stood up and moved over to a cabinet off to the side to pull out a scale and a tape measure. We measured my weight and height—it was what I expected, as it hadn't changed much since my second year of college. I opted to tell her my clothing and shoe sizes, only hesitating for a minute when she asked for my bra and underwear size. She asked so nicely and nonchalantly, so I told her.

There were a few more questions about my diet—she didn't look impressed—and then we were done. Jordan handed me a lollipop in a crinkly, clear plastic film and jokingly said that I had been a very good patient today. The exchange made me smile and almost made me forget the weirdly specific questions. I happily popped the red lollipop in my mouth as I walked back to my desk.

I HAD MADE it almost to the end of the day. Paperwork was filled out. Laptop was set up. I'd worked with Annie to get the files started. I had my checkup with Jordan. And I'd skimmed through some of the documents in the shared drive. A good and mostly typical first day at a new job.

Before heading home, I wanted to get my notes typed up so I could add anything I may remember but had forgotten to write down. It was a quick write-up. Reviewing it to ensure it made sense, I realized that not once had anyone mentioned anything about trees or the woods before I asked about searching them. So much for good first impressions.

6

______

The sun woke me up. It wasn't supposed to be sunny this time of year in Seattle. Why was there a sunbeam right on my face? I thought I had secured the curtains before bed to block out any light. Ilka wasn't too impressed with the sun either, and she grumbled about it under her breath like an old man as we both made our way to the kitchen.

She and I were both born and raised in the Northwest. We had come to love the sun during the appropriate time of year—two and a half months in the summer. Other than that, the gray suited us better. This sun was adding an extra layer to the overthinking-hangover mood I was in from so much happening yesterday.

I had decided to accept that the world I knew had more to it. At least I'd believe it for now. I really needed to learn the appropriate terms to use. Maybe the documents Annie had shared yesterday had a summary I could read through. Regardless, there were things about this world that I needed to learn.

Accepting there was more to know was okay; not immediately knowing everything I needed to was not okay with me. It had been an aggravating drive of mine since childhood. My mom had tried to help me find peace with not knowing, but it didn't stick. The day that we can download information straight to our brains like some science fiction movie could not come soon enough. I'd be the first to sign up to have some mad scientist try it out—well, maybe the second in line.

There hadn't been any more talk about memory-wiping pills or stern warnings that I couldn't leave. In fact, with the thirty-day probation, they might make me leave. They didn't seem like the type of people to hold anyone hostage. If it turned out they were just a bunch of rich cosplayers who wanted to pretend there was another world hidden from the rest of us, then I could play along for a while too. I'd had weirder team members at other jobs. And so far no one at the OPT Agency had yelled at me or made me cry, so that was a plus.

Ilka stretched, and I could tell by her feline version of resting bitch face that if I didn't stop dwelling on this and get breakfast for her soon, she would try to make me cry. The kitchen was bright as well and beautifully clean thanks to my frantic efforts last night that helped to calm me down. I loved waking up to a clean kitchen.

The only thing missing from the kitchen this morning was my mom at the table with her coffee, scrolling through her phone and chuckling quietly to herself when she got to a funny video. She'd then send it to me and watch my face as I watched the video, frowning dramatically if I didn't laugh at all. Or teasing me that I'd think it was funny when I was as old as her if I didn't give the appropriate level of laughter.

Grief is a funny thing. I don't think it ever gets smaller. At least it hadn't for me. But it did hide in corners, ready to jump out in all its big, shadowy glory when I least expected it. The emotional jump scares were lessened when I was busy, and I had gotten good at recovering quickly from the startle of emotions. That morning it had pulled me back to the day of my mom's death.

I had been at work. It was a normal day, some light rain earlier in the morning but the afternoon was clearing up. I remember feeling glad that I wouldn't need to wait for the bus in the rain. It was almost time to pack up and I was finishing a few last-minute tasks when I suddenly doubled over. A pain, like a punch to my chest, hit me out of nowhere. Sharp, sudden, and then gone. The pain made my mind go blank and my heart race.

The urge to run came right after. I felt like I'd explode if I resisted it, so I rushed to pack up my bag and left with work still undone. Normally I would wait for the bus, but instead I ran, ignoring the looks of confusion from people I passed on the street. I remember counting my steps as they slapped on the sidewalk and kicked up rain from puddles, using the counting to try to control the rising panic. I dodged people and bumped into a few, continuing without looking back. Luckily I caught up with a bus before I hit the hill that I'd need to climb to take me home.

I stood by the back door of the bus, frantic energy making me dance in place. I bolted off the bus as soon as it hit my stop. My body was pushing me to get home. I crashed through the door of the home that I shared with my mom, not sure what to expect. It was quiet. Not even Ilka was making her presence known. The house was dark. I was alone.

The next hour I spent sitting on the couch in the dark. Not moving, not really thinking. Just breathing and trying to make sense of why my mind was blank and my heart was racing. My mom wasn't answering her phone. The knock at the door startled me out of a trance.

I opened the door to two officers. They didn't need to say anything. The blankness left my mind at that moment, and all I could picture was my mom in an emergency room, doctors and nurses unhooking tubes and lifting the sheet up and over her face. I knew what they would say before they opened their mouths. Almost always I can replay conversations I've had, but I don't remember this conversation, only the gist of what they had said.

They told me that she had collapsed at the grocery store. Someone had called 911 immediately and a worker at the store had started CPR. Even with the prompt lifesaving measures, they weren't able to revive her. She was pronounced dead at the hospital. They said that with a heart attack like this it would have been quick. She wouldn't have suffered. I never went back to that grocery store.

Shaking my head free of the images of my mom and that day, I got Ilka her breakfast and made a cup of coffee for myself. Ilka, uncharacteristically and as if sensing my grief, wound her way between my legs, offering a brief comfort before disappearing out of the room. I watched her go, wiped the tears from my eyes, and then steeled my nerves for day two of my new job.

I WALKED UP to the house-slash-office and opened the door without hesitation, deciding that confidence would be key for getting through the day. Smells of cinnamon and baking bread greeted me and reminded me of one of the primary perks of working for this agency: free food.

Delicious free food. I followed the smell and walked softly into the kitchen. Yesterday whenever I had entered it had been empty of people but filled with treats or food for lunch. I had eaten lunch quickly by myself, not wanting to make a fuss and not yet ready to reach out to anyone for that type of social interaction.

This morning a stout and lovely older woman stood between the island and the stove, spreading icing on top of cinnamon rolls. Her silver-streaked brown hair was tied up in a bun, one large streak of gray sweeping from the middle of her forehead to the left and swirled up in the bun. Flour dusted the front of her apron, two distinct handprints wiped on the sides. A soft hum of a tune I couldn't place floated from her mouth. I couldn't help but smile. She reminded me of my mom. Or what I imagined my mom would look like had she had more years of living. I felt drawn into the tableau and walked up to the island counter opposite her.

I must have startled her with my entrance. She let out a soft "oh" and looked up, making eye contact. She smiled gently at me, recovering quickly from being startled. "The cinnamon rolls will be done in just a minute," she said in a soft but somewhat gravelly voice.

We hadn't met yesterday as Helen had suggested we would; the new case had taken up everyone's time. But I was pretty certain this was Mrs. Clark. She motioned for me to have a seat.

Settling into a bar stool at the island, I introduced myself. "I'm Linda. The new EA. I just started yesterday." I tried not to drool over the lovely baked goods that would be my breakfast. And maybe my lunch if there were any left.

"Oh, that's right," she replied. "Helen mentioned you'd be starting. Everyone calls me Mrs. Clark. Welcome to the team."

"Thank you," I replied and then paused. I got the feeling that Mrs. Clark didn't want to chat much. Silence was okay with me. It didn't feel strained or forced. She continued to frost the cinnamon rolls and I looked out the doors toward the garden.

"Do you know what they plant in the garden?" I asked almost absentmindedly. It was clear that the space was well taken care of by someone.

"I mostly plant vegetables and berries. We have a few apple and pear trees too," Mrs. Clark answered and confirmed that she was the one who tended to the garden. I bet the food from it would make an appearance in the meals she prepared. I couldn't wait.

"That sounds lovely," I said wistfully. I wondered if she would mind having someone help from time to time. I wasn't as good at gardening as my mom had been, and I bet I could learn a lot from helping out.

Mrs. Clark finished up the cinnamon rolls and then served one on a plate for me with a fork and napkin. She turned to fill a mug with coffee and then placed that in front of me too. I dug into the cinnamon roll with no prompting and let out a sigh of food-based pleasure.

"That's always a good sign," Mrs. Clark said quietly. I chuckled through my cinnamon-roll-full mouth. She placed the pan in the middle of the island alongside some small plates and napkins, then quickly cleaned up a few crumbs and walked out the back door to the garden without saying another word.

She wasn't exactly rude, but I was certain now that she wasn't one to sit and talk, or maybe she just needed to warm up a bit more. It was good to meet her and hopefully make a good impression. I wasn't going to complain about the short conversation. Maybe she was just an introvert. Anyone who could make food this good could be whatever they wanted to be. Her care for the team was spoken through the food she made.

CINNAMON ROLL properly devoured and my second cup of coffee of the day downed, I gathered up my work bag and headed upstairs. I'd heard voices while I was eating, so I knew I wasn't the only one in the office, but it was still earlier than Helen said people generally got in. I had purposefully come in a bit earlier than was required so that I could get a handle on when other people arrived.

Making my way up the stairs, a movement to the right caught my eye. Hank was opening the door to the middle office on that side of the hall. I didn't think that was where his office was, but maybe I had misremembered. Or maybe he was meeting with someone. I squinted to see the name on the door after he had closed it. As I had thought, it was Jordan's office, not his. Glancing around the space, I didn't see any other people. They had either already made their way to closed rooms or Hank had been talking to himself.

I settled into my desk where I could face out through the double doors that I had left open, giving in to an urge to keep an eye on the office space. Helen's doors were closed and I didn't hear anything coming from her office—likely she wasn't in yet. With my view out the first set of double doors, I could see most of the conference room and the stairways. The office doors were just out of sight. It was quiet with just the low hum of the air in the vents filling the space. I tried not to make too much noise so I could hear anything happening outside my view of the office.

I'd like to lie and say I'm not a nosy person, but I am. You'd probably find me keeping an eye and ear on the office anyway. But Hank's odd behavior of sneaking into Jordan's office heightened my need to know what was going on. Trying to do something productive while still being able to keep tabs on what was happening, I set to work tidying up my desk.

Yesterday I had rummaged through the drawers to see what treasures I'd find and then stowed the supplies that had been left on my desk. I didn't need to rearrange much of anything. Whoever had set up my desk for me had similar office supply sensibilities. They understood that writing utensils go in the drawer to the right and notepads on the left. I decided to start the morning off with the general briefing documents I'd been given to get up to speed on this new world. Also, reading would be a quiet activity to start off the morning and keep me alert to sound or movements outside my office.

I WAS JUST STARTING BACK in on the general brief on vampires when the sound of someone walking up the stairs caught my attention. I looked up in time to see Jordan with her work bag slung over her shoulder. If she was just getting in, that meant Hank was in her office without her. Hank's odd behavior had now escalated into suspicious behavior.

Jordan plopped her bag onto the conference table, gave me a little wave when she saw me looking at her, and then turned around and walked back down the stairs. I strained to listen to what was going on outside of my current view. A door, which I'm pretty sure was Jordan's office, opened softly and then closed just as softly, as if someone was trying to conceal the movement. A few moments later Hank came into my view.

I wasn't not sure why—I wasn't doing anything wrong —but I ducked down below my open laptop screen and pretended like I was reading. Hank's footsteps walked past the double doors and then down the other side of the room. A door opened and closed at a more normal volume. I presumed it was Hank going into his own office this time.

That was all very strange and he seemed really suspicious. But I was brand new to this office. Maybe they weren't precious about their spaces and he was just borrowing something from her office or returning something to her. They seemed like a tight-knit group; I could have been making a big deal out of nothing. I noodled over the problem but ultimately decided I'd keep it to myself, for now.

A STEADY STREAM of folks came upstairs and into their offices. Starting a bit before nine o'clock, everyone made their way, breakfast in hand, to the morning staff meeting. Luckily I had checked Helen's calendar, so I knew this was happening. No events had been added to my own calendar yet. I hesitated for a minute about joining, but it did say it was an all-staff meeting. So I joined the group, taking the same seat I had occupied yesterday morning.

Helen started the meeting promptly at nine. No one seemed surprised that I was there, so I felt comfortable with my decision. We started with updates on the active case. We went around the table and everyone said what tasks they had completed and what they were going to tackle today. My update was the lightest, but no one seemed to think anything of it since it was only my second day. Circling back to Helen after everyone had taken their turn, she brought us up to speed on the meeting with the family from last night.

"The family was able to fill in some gaps and answer some questions we had about the timeline and Jane," Helen started off. Everyone was leaning slightly forward with laptops open and engaged in the conversation. It was a rare sight for me to see this many people without one or two clearly multitasking during a meeting. I realized I had mirrored their behavior unconsciously, excited to hear what they had learned last night.

"The family disclosed that Jane's adopter, Ms. Wadsworth, had also been attacked," Helen shared.

Every face snapped up to meet her with shocked expressions, mine included. This was important information and I think we were all surprised to just be hearing about it. Helen looked around the room and then cut off questions by telling us firmly, "I'm not going to theorize why this wasn't initially disclosed, but now we know. Ms. Wadsworth was found just outside the grounds while they were searching for Jane," Helen continued. "She was unresponsive but is doing fine. They believe that whoever took Jane drained her adopter of almost all her blood."

Jordan let out an audible gasp at this news. "And Ms. Wadsworth is recovering?"

"Yes," Helen said. "The family believes she'll make a full recovery."

"Oh, good." Then scrunched up her face when she asked, "Would that blood sustain Jane if it's not fresh?"

"It's unclear," Helen said sadly. "This is very unprecedented. But it does point to the abductor being familiar with adoption processes and the need for Jane to have her adopter's blood."

"If the family will permit us to have a sample of Ms. Wadsworth's blood, once she's recovered, I can run some experiments to see if we can find out if it keeps the properties needed when outside the body," Jordan offered up.

"I'll call the family right after this meeting. I'll let you know," Helen answered.

Jordan nodded her head and went back to typing up notes.

"We were able to speak to Ms. Wadsworth," Helen continued. "Unfortunately, she did not get a clear view of her attacker and she remembers very little of the incident. We'll follow up as she recovers to see if she remembers anything more." She gestured in Steve's direction.

"We were able to narrow down the timeline to a thirty-minute window when the two were left alone in the side garden of the estate," Steve said, taking over the update. "Jane's attendant had gone back inside to get her a requested refreshment. She was delayed inside for about thirty minutes. The attendant did not share this information with the family right away. The two were discovered missing an hour and a half later by another family member."

Everyone nodded in understanding, and I felt like I was missing something.

"Why didn't the attendant tell someone sooner?" I asked before I could stop myself.

Everyone looked in my direction. I sank down in my chair. Helen smiled politely. "Attendants are human and are often in line to be considered for adoption. The families have strict expectations for them. Leaving Jane unsupervised for that long, even in the company of her adopter, would be against protocol and would, at the minimum, result in being moved to the back of the list for adoption. At worst, they would be completely expelled from the estate and their employment. I think they were hoping to find them or they would return and not need to tell anyone about the lapse in protocol," Helen said with sympathy. "We weren't able to talk to the attendant to confirm this."

Steve picked up the thread from Helen again. "Even with the thirty-minute window, it's unclear how they were attacked and how Jane was removed from the estate. We were able to find some gaps in the estate's surveillance. They mostly watch for people coming into the estate through designated entrances, not all potential entry points. So not all the grounds are covered thoroughly. Helen, I assume you want to inform the family of these gaps?"

I was surprised they hadn't told them yet. Glancing around the table, it seemed like I was the only one who was surprised.

Sounding unhappy about the task, she responded, "Yes. Prepare a formal report and I'll set up time to let the family know. They are not going to be happy about this."

If the family would get so upset about someone being left alone for thirty minutes, I supposed they'd also be pretty upset about gaps in their security. Nothing had come up in my readings yet on why the family's estate would need so much security for intruders. It's hard to imagine anyone knowingly wanting to mess with them, so maybe it was primarily for theft prevention.

"Do we know what or who delayed the attendant?" Cam asked.

"We were told that they were delayed with a personal phone call," Steve answered somewhat vaguely.

"The family did not wish to share with us who the call was with," Helen added. "They assured us that they had investigated that thoroughly and it was not of interest to this case."

"And do we believe them?" Jordan asked what I had also been thinking, luckily faster than I could blurt out again.

"We should note the lack of information from the family," Helen responded, "but for now we won't press them to be more forthcoming." She changed the topic slightly: "Steve, any luck on Jane's background and financial records?"

"Yes, we were able to get the standard background check back already. Nothing different from the family's file or anything unusual in the report," he responded quickly and then looked frustrated. "No luck on the financial accounts." He lowered his voice slightly like he didn't want to admit to it. "The family said she would have some, but we are having trouble tracking them down. We'll keep pushing to find them."

"Alright," Helen said calmly. "Keep trying and keep me posted."

"Will do," he said with a nod.

A few smaller updates were shared. Task assignments

were amended or added. And the morning meeting wrapped up. Helen reminded everyone to send an update in the group chat right away if they found anything interesting.

Yesterday Cam had helped me set up the chat tool that the team used on my laptop and phone. It wasn't one of the normal corporate tools I was used to but pretty similar in style and how it worked. She'd explained that this was the primary means of real-time updates and talking about stuff when folks weren't in the office. We didn't use normal text messaging on our phones for anything work related.

Also, if the person you needed to talk to was around, it was more common to talk to them face to face. That was a relief—it always felt weird to text people who were sitting within shouting distance. Not that I would shout in an office, or at least I didn't that often.

I gathered up my laptop and headed to my desk to dig back into the vampire briefing document. The list of questions I wanted to see if I could find an answer to was growing faster than I was crossing questions off.

"LINDA, I need your help with something," Helen said, setting her cup down in an empty spot at my desk later that morning.

Eager to be more involved, I was hoping that *something* had to do with the case that the team was tackling. "Happy to help with anything," I replied, my eagerness clearly showing through.

"We have a retainer client, the Northeast werewolf pack

near Boston. Normally I wouldn't have taken on this project right now, but I had already committed before the family's case came in and I don't want to postpone the work the pack needs done."

I nodded along. It was reasonable for a retainer client to have projects they needed done in a timely manner. Keeping retainer clients on the books often relied on having a prompt response to their smaller requests. Even though this was a small agency, they probably had a lot of clients paying retainers. Based on what the office was like and what they were paying me, they would need them.

"We have a list of six individuals they need vetted," Helen continued. "We need to complete a detailed report for each one. I'll email you the list of names and the template we follow. We also have some initial information from the pack to help get things started. I'd like you to organize that information and then do a first pass on the research and fill in what you can. It doesn't need to be perfect, but anything to get us started would be great.

"These are all humans so you should be able to find information about them through the normal means," she instructed. "Cam can give you access to the government databases we have access to, if she hasn't already."

I remembered Helen said in the interview that I wouldn't get in trouble with any government agencies, so I assumed we had permission to be using these databases. I have to admit, other than the werewolf pack part, if that was true and not part of an elaborate cosplay, this sounded pretty standard and within my skill set.

"I can do that," I said, trying to sound convincing, probably trying to convince myself more than Helen. I really wanted to do well, and it could be a clear contribution during my thirty-day probation to prove I could do this job. "When do you need this done?"

"End of next week would be fine for the first pass. But if you get stuck on anything before then, just let me know." She smiled and walked back into her office, leaving me to get started.

The emailed list was six people, like she said, but the template was eight pages of questions with very little space for answers. Most of the questions were asking for short answers, not true-false, fill-in-the-blank, or single-word answers.

Helen had also sent a report from the last search they had done as an example. They had full-paragraph responses. Or, on some questions, pages of text. Two weeks. Six people. And at least eight pages per person. So sixty-four pages in two weeks. With a whole lot of research fun sprinkled in. That might sound horrible for some people, but I actually really enjoyed research. If this was a test, I could do it, and I could do it well.

7

———

The morning had gone by fast thanks to the task I had to focus on. I made a lot of progress on the research of the six individuals for the pack. The people I was collecting information on all seemed rather boring, nothing criminal or even overly important or exciting in their background, which I guessed was what the werewolf pack was probably looking for.

I had scanned the werewolf folder in the shared drive to have a little more context about them and how those groups worked. From what I could make sense of, these six people were recruits being considered to join the pack.

Deserving a break for the progress I had made on only day two, I went down to the kitchen to see what there was for lunch, determined not to eat at my desk even though the research tasks were still calling to me. Mrs. Clark scurried out the back door as I walked in, like she had almost every other time I'd come into the kitchen. At least she had already finished the lunch spread on the kitchen island, so

I hadn't disrupted her work. It looked like I was the first down for lunch today. I filled the kettle and set it to boil so I could have a cup of tea with my lunch.

Before the water had hit a boil, Annie and Cam came in chatting excitedly about something. They both saw me near the kettle, stopped talking, and smiled. It was time for me to be social and make friends. At least it was the two people I had already hoped to get to know more first.

"Hey, Linda, do you want to eat with us today?" Annie asked, and Cam smiled in clear agreement with the invite.

"Yeah," I responded, trying not to sound like I was in middle school and had no friends.

"Are you getting tea?" Cam gestured to the kettle that had started to make some bubbling noises.

"Yes. I've already had two cups of coffee, so switching over to tea. Trying to be healthy." I shrugged playfully. They both laughed a little, thank goodness. "Do you want a cup?"

"That'd be great," Cam replied.

"I'd love one too if you have enough water," Annie chimed in.

"For sure," I said, glad that I had filled the kettle enough. I brought the kettle and a trivet over to the table for the three of us and grabbed the box of tea to bring over as well. We all gathered our plates filled with salad and the most perfect club sandwiches you have ever seen, then settled around the table.

"Linda, tell us a bit more about yourself," Cam started things off as she poured water into her mug.

I gave myself an internal pep talk: *No pressure, be your-*

self, and they'll like you. You're likable. "I grew up here in Seattle with my mom. She died about two years ago." *Nice, I started off with the dead mom, that's always a hit,* I thought sarcastically. *Just keep talking.* Maybe they wouldn't dwell on that fact. Or worse, ask for details and turn this lunch into a "Feel bad for Linda" meeting. "I'm twenty-seven and live in Queen Anne with my mom's cat, Ilka. Well, she's my cat now." I could have kicked myself. Did I not know how to talk to strangers anymore?

"Ilka, what a great name for a cat. What kind is she?" Annie rescued me with a question and a redirect to safer topics.

"She's a Norwegian forest cat. She's big and fluffy and thinks she is the owner of the house. I'm not sure she likes me, but I feed her, so I'm at least tolerated."

Cam and Annie both chuckled at my joke.

Okay, I sighed internally with relief. *This could work, they at least got my humor.* "Random question," I threw out to make it seem like I hadn't been thinking about everything so obsessively for the last five days. "What does *OPT* stand for in the agency name?"

"It's the names of the agency founders," Cam said between bites. "There were three founders, Owens, Pendleton, and Truly. It's just Helen now, but she kept the name."

"Cool," I responded, one mystery down. "So tell me a little bit more about you two."

"I'm from Utah," Annie started off. "I'm thirty-two. No pets, but I'd love to meet Ilka."

"We can make that happen," I said with a smile.

"I live over in Magnolia," she continued. "It's fine. It's a lot of little old ladies who love to go for walks. And young families who love to go for walks. I don't like to go for walks."

Cam and I both laughed at her seriousness in that statement. I added a point to the friend column in my head for Annie. While I walked most places out of necessity, I wouldn't say that I loved to go for walks. The laughter faded and both Annie and I looked at Cam for her introduction.

"I'm also thirty-two. Annie and I are actually only about a month apart in age. She's older," Cam joked.

Annie responded playfully, "That's right. And don't you forget that I'm your elder."

Cam continued after we had a chuckle at Annie's joke, "I live in the city near Pike Place."

"You should see the view," Annie added. "Cam's place is gorgeous. She has great taste and everything is so high-tech that it feels like you are in the future."

"Thanks, Annie," Cam responded genuinely. "We'll have to organize a dinner again and have folks over."

"That would be fun, I'm in," I agreed quickly and gave myself some props for being social and working toward my goal to make friends again.

Both of them had great senses of humor, a bit dry like me and very witty. We bantered easily back and forth and the conversation flowed. I could tell that the three of us would get along great. I wasn't quite ready to ask them about our other colleagues—I didn't want to seem overly nosy. And I definitely was not ready to ask them to spill any tea about Helen, our boss.

But I was only five days old to the otherworldly supernatural, and this felt like a chance to see how far the conspiracy went. I'd been swinging wildly between deciding to believe and not believing at all. Having seen no direct evidence of this world, I was curious to see what these seemingly normal and smart women would say.

"So, otherworldly supernaturals, huh?" I asked, starting off strong and then took another bite of my sandwich so I'd stop talking.

Cam laughed, spitting out a bit of her salad. Annie looked sympathetic as she responded, "Yeah, it's a bit of a shock to learn that things aren't what you think. But you'll get over that, and it's kind of cool to know this big secret that most people have no idea about. And you get to learn about all these cool things. You really start to see the world and your place in it differently."

She seemed very sincere and I could feel my doubt chipping away. I liked what Annie had said about seeing your place in the world differently now that you had this knowledge. That could be a really good thing for me at this stage of my life, and I made a mental note to give it some more thought later. For now I wanted to learn more about this new world, not get philosophical about our place in it.

I also wanted to learn what sauce Mrs. Clark put on these sandwiches. It was tangy and sweet, like a cross of mayo and honey mustard, maybe with a touch of vinegar. I had licked it off my fingers four times already, but only when Cam and Annie weren't looking.

I prodded gently, not wanting to bias any information:

"Helen wasn't too specific about things or what is real versus not."

"Basically, if you've read about it, seen it on TV, or in a movie, there is likely some truth to it," Cam offered as Annie had a mouth full of sandwich. "Humans aren't as creative as we'd like to think. Everything is rooted in some form of truth. It may be misunderstood or sometimes grossly misrepresented, but it's still anchored in something real."

"Does that mean that people we thought are humans may actually be part of the otherworldly supernatural community?" I asked.

I had been turning this question over in my head all weekend, thinking through all the strange interactions I'd had with people throughout high school, college, and working. For a few of my neighbors, being supernatural would go a long way to help explain some behaviors. Nothing that bad, I'd had a pretty sheltered life, but there were definitely some characters in my past and present.

"Yes," Cam responded. "I mean, they're all around us even though their numbers are very small. Most live really long lives, so they try to stay out of the spotlight. Historically, becoming even slightly known to humans has never worked out well for them."

"Also," Annie interjected after swallowing her food, "their numbers stay small so it's easier for them to stay under the radar, and there are groups like ours in place to help support them if interactions with humans get out of hand."

"Why are there so few of them? If they live so long,

you'd think there would be more of them." It didn't make sense to me.

"Jordan has some theories about that," Annie said thoughtfully. "But essentially, all the ways that the different groups reproduce have very low success rates. This has kept the populations small while the human population has grown due to our reproductive success. We are basically the rabbits of all the humanoid species."

Flashbacks of Biology 101 came back to me and that theory resonated with what I'd been taught. If a species can't reproduce effectively, they are on their way to extinction. It's one of the reasons pandas were considered vulnerable and there were conservation efforts to boost their numbers. It seemed rude to ask if supernaturals could take on similar conservation efforts. I decided to stick to easier topics. "So how do you know who has magic or who is supernatural or not?"

"In some cases it's pretty obvious if you know what to look for," Annie responded. "In other cases you'll likely never know. People with magic tend to hide it and supernaturals are pretty secretive. For good reason."

"Is there anyone I'd know who is otherworldly or supernatural?" I asked.

"Not likely," Cam replied. "Maybe some historical figures before the groups and the Council all became stricter about discretion. But that would have been centuries ago."

"I have a theory about a few," Annie ventured to our small group. "I think Nostradamus, Cleopatra, Joan of Arc, and Leonardo da Vinci were all supernaturals. Oh, and Taylor Swift."

Cam and I both stopped mid bite and chuckled. "Taylor Swift?" I asked. "I could see the others, but why her?"

"Well, she is magic with her lyrics and she has amassed a huge fan base. She could be a siren. Or at least a partial siren," Annie defended her statement.

"I could see her having some siren genetics, maybe," Cam conceded playfully. "But if she were enough of a siren to be on the Council's radar, there is no way she'd be allowed to have the career she has."

"Okay," Annie said, a bit defeated but still keeping the playful tone. "But I still love her and would follow her anywhere."

We all had a good laugh and agreed on that point. We talked about other historical figures who may have been supernatural. We stayed away from the topic of any living celebrities. I had more questions I wanted to see if I could get answers to before ending lunch, so I switched the topic.

"Another thing I don't understand is why people with magic or supernaturals need our help," I said. "It seems like they'd be able to handle things better than we can."

"That's a good question," Cam said, and I felt better about bringing it up. "Agencies are in place to help with two main things. Like Annie said earlier, we help when interactions with humans get out of hand. And when there are conflicts between groups. Like with the case we have now."

"Most of the supernatural groups have some pretty

strict rules and cultural norms they follow," Annie added. "Working with us lets them technically not break those rules because we aren't held to the same standard."

"Even if they could handle their own problems, we help them skirt the rules and hopefully keep them off the radar of the Council," Cam said.

"Also, even though agencies are useful, there are now only like five still active globally. So we stay pretty busy but rarely work with the same clients on big cases. Right, Cam?" Annie said.

"Yeah," Cam said, swallowing a bite. "I think there used to be way more before the Council became more active."

"That makes sense," I responded. Although I still wasn't sure it all made sense.

I made a note to look through the shared documents for the folder on the Council, if there was one. I hadn't wanted to shift the topic by asking what that was even though I'd heard it mentioned several times.

We cleaned up our plates and made more tea to take back to our desks. I was glad to see that I wasn't the only one who constantly needed a beverage available. We also made an agreement to try to have lunch together when we could. Annie and Cam assured me that they would answer any questions they could during our lunches as I learned more about this new world and the work we did at the agency.

Back at my desk I set aside the research assignment for the pack. I set a timer so I wouldn't spend the whole afternoon lost down a research hole, but I wanted to get some of my questions about the vampire families and the Council answered.

First up, I looked more into the vampire families. I found a document that detailed the list of families and their current members. It turned out that there were only seven families, and other than the London family, they all seemed to be in bigger areas of the world. Each family was named based on the region of the world they occupied; the London group was the only one named after a city.

There were only two families in North America: the Northwest family, our current client, and the Southeast family. Their territories didn't conform to government boundaries and ranged far into Canada and down into Central America. It was also interesting that the boundaries of families didn't bump up against each other. There were big areas of the world with no families at all. In the States, the entire Midwest didn't have any family territory claimed. It was unclear if that meant they didn't have vampires.

The total population of vampires was barely over one thousand. Much fewer than I would have thought. The families all had similar membership numbers. The largest family was the Northwest Americas family with two hundred and eighty members. The smallest was the London family with one hundred and thirty members. This file had links to documents on each of the listed vampires. I had to stop myself from spending the rest of the afternoon reading through the individual files. My timer was almost up and I wanted to see what I could find on the Council before I needed to get back to my assignment for the pack.

Navigating back to the top folder structure in the drive, I scanned for the Council. There was only one document listed, not even a folder. I clicked into it and was immediately disappointed. It was barely longer than a page of information. At least it would be a quick read.

The summary of the document is that the Council was established in the sixteen hundreds. They create rules and guidelines designed to protect all otherworldly community members from detection and persecution. There was a link to a document that looked to be a very lengthy legal-looking write-up of those rules and guidelines. I tagged that to come back to another time.

There were several paragraphs that spoke about key events forming a bit of a timeline from their start to now. A few stood out to me, and I made notes of the links to check them out later. One spoke briefly about territory disputes in the sixteen hundreds, with a link to a folder. Another talked about the witch hunts in the seventeen hundreds and the Council's involvement to curb them. A quick glance at the linked document was interesting, so I made a note to come back to it.

The last one that stood out was a short paragraph on something called the Oracle Accords. The link to the corresponding file was broken, resulting in a "Document Not Found" message. Without the linked document, all I could make sense of was that it was the most recent otherworldly community-wide intervention that the Council had been involved in during the early nineteen hundreds.

I added another note to my list to look into the broken link.

Reading through the short document again, I was surprised by what I didn't find. There was not a list of who was on the Council or even how many people made up their ranks. There was not any indication of how they met or were organized. They clearly did stuff, but how or what was very unclear.

Where other files had annotations from the team members with highlights, context, and links to other documents with helpful notes, this file had no annotations and was very vague. It was basically useless and didn't give me much more information than I had already gleaned from the conversations where people had mentioned them. Unsatisfied, I didn't tick off the line to research the Council on my to-do list. I'd need to keep digging into that later.

My timer hadn't gone off, but with the frustration from not learning anything interesting about the Council, I decided to get back to the pack assignment. That research was easy. I had organized the information from the pack into the forms and was now looking at filling in the gaps. Some easy searching through Google and social media filled in some interesting information on the first person.

The government databases looked very official and outdated in their design, so I believed that these were actual government tools. I didn't dare copy and paste from them. Accidentally editing a government database would probably be bad news. Even though I'm sure Cam would have warned me if that was possible, I wasn't going to risk it. So I rewrote the information into our documents instead.

It was only three o'clock and I had made good progress. The basics and several of the gaps were completed for the first two individuals. I'd do another pass to see what more info I could dig up after I'd gone through all of them to get the easy stuff in first.

Feeling good about that plan, I wanted to look at the shared case file for Jane to see if the team had made progress on anything. Nothing had come up in the chat, but I wanted to stay up to date and didn't want to wait for the morning meeting.

Unfortunately, there wasn't anything too interesting in the files. The team had clearly been making progress. Mostly they knocked out to-do items, but everyone seemed to be bringing up more questions than answers. Several new folders had been added along with documents. Needing a change of pace, I decided to go see if there was anything I could help Annie with. If not, at least I could grab a snack in the kitchen and have a change of scenery for a bit.

8

———

I found Annie sitting in the living-room-slash-waiting-room on the first floor. She had her laptop set up. Papers were spread out on the coffee table with a mug and a plate with half-eaten cookies.

"Is there anything I can help with?" I asked Annie, getting her attention.

"Yeah. Do you want to help me go through these contact sheets?"

"Yes. Happy to help."

"Cool. Have a seat and I'll show you where to find the files," Annie said.

I moved to the seat she gestured to next to her on the couch. We set up side by side so we could see each other's screens.

"Find the file labeled *Contacts Review* in the case file," she instructed.

I opened up the case file and quickly found that folder.

"Helen and Steve got the estate's visitor logs. And they

got the family at the estate to fill out information on any contact they've had with anyone outside of the family or their employees in the last two months," Annie explained as she opened up a document in the folder to show me. "These just came in and we need to review them and flag anything that looks off. We'll then decide which ones to follow up on."

"Anything specific we're looking for?" I asked, unsure of what exactly she meant by *looks off*.

"Patterns, one-off meetings, things that make you raise your eyebrows," she said vaguely. "Basically, be suspicious and nosy. It's better to flag more things that turn out to be nothing than to have too few. Also, we're just the first pass. The rest of the team will take a look too. So no pressure," she reassured me.

"Okay. That's good to know," I said with relief.

"The logs of estate visitors will probably be easiest," Annie said, pointing to a file on my screen. "Why don't you start with that one? I'll work on the individual lists—they tend to be sloppier."

Ready to get to work, we both tucked in to our individual screens when there was a knock at the front door. Annie looked up, startled, and furrowed her brow.

"We weren't expecting anyone today," she said as she got up.

Annie placed her laptop on the couch where she had been sitting and then walked over to the front door. Luckily, I was in easy hearing distance and I was positioned in view of the door, so I only had to lean a little bit to see what Annie was doing.

"Hello," Annie said very professionally to the stranger standing at the door. "How can I help you?"

"I have a delivery for Mrs. Clark," the stranger responded. Her voice undulated in a way that made it sound like there was a trio harmonizing with each word she spoke. It was mesmerizing and I instinctively leaned closer, trying to see who the voice belonged to, but Annie was blocking the person at the door.

"Was she expecting this?" Annie asked, still professional but now with a bit of an edge.

"Yes," the musical voice responded. I scooted closer to see if I could get a view of who was at the door. My knee bumped the coffee table, knocking over the mug with a clatter. I gasped and reached out to correct it and prevent all the papers under it from being covered in tea. I sighed in relief to discover that the mug was already empty before I knocked it over. The noise of the mug and my gasp must have caught the attention of Annie and the guest at the door. I looked up and made eye contact with the woman behind the musical voice. She was beautiful and wild. Her hair and dress flowed on the breeze as if they were in water. Her eyes were a piercing blue. But her mouth was set in a firm, unhappy line.

"Who is that?" the woman demanded. The words came out like a discordant chorus.

Annie replied sternly, "That is none of your business. She works here now. That's all you need to know."

I shrank back in my seat, confused at the exchange. The woman let out a scoff, but Annie's words must have persuaded her to not press the issue. The woman shoved a small, brown, cardboard box toward Annie.

"Just give this to Mrs. Clark," she said, the words not so discordant but not the same melody it was.

"I will. Thank you," Annie said brusquely, taking the box from her, and then closed the door behind her.

Annie placed the box on a small side table in the entrance. She grabbed a sticky note and marker out of a drawer, scribbled something on it, and then placed the note on the package. She walked back into the room with her face blank, not giving away anything.

"Sorry about that," Annie said, picking up her laptop, and then settled back on the couch. "Where were we?"

"Um. Who was that?" I asked with a mix of awe and confusion.

"That was just someone dropping off a package for Mrs. Clark," she replied.

"I gathered that part," I said. "And?"

I let the question hang in the air, not sure how to ask. Annie looked at me with eyes trying to convey innocence. It didn't work. I stared at her and raised my eyebrows.

"Oh, right," she said. "I need to send Mrs. Clark a message to let her know it's waiting in the hall for her."

"Annie," I said with mock exasperation. "Are you going to explain to me who that was?"

"Alright," she finally said. "I guess it's okay for you to know. Just maybe don't mention this to anyone. Helen wanted you to have a slower, more controlled exposure to otherworldly people."

"So that was someone otherworldly," I said with a bit of

skepticism. Up until this point, I still wasn't fully convinced that this wasn't some shared delusion.

"Yes," Annie said and then added quietly, "That was a siren. I didn't realize we were expecting them to drop something off today."

"A siren. Like the women who live in the oceans and draw people to their death with their singing," I said more than asked.

"Well, technically," Annie responded coyly. "But they don't really do the death part anymore. Most often it's just simple mischief that they are getting up to. Usually harmless."

I knew my mouth was hanging open; I was having trouble keeping it closed. I had mentally already decided to just accept the idea that supernatural and otherworldly people existed. But seeing one in person was entirely different. Maybe this was really true. I thought back to the conversation I had with Annie and Cam at lunch and then couldn't help letting out a small laugh. Annie looked over at me, confused.

"I can see what you were saying about Taylor Swift being a siren," I said, getting control of myself. "I'm on your side now."

"Right!" Annie proclaimed happily. "It makes sense. Please tell Cam next time you see her."

"I will. I promise," I said with a smile.

We both laughed a bit more and then decided it was time to get back to work. I wanted to keep talking about sirens and other things in this new world, but we had work to do and Annie was already clicking and typing up notes in her document.

I turned to my computer and opened up a document that looked like a ledger. There were tables with clear dates, times, names, and notes. It looked like the estate had anyone who visited sign in and out. The most recent visits were at the top. I scrolled down to the bottom to find that they had sent over exactly the last two months of the log.

I decided to start at the bottom of the list and work my way up. It shouldn't take me too long. There weren't that many visitors a day, and several days didn't have anything listed. Most of the names repeated and the purposes seemed reasonable. A lot of food and grocery deliveries. It took me a minute to remember that humans lived on the estate too and would need to be fed.

There were a few companies that signed in. It looked like they were maintenance-related items. I searched for the company names to see if they had websites and whether they matched what was listed on the log. Everything seemed to be a match and legitimate, but I flagged them anyway because they were all one-offs. Someone could have used a maintenance request as an opportunity to scope out the place.

Almost through the document, I had only flagged those few maintenance visitors and an individual's name that came every week at the same day and time. Those visits just had the note of *private visit* listed each time. Then on page two a new name written like a signature from the Declaration of Independence showed up: Mr. James Winthrop.

He had come to the estate less than two weeks before the abduction. A quick scan ahead showed that he had only visited once during the two months I had access to. He was there for one hour to visit Ms. Wadsworth, Jane's adopter and the other victim of the attack. No other notes about the visit.

My hairs immediately stood on end and a pull in my gut almost made me gasp out loud. This had to be something.

"Annie, I think I found something," I said, unable to just flag it and move on.

"What?" Annie said, genuinely interested as she leaned over to look at my screen.

I started talking too fast in all my excitement of finding something interesting. "Someone named Mr. Winthrop came to visit Ms. Wadsworth two weeks before the attack. And he only showed up this one time."

"Winthrop. Winthrop." Annie repeated the name mostly to herself. "That name sounds familiar. Let me check something."

She went back to her own laptop and started clicking through folders. I leaned over to watch as she went into a folder that looked like bios of individuals. She entered *Winthrop* into a search bar and one item returned. We both let out our held breath.

"Mr. Winthrop is a vampire." Annie said, "but he's not a member of the Northwest family. He's a member of the Southeast family."

"Why didn't the family tell us about this visit already? They had to have known," I asked.

She turned toward me with a smile. "I'm not sure, but this is a good find. That could really be something." The way she said it matched my excitement. "Flag that one as urgent in the document."

I flagged it and then finished up the rest of the document. Nothing more to flag. I was about to ask for another document when the phone buzzing on the coffee table startled both of us. It was a reminder that I had an end-of-day meeting with Helen.

"Sorry," I said softly, not wanting to disrupt her work. "I have a meeting with Helen in five minutes."

"Oh, that's alright. Thank you for the help," Annie replied. "If you get a chance, mention your find about Mr. Winthrop visiting the estate to Helen."

"I will, thanks," I replied. It was kind of Annie to call it my find. I was sure anyone would have noticed it in the log. I just happened to be the first one to review it.

HELEN'S OFFICE doors were open, so I hovered in the doorway at the set meeting time. She glanced up, smiled, and motioned for me to have a seat. I settled into the wing-back chair on the right. I'd brought my laptop with me to take notes or to show her the pack assignment if she asked. It sat comfortably in my lap.

"How are you settling in?" she asked to kick things off.

"Great," I replied. "I'm making good progress on the pack assignment, and the general briefing documents have been useful to fill in any questions that I have."

I held back from mentioning my frustration with the

Council's briefing document. She had said I could look through any of the files, but for some reason I felt a bit of hesitation to admit that I was reading about the Council.

"That's good. And how is the rest of the team treating you?"

"Good," I replied sincerely. "I had lunch with Annie and Cam today. Everyone seems very kind and competent and willing to answer questions I have."

Again I held back from sharing anything negative. It didn't feel like my place to bring up Hank's strange behavior from this morning. If there was something wrong or missing from Jordan's office, I was sure she'd bring it up to Helen.

"Great," Helen said. "I wanted to follow up on our conversation yesterday about your thirty-day probation."

I swallowed a lump in my throat and just nodded.

"I apologize for being vague yesterday. It's been a while since we've had a new team member join and I'm a bit out of practice with onboarding someone new," she admitted, and I smiled in response. It was a good sign that my new boss was self-aware and willing to apologize. "The basic thing that we'll be looking for in the next thirty days is a fit with the team and the work we do. As you can probably see already, we all tackle cases together, and they can be critical and stressful. It's important that we have trust and respect within the team.

"Specifically, I'll be looking for examples of you working with team members, speaking up in meetings, and being free with information." She paused after that as if to give me space to respond.

"That makes sense," I said simply. I made a mental note to write that down and be intentional about doing those three things over the next several weeks—not that it was outside of the normal for how I'd like to work.

"Also, at the end of the thirty days, I will be asking everyone to fill out an evaluation for you," Helen said, and I tried not to let my face drop.

Past experiences with peer feedback had not always been great. There had been a few cases where it felt like someone had a personal vendetta against me. Or it seemed like someone thought that being overly critical of me would make them look better. It was not my favorite form of evaluation.

"Okay," I said, but I made another mental note to get my hands on that form to see what they would be asked.

"Perfect. Any questions for me about anything?" Helen asked.

I knew that she was probably going to ask this. No questions about my assignments came to mind, but this was an opening to mention what Annie and I had just discovered in the visitor logs.

"Not a question really, but I did want to bring up that there was one person who stood out in the contacts review Annie and I were just working on. I flagged it in the file and mentioned it to Annie, but I'm not sure you've seen that yet."

I was hedging a bit, wanting her to know that I was following directions and not going rogue. She nodded her head to encourage me to keep going.

"He's a vampire with the Southeast family, Mr.

Winthrop," I offered. Helen tilted her head and narrowed her eyes in interest, so I kept going. "He visited Ms. Wadsworth at the estate about two weeks before the attack. There weren't any details about why he was there."

"Interesting," she responded sincerely, and a weight lifted from my shoulders. "Good work. We'll want to look into that more. I'm also glad to hear you are helping out on the case. Feel free to assist or shadow anyone, it'll be helpful for the case and a good way for you to learn more about what we do.

"Also," she continued, "there is a lot of information that may not make sense, especially early in the case. I encourage everyone to speak up if they have any theories, even a hunch."

Helen's words were encouraging. I don't like to think of myself as a people pleaser, but everyone likes to have their boss tell them they are doing a good job. It was also nice to have her permission to work with everyone else on the team. I wanted to do that anyway, but now I felt like it was expected.

We ended our meeting with an update on the pack research. She was pleased with the progress and reminded me that I had a couple of weeks so no need to rush through it. Also, I only needed to do a first pass so not to worry if I got stuck on anything that I couldn't find, just flag it and move on. I nodded my understanding but secretly I wanted to do more than what was expected on my first assignment. It felt like the best way to make a good impression.

9

————————

My third day in the office started much like the second. I stopped by the kitchen to grab some coffee and a lovely breakfast pastry that Mrs. Clark had prepared. Okay, it was two breakfast pastries. How am I to be forced to choose between a sweet and savory option? This was the third day in a row that there had been fresh-baked pastries. I didn't want to get my hopes up that this was an everyday thing, but I would be pleased if it was.

Settling into my desk and opening the laptop, I clicked through my normal start-of-day tasks on autopilot. First my emails. No spam to delete, which was weird but I guessed this was a new email address that folks didn't have. A couple group emails notifying everyone that documents had been added or edited in the shared case files. I tagged a couple to come back to after the morning meeting.

Next, Helen's email. I wasn't up to speed enough to

handle responses for her yet, but I could at least clean out junk and organize any emails that had come in recently. No spam here either, just a few inquiry emails I added to an existing folder her prior EA must have set up. I added the case notes emails to the folder I had created in her inbox for the new case yesterday.

Helen's calendar was pretty empty—a few recurring holds with very little information on what they actually were and the regular staff meetings for today. Very different than what I was used to, but this team seemed to be a one-big-case-at-a-time establishment. That didn't bother me.

Staff meeting would start at nine o'clock. I was there ten minutes before with my laptop ready to go. Both pastries were already consumed and I had a half-full cup of coffee to finish. I was determined to be first to the table and to contribute positively today. It was important to start checking off the goal of speaking up in meetings.

Everyone else filed in and made their way to what was becoming clear were unspoken assigned seats. This made it easier for me, and I liked the routine that the team clearly had. I opened the staff file I had started in my personal drive and added more notes about the team that would help in the future.

I was starting to see patterns in what their morning drink of choice was, if they brought breakfast with them or grabbed something from the sideboard set out by Mrs. Clark, noting if they were a sweet or savory breakfast person. I was glad to see that the majority were both. I wouldn't feel bad about bringing both options to the morning meeting in the future. It was common for everyone to have food or a drink at the meetings; this team loved their food.

I also noticed who from the team was early and who came in just in time. Annie was an early person. I saw her surprise when she got to the table and I was already there. Jordan and Hank came in with plenty of time to scope out the food options. Cam and Steve brought something with them and arrived right on time.

Helen arrived right on time as well, though I couldn't figure out her food pattern just yet; she seemed to mix it up every morning so far, although she did eat during the meetings along with everyone else. It was encouraging and a bit odd that no one had been late to a single meeting yet.

The little things that didn't really matter that much to most people mattered to me. It was fun to find the patterns. But I also believed those patterns could be helpful in the future to anticipate what the team might need. I was Helen's EA, but I also wanted to be a good team member, and little gestures of care were the best way I found to do that. Not in a creepy way—there was a line. Pattern finding was also a strategy I learned to help to calm my nerves and quiet the daydreaming that I tried hard to control, often with no luck.

Almost like magic, everyone had settled almost precisely at nine o'clock and Helen started the meeting.

"Per normal when we have an active case, we'll split morning staff into two parts, general and then case specific. Due to the urgency of this case, we'll start with the case-specific items. If we don't get to all the general items, we'll discuss async or regroup on them tomorrow." Helen kicked off the meeting with the introduction that was most likely for my benefit. "Steve, start us off please."

"As everyone knows, we met with the family two nights ago. They were able to provide more information about the search they conducted, the security measures of the estate, and the timeline of events. I've updated all of those write-ups into the shared case file." Turning to Helen, he continued, "The security report for the family will be in your inbox after this meeting. Let me know if there is anything you want changed on it."

Helen tilted her head slightly. I had learned that that was her normal way of indicating her understanding.

Steve continued his update: "The family seemed surprisingly forthcoming with most information this time—aside from the items noted yesterday revolving around why the attendant was delayed. However, everything matched what we expected, no big surprises. Signs do point to an external party involved based on the tracks discovered the next day and the unlikeliness that Jane would have attacked her adopter and left on her own. But we haven't ruled out an inside job yet." This wasn't new information from yesterday. It seemed like he was a bit disappointed not to have anything new to share.

Jordan, sitting to his left, picked up the thread. "Based on what the family confirmed about the blood replenishment needs of a five-month-old adoptee, we expect that whoever has Jane would need access to a blood bank or a large population of people who wouldn't, or couldn't, report blood loss. Or we'd see an uptick in emergency room visits or police reports if it was a rogue adoptee."

The last part seemed most ominous, and I made a mental note to keep a closer eye out walking home from the bus stop tonight.

"That's in addition to the blood that we think they have from Ms. Wadsworth," Jordan added. "Helen, did we get permission from the family to study Ms. Wadsworth's blood?"

"I was able to speak with them, but they said they'd need to get back to me," Helen answered. "I'll call them again after this meeting. But I don't think it's likely. Sorry."

"That's alright, I understand," Jordan said, a bit disappointed.

Everyone seemed to nod their heads knowingly, frustrated that the family would be keeping information from us that would be helpful. The family had asked for our help, but they picked and choosed how much they would help us.

"Anyway, she'd still need fresh blood, and we haven't seen any unusual upticks in ER visits in the areas that we think meet the potential paths of travel," Jordan continued, much to my relief. "So we are tentatively ruling out that Jane is on her own without support. Cam and I are going to expand the potential paths of travel and incorporate a factor of blood bank levels to see if we get a ping on any unusually low levels or usage volume." Jordan looked toward Cam to go next.

Cam continued the roundtable updates: "As Jordan mentioned, the paths of travel model is active and we'll continue to add new factors that may help narrow in both travel paths and areas that could hide Jane and support her blood replenishment needs. Right now we are focusing on the northwest, along the coast, as the most likely areas. The Rocky Mountain area seems too rural to get the blood they would need without detection."

Something nudged me. That all made logical sense, but something seemed off. But it wouldn't be helpful to just say that seemed wrong, so I kept it to myself.

"Excellent," Helen responded and wrote a quick note on her laptop. The group paused, letting her finish typing. "Hank, your update?"

"We've got the surveillance plans mapped out for the family and are ready when you give us the go," Hank said, looking at Helen. Steve had mentioned that they weren't ruling out an inside job yet, so it made sense that they'd want to surveil the family.

"Based on what we know right now, I do think we should start the surveillance. Any objections?" Helen queried the table.

Everyone seemed to consider the question and then shook their heads. I was surprised and intrigued that Helen asked the team that question. Historically, I've only ever seen bosses give orders and direction, not ask for consensus or general objections.

"Great. Hank, please keep us posted, normal update frequency and method for now." Helen nodded to Hank and turned toward Annie for her update. "Annie?"

"Linda and I updated and uploaded the files of both families to the case folder. We also did the first pass on the visitor logs and contact sheets." It was generous of Annie to include me in the update. Working with Annie had been great, but I had only reviewed one document and mostly I was organizing files. She had added in the information and pertinent questions that the team was now tracking down answers on.

"All of you have already started adding responses to the open questions and visitors we flagged. Thank you," Annie finished up and turned toward Helen.

The team continued to provide updates, going back and forth in a clearly practiced cadence. Helen would often prompt for more details or give direction on a task. Everyone took on tasks and offered assistance to each other when they felt it would be helpful. There was a steady ease and comfort that came from watching a well-running team work together.

"Thank you all. From reviewing the information, I think we are narrowing in on a potential individual." Helen left that hanging for a minute, not that I think she was the type to do dramatic pauses on purpose, but if she were, this was it.

"Linda, could you share with the team what you and Annie found in the visitor's log?" Helen asked, turning toward me.

"Oh, yes," I said, slightly startled. Annie had already covered our update. "We noticed that someone visited the estate about two weeks before the attack. They were there specifically to see Ms. Wadsworth." I looked at Annie for reassurance. She smiled and nodded her head. "The individual is James Winthrop. And he is a member of the

Southeast family" Quick glances around the table showed that no one was surprised, but they almost all had encouraging looks on their faces.

"Thank you, Linda," Helen said with a smile. "I know we haven't officially started surveillance, but it seems like we should start primarily with Mr. Winthrop."

I was startled a bit at her statement. I wasn't sure what I expected from sharing that name with her last night, but I didn't think it would become a primary lead for the whole group.

"A quick review of records yesterday showed that he has had some significant behavior pattern changes in the last few years and specifically in the last six months," Helen clarified to the group. "Also, we discovered last night that he recently purchased several pieces of property that aren't included in the Southeast family's estate portfolio. We need to double confirm, but it appears that there is one property that is within the Northwest family's territory."

There were at least two gasps around the table, indicating that having property in another family's territory was at least not common and more likely strongly against the rules. No one clarified for me, so I made a note to dig into that question later.

Helen continued on this lead, "While the property purchases and his known movement don't fit our timeline exactly, there is likely information that we don't have yet and need to get. He also has a history of strange actions that border on rule breaking according to most vampire customs. It seems more likely that a single family member could be culpable than the whole Southeast family. And his visit with Ms. Wadsworth prior to the attack is suspicious.

"Steve and Hank, please amend the surveillance plan if needed to give priority to Mr. Winthrop," Helen instructed, and all the heads nodded. The vibe in the room had shifted to the positive now that we had what looked like a promising lead.

TALKING over a lunch of quiche and salad that Mrs. Clark had masterfully prepared, I was grateful that I could pepper Annie with questions.

"Help me understand why vampires have territory but also houses in other territories. Seems like that wouldn't work," I asked between bites of my salad that I was trying to eat quickly so I could savor the quiche.

"The families established territories several centuries ago. I think the last time they changed was sometime in the eighteen hundreds," she replied. I nodded as I ate more of my salad so she would continue. "All the families have a lot of money, most of it in trusts so that it doesn't raise suspicion with governments, and they like to spend it. New family members are mostly considered because of their service to the family, but sometimes they adopt someone with wealth to bolster their holdings. It looks like this was the case with Jane."

"So Jane wasn't working for the family before her adoption?" I asked. This was probably in the case notes, but I couldn't remember.

"No, not for long," Annie confirmed and then added in

a bit of a whisper, "Her adoption was rushed. The paper-work just says 'extenuating circumstances.' But, it's pretty obvious that it was due to money."

"Interesting" was all I could say as I turned over that information in my head.

"She probably signed a lot of her portfolio over to the family," Annie continued, "if not all of it. It'd go into the trust and be used for the family, so any family member and many of their most trusted staff can basically get anything they want. They just need to ask."

I must have looked confused, but she took a small bite, so I filled the gap. "So the families have a ton of money," I said, summarizing what Annie had just explained. "I still don't understand why they'd be buying houses in another family's territory."

"If you were hundreds of years old, you'd run out of interesting property within your territory and things to fill said property pretty quickly. The families have an agree-ment that as long as you ask for permission, you can buy properties within others' territory. Think of it as little embassies throughout the world."

"Okay," I said, putting down my fork and leaning in. "Then why is Winthrop buying property outside of the family's portfolio a big deal?"

"It's just that it isn't usually done that way," she said, and I gave her a minute to take another bite before giving her a confused look. "I checked both the family records and the Council rules for Helen after the meeting this morning, and there doesn't seem to be anything techni-cally against the rules for Winthrop to do that. Assuming he's asked the Northwest family for permission," she concluded and started into her quiche.

I puzzled over it as we both ate more of our lunch in silence for a few minutes. For Mr. Winthrop—or just Winthrop as Annie and I had started to refer to him—to have property that was not purchased by and within the family's portfolio was very strange but not necessarily against the rules. It was also very strange for someone who just needed to ask for what they wanted. We still weren't sure if the Northwest family had given him permission to be in their territory.

"Why do you think he is buying property on his own?" I asked after Annie had a chance to finish her lunch.

"If he's getting property outside of a family's territory, it may be that he's working toward a division of a family," she replied factually, and I made a mental note to look up divisions. "But that hasn't happened in over three hundred years. I also don't think any of the families are big enough to divide like that."

I shrugged in reply—I both had no idea what a division was or how big a family needed to be.

"Whatever he is doing, it's likely not going to end up good." Her ominous reply was followed by her getting up and coming back with two slices of chocolate cake as I sat and thought through it.

I'd been doing more reading up in general about vampires between the morning meeting and lunch. The documents included useful information such as the fact that vampires did not have to avoid the sun at all costs. And older vampires, such as Winthrop, could withstand relatively normal amounts of time outside on a summer day. New adoptees had to be more careful because it took time for them to develop the tolerance.

The chocolate cake called to me, and I let the topic drop so I could dig in. There were three layers of the lightest cake sandwiched with rich, but not too sweet, chocolate frosting. The whole thing was then covered with a chocolate ganache. Some may say that was too much chocolate, but not me. It was the perfect ratio of cake to frosting. It was bliss.

After several bites of cake and a restrained sigh of satisfaction, I dove into another topic I couldn't make sense of: "The sun thing."

Annie laughed. "Yeah, the sun thing. Not what you thought, huh?"

"Vampires can be in the sun, but they don't like it," I summarized what I had learned earlier in the day.

She nodded and kept eating her slice of cake.

"And younger vampires, like Jane, would need to be more careful," I continued.

"Yep," she responded after licking the chocolate off her lips. "It's a skill that takes some time to learn. From what I understand it has something to do with how they can block or bend light. Jordan would know more if you're curious."

I gave her a puzzled look and my forkful of cake froze midway to my mouth. "That's alright. Just good to clear up some misunderstandings that I learned from popular culture."

"Yep. There's a lot of that," she said with a sigh.

"But they do consume human blood, right?" I asked.

"Not always just human blood, but yes," Annie said quite calmly. "But as you probably read already, the killing of humans for blood went out of favor in the sixteen hundreds."

Similar timing to when the Council was formed, I noted in my head, surprised that it wasn't annotated in the document by someone already.

"Donors are now generously compensated by the families—you can buy anything with enough money," she continued and then leaned in and whispered even though we were the only two in the kitchen, "Not that I'd recommend that lifestyle."

I just nodded and drank the last bit of my drink, and then a thought from Jane's case popped into my head. "If they don't kill humans anymore, why would Jane not being with the family potentially lead to killings?"

"Well, fully grown vampires can control themselves and not kill. Newly adopted vampires don't have that self-control yet."

My wide eyes and slight terror on my face just made her chuckle a bit.

"The last recorded killings by a vampire were in the late 1880s around London. That was due to a rogue adoptee during the early months post adoption," she shared as if that would soothe me. "The family had adopted and then 'lost' the adoptee."

"The air quotes you put around lost are not reassuring," I said, only somewhat jokingly.

"There are some rumors that it wasn't an accident but

an experiment to see how the government there would respond," she explained.

"And how did they respond?" I asked when she paused. I wanted to know more.

"Well, not great," Annie answered. "It started a period of vulnerability for all supernaturals, not just vampires. And the London family was severely punished. They are still working to reestablish their reputation, hence the lowest membership count of all the families. And why they are the only family known by the city they live in. Their territory was restricted to only London and they haven't grown enough to ask for an expansion."

Hank and Steve came into the kitchen before I could ask a follow-up question. Seeing us at the table, they both stopped talking. They silently served themselves some lunch and then walked out balancing their plates and drinks a bit precariously. I wasn't too concerned about it until Hank gave me a side-eyed look on his way out.

"Don't worry about them," Annie said, probably sensing my confusion. "They get a bit anxious and secretive when they are planning surveillance. They'll loop in anyone who is going with them, but they have a theory that surveillance plans are on a need-to-know basis. You and I will likely never need to know. But we will get the update at the morning meeting tomorrow."

This didn't help to change my feelings toward Hank for the better. I still hadn't forgotten about his snooping in Jordan's office. And I was still not able to place why he seemed familiar, and not familiar in a good way like Mrs. Clark was. No one else seemed to have a problem with him, although I hadn't seen him interact as freely or easily as the other team members did. I'd be keeping an eye on him and I'd try to find a way to learn what he had been doing in Jordan's office.

Annie didn't seem bothered by the secretiveness of Hank and Steve, so I didn't push her to talk about it. I tried to move my mind onto other important matters, like what Mrs. Clark would make for us to eat tomorrow.

THE REST of the afternoon was pretty boring for me. Everyone was busy with their own tasks. I read more about vampires, and everything confirmed what Annie had shared with me.

I watched the clock and didn't feel any guilt about packing up right at five to head home. The office was already pretty quiet. I said a quick goodbye to Helen to let her know I was heading out. She was on the phone and gave me a smile and nod. Everyone else was either in their office behind closed doors or already gone for the day.

As I made myself dinner that night, I thought about what I'd learned. The life of a vampire didn't sound so bad. Thinking about the state of my bank account right now, I wondered what they looked for in adoptees. But then again, I don't think I could drink blood even if I didn't have to kill for it. The frozen chimichanga I was heating up suddenly sounded delicious.

10

It turned out Annie was right: I wasn't need-to-know in terms of the surveillance plans. And I certainly wasn't on the surveillance team with Steve and Hank. So I wasn't looped into the plans that were being formed all afternoon yesterday. After dinner the rest of my evening was spent daydreaming about what the two of them were up to on the other side of town as I tried to watch TV.

After the general updates on the case in the morning meeting the next day, they gave the update on the stakeout. It seemed like Helen liked to save bigger updates for the end. This helped to keep people moving through everything still in progress and not get stuck on the new shiny thing in front of them.

The update from Steve and Hank was fairly bland. Neither of those two were keen on providing color commentary on the night nor had a flair for storytelling.

But based on their retelling and some light daydreaming of my own sprinkled in, this is how I imagined it went.

Picture Steve and Hank in a dark paneled van, but a really nice one. I can't imagine Helen would let them out in something dingy. It probably even had a mini fridge stocked with drinks and treats. Shelves and a pegboard on one side full of gadgets supplied by Cam. Maybe even a bank of monitors that they could use to watch the video feeds from cameras they'd placed. And those big over-the-ear head-phones to listen in on the bugs or wiretaps they'd planted. Basically anything you'd think of from a spy van in a movie.

The night is dark, cloudy, and a light mist settles over the street. It's Seattle in the fall, this is every night here, but I like the air of mystery it gives for the setting. From their report, they park up the hill a bit from the apartment that Winthrop had purchased about six months ago. They're positioned to have a good angle on anyone who may be coming or going.

According to them it's a stoic and no-nonsense stakeout for a reasonable amount of time. I like to picture them chatting about sports or movies. Maybe talking about a good book they've both read and what was next on their to-be-read lists. All the while passing binoculars between the two of them and pointing out things that may be of interest. Making notes on little flip notebooks like the investigators in TV shows carry.

Also, they are snacking on sandwiches and potato salad provided by Mrs. Clark. Obviously you'd have food on a stakeout. Even though they didn't mention that in their report. I've seen how they both eat. I can't imagine them going through the evening without dinner and snacks. Oh, and likely they had some of those chocolate chip cookies that we had for our afternoon snack yesterday.

Everything was still professional of course. They weren't the unprofessional type. But I bet it was a bit livelier than they described to the group sitting around the table. At least for their sake, I hope it was.

Skillfully, and also with a bit of luck, they spotted a redheaded woman walking up to the apartment's main entrance. She looked behind her and paused as if she was expecting someone. Shortly after she entered the apartment, our Mr. Winthrop followed her in.

They spotted both the redhead and Winthrop in a window of the apartment building. The two were talking and seemed amicable. The window shade was drawn before too long, so they don't know what happened next. There was no sign of other people and no sign of Jane.

Steve and Hank had taken some photos that they passed around the table. I was only going to give them a passing look as they came to me, but something caught my eye. The woman seemed tired. Not just that *it's raining and it's the end of the day* kind of tired. But a heavy tiredness, like they'd been carrying around a heavy weight for far too long. I didn't know this woman, and she may have been involved in a kidnapping, but an overwhelming sense of compassion for her hit me in the chest.

The image of Winthrop was more obscure. It was clearly him, even though you couldn't see his face. You could tell by his height against the doorframe, and it was almost like the rain illuminated by the back lighting in the picture was repelled by him. Also, the outfit felt like a dead giveaway—no pun intended. He was in layers of dark fabrics tailored to fit him perfectly, the collar of his black trench coat popped in the back to keep the rain away. I was a newbie to the existence of vampires, but how anyone thought Winthrop could be just a normal person was beyond me.

"We checked the paperwork on the apartment," Steve shared with the team. "It's just one of Winthrop's aliases. No second names are mentioned."

"We also cross-checked the woman's description with known associates and staff of both families," Hank chimed in. "No one who matches that description."

"Steve, can you reach out to some of your contacts to see if they can help us identify the woman?" Helen asked, turning toward him. Steve nodded his head and made a note. I was curious about who those contacts could be, but there was no time to ask. Helen was moving right along with the meeting. "Good work. Let me know when we get a name on the woman. But I think we have enough for me to politely ask Mr. Winthrop to come chat with us."

Steve and Hank both nodded. Then Steve offered, "There is a silver lining for us that the word has gotten out to all the families about Jane. They would expect us to make some contact about the matter, and Mr. Winthrop is technically outside of his family's territory, so it won't seem odd that we'd like to talk with him."

The news that Jane's disappearance had been

spreading through the families had been shared first thing in this morning's meeting. I wasn't surprised. While everything I read and heard from Annie about vampires made it sound like they were a dignified, old-money type of group, they also sounded like a bunch of gossips. Nothing stayed secret between the families, and that had clearly led to conflicts in the past. I guessed when you lived so long, anything new or of note would be interesting to talk about.

Heading downstairs to freshen my tea after the conclusion of the morning meeting, I couldn't help but smile a bit when I overheard Steve compliment Mrs. Clark on the potato salad, sharing that he especially liked it with the extra pickles she had added this time. I knew there was food involved in their stakeout.

THE OFFICE WAS in a buzz with Helen's decision to bring Winthrop in for questioning. Apparently hosting a vampire in the office was an anomaly and had some protocols that needed to be followed. Annie assured me that she and Mrs. Clark had a handle on it and would let me know if there was anything I could help with.

With all the commotion, I didn't have a chance to talk to Jordan. Probably for the best—I wasn't sure how to bring up the fact that Hank was in her office without sounding paranoid, so I'd let it go for another day. But I was still keeping my eye on him.

Annie and I got to work in the small back conference room, moving out the small table and chairs. Nicer arm chairs, a rug, a coffee table, and some side tables were brought in along with other decor that came from the upstairs suites and the basement. Additionally the heavy drapes were pulled closed.

"Just because they can be in the sun doesn't mean they like it," Annie had informed me as we finished setting up the room.

Helen walked by while we were completing the finishing details. "This looks great. I like the new setup."

"Thank you," Annie replied for the both of us. I smiled my thanks. Annie had done the bulk of the work. I was just another pair of hands.

"I think we should keep it this way," Helen declared, surveying the room more closely. "It'll be nice to have a space that is a little more informal for interviews. Not so business-y."

"Well," Annie started with some hesitation in her voice, "we did pull a lot of this from rooms upstairs."

Helen just nodded her head and walked around the edge of the room. We moved into the middle so that she could continue walking around and thinking.

"I guess we'll need to do some redecorating upstairs then," Helen said, and Annie grabbed my arm in excitement. "The rooms needed some updating anyway. Annie, do you think you have capacity to take that on? Maybe after the current case?"

"I would love that!" she said and squeezed my arm tighter.

"Send me a budget proposal before you buy anything," Helen concluded on her way out the door.

Annie finally released my arm and moved to stand

right in front of me. She scrunched her nose in excitement. "I love spending the company's money redecorating. Helen never seems to care about the budget in the end. Do you want to help?"

I was a bit taken aback. I had never worked for a boss that didn't care about the budget. I'd also never gotten to redecorate an office, let alone a suite of bedrooms in an office-slash-mansion. Having not seen them yet, I wasn't sure what I was getting myself into, but I wasn't about to turn down this offer.

"Yes, of course," I said, and Annie squealed a bit.

"Great. Everything looks good in here," she said, turning in a circle to take in the room. "Let's go see if Mrs. Clark needs help with anything."

MRS. CLARK WAS in the kitchen. She had pulled out a unique glass tea set, and I sat with her and Annie to help give it a quick polish, ensuring that there were no finger-prints to be found. Hank had been sent out on an errand to gather what Annie would only refer to as *refreshments* that would end up in this glass. We all clearly knew what it was, and I was determined to assume it was from a blood bank and that we didn't have donors on retainer. As we started polishing, the conversation turned to what I'd been learning about this new otherworld.

"What has been the most interesting thing you've learned?" Annie asked to start up the conversation between the three of us.

"Probably how rare vampires are." I started off with an

easy and not conspiratorial opinion, not ready to share any real concerns or big questions I had yet. Surprisingly, Mrs. Clark made a small snort of what I think was disgust in reaction to my answer.

"Yeah, there aren't as many as you'd think," Annie responded, either not hearing Mrs. Clark's snort or deciding to ignore it. I searched Mrs. Clark's face to see if I could make sense of her displeasure. Her demeanor had settled quickly back into her normal calm.

"What else?" Annie prompted.

"I guess also that their territories don't touch," I offered. "It seems strange that the different families haven't claimed all the territory they can."

"Vampires don't rule the globe," Mrs. Clark said, sounding offended.

"Oh, I'm sorry." I backtracked as fast as I could. "I didn't mean to imply that. I'm not sure how it works."

Annie took pity on me and intervened. "You haven't had time to learn about the other groups, and we probably don't have a comprehensive map of territories that overlays everyone. That would actually be a fun project —we should look into that together when this case is over."

"It's taken centuries, but we have come to a balance," Mrs. Clark told us, her usual motherly patience back in her tone. "The vampire families do take up a lot of space in the world. They are a very powerful and influential force. But when you learn more, you'll see that everyone should have what they need to prosper."

"Does the Council help manage territories?" I carefully

threw out this question, hoping not to offend but also trying to learn more about the Council.

Mrs. Clark didn't look offended, and Annie kept a straight face. But there was an uncomfortable pause after my question. Finally Mrs. Clark answered, "They can be called on to handle disputes if necessary. And, I suppose they were instrumental to the balance in the earlier days of their existence," she said calmly. "But nowadays everyone tries to manage between themselves. Without the Council's interference."

The last line was said as a forceful statement. Not so much for my sake, but almost as if Mrs. Clark was asserting her own right not to have the Council interfere. It already felt like I had danced around a line of questioning that was sensitive for her, so I decided not to push the issue further. We finished up polishing quickly and in mostly comfortable silence.

WINTHROP ARRIVED PROMPTLY at the designated time of eleven thirty that morning. He was driven up to the front walk in a sleek black car. Cam whispered to me with a touch of awe that it was a Rolls-Royce Ghost. She seemed impressed, so I responded with the appropriate oohs and aahs.

Cam, Annie, and I were trying to watch discreetly from the second-floor window over the front of the house. Cam's idea, not mine. She said this would be a great chance for me to see if I could figure out what made a vampire stand out now that I knew he was one.

My heart was racing—this was finally a chance to see if this was all some group delusion or if this was real. The back passenger door of the car opened and a tall, dark-haired man dressed very modernly in all black walked up to the front door. The outfit matched what I expected and what was likely his normal style. Even at this distance you could see that they were all dark colors, tasteful, tailored, and quietly expensive.

He looked like his pictures, but what I can only describe as more. He seemed to pull the light outside toward him, creating a glow. I thought about how silly I thought the books were that described vampires as glittering, but I could now see how this could be interpreted as that.

Helen already had the front door open before he hit the first step. Winthrop's gaze tilted up as he climbed the stairs. He looked up to the window that the three of us were standing at, made eye contact with me, and smirked. The three of us all ducked down like we were teenagers who had been caught spying.

We weren't told we couldn't observe from upstairs, so I didn't feel too bad, but I was embarrassed. I could feel my ears going red and I was a little flushed. Cam and Annie didn't seem as affected based on the laughing that they were trying with little success to control.

The driver moved the car a little ways up the street to park as soon as we heard the front door close. Helen was only permitting Steve to join the interview of Winthrop. She said that we'd all be briefed after the conversation.

Additionally, no recording would be made—as was protocol, Annie reassured me.

The three of us hesitantly made our way back to our respective desks. It was clear that we all wanted to know what was going on and, given the chance, would have continued our not-so-covert spying efforts. Unfortunately, I was nowhere near close enough to accidentally overhear any conversation happening in the back conference room, now affectionately called the back parlor by everyone but Hank.

After the quiet laughter died down and I had settled behind my desk, I realized that the vibe throughout the office was pretty tense, likely both because we had our first solid lead and because there was currently a vampire on the premises. I focused all the attention I could muster on my research assignment for the pack. I was making good progress and hadn't hit any major walls yet.

To get through it quickly, I had decided to fill in all the easy sections or anything I could uncover quickly, tagging anywhere that would take more effort to come back for later. This was so I could get a better sense of how much in-depth research work would be needed and plan out the rest of my time on the project better.

I had just finished up the fifth individual, and the picture of these individuals' lives and what I then assumed the pack looked for in recruits was becoming clear. They were all over thirty; the oldest so far was forty-seven. Everyone had a steady employment record, though their industries varied widely. Nothing too flashy for jobs, no

CEOs, politicians, or pop stars. Everyone also had very little social media presence.

That was normally my go-to for finding small details about someone. But all of these folks either had no social media to speak of, or they had profiles that only contained things like the occasional happy birthday wall posts clearly from more distant relatives and friends from high school.

No one on the list had any criminal records, not even unpaid parking tickets. They all had library cards for various Boston and small-town libraries around the area, an insignificant detail but something that I found interesting. Bank records were also clean; those had been part of what the pack submitted.

Bank databases were not one of the government databases that Cam had set me up with. All of the transactions seemed normal. No wild swings in outgoing or incoming money. No extravagant spending habits. No weird recurring payments that could signify blackmail or bribes. The money side seemed like it would be the most interesting, but they were all clean.

There was one strange thing about all of these folks that made sense as I thought about it. It also made me sad. No one on the list had living parents, siblings, or nieces and nephews. And no one was married or had children of their own. If my life continued the way it was going, I may be an ideal pack recruit candidate in three years.

. . .

I was just starting to dig into the sixth and final individual when I heard the now familiar clicking of Helen's steps walking toward my desk. My smile of excitement to hear about how it went faded fast when I looked up and saw that she wasn't alone. No other footstep sounds had accompanied her, but Winthrop was walking just two paces behind. Upon seeing him walk in, my ears went red hot and I felt flushed again.

"Linda, I need you to come in and be an official recorder for Mr. Winthrop and me," Helen said calmly and firmly. My palms started to sweat but I gathered my things and followed them into her office.

11

Helen settled gracefully behind her desk. Winthrop had taken the chair on the left. I sat in my normal chair on the right facing Helen's desk. I was getting a flashback of the conversation in this room from last Friday. It was hard to believe that hadn't even been a week ago. So much had happened and now I couldn't deny that there were otherworldly beings in this world. Sitting next to Winthrop, I tried to control my breathing as I snuck glances at him to take in what I could.

Winthrop was taller, darker, more handsome, and much scarier than Steve had been sitting to the side of me last week. It was even clearer now sitting close to him that he impacted the light around him. It pulled toward him subtly and made a slight glow encircle him. He sat up straight but looked completely relaxed. He looked ahead of him but didn't seem to focus on anything specific. His body didn't move and I couldn't see any rise or fall of his chest. The only movement was a slight clenching in his jaw every thirty seconds or so.

Helen didn't seem to be in a hurry to get started. She let us settle in and moved some papers around on her desk like she was waiting for something. Winthrop and I both sat frozen as she prepared her desk and her thoughts. It turned out that she had been waiting for Annie.

Annie rolled in the tea cart and served Winthrop a small glass from the set we had polished earlier and a cup of tea to Helen. She gave me a conspiratorial and secret nudge as she set some tea down on my side table. We made eye contact as she backed the cart out of the room; she looked excited. I can only assume I looked terrified. I was sure I'd have some stories to tell her after this meeting.

"Mr. Winthrop, thank you again for agreeing to move the rest of our conversation to my office," Helen kicked things off now that we all had refreshments. It was clear that she was strict about refreshments when hosting someone. "And Linda, thank you for joining us." She gestured slightly toward me. "With Steve needing to step away, I've asked Linda to come record notes as I do not allow recording devices in my office."

I was pretty certain Steve's calendar was clear and I couldn't think of anything that would have taken him out of the meeting with Winthrop. Helen had said during the interview tour that clients didn't usually come up to the second floor, but I guess exceptions are made for vampires. The confused look on my face must have caught Helen's attention. She very subtly shook her head, and I straightened out my face.

"Thank you for having me," Winthrop responded in a guttural, deep, and—not to be too cliché—dripping with sex voice. I didn't realize that he hadn't spoken around me yet. I also didn't know that my vagina could be voice activated.

Generally I romantically leaned more toward women, nonbinary folks, and more feminine men, but his deep voice did things to me that I shouldn't even have been thinking about while I was at work. Helen looked my way, and I swear she knew what I was thinking and that she was smirking at my reaction. Shaking my head to clear it, I focused on my notepad, ready to take notes.

"Now, can you help me understand why you were visiting Ms. Wadsworth two weeks ago at the Northwest family estate?" Helen asked in a way that wasn't a question but a demand.

Winthrop squinted his eyes in a slight reaction. "Ms. Wadsworth was offering me recommendations on property in the Northwest territory to consider," he replied calmly. "She has exquisite taste and I'm looking to move to a more rural location in the area."

Helen didn't react. I tried hard to control my face. His answer came across as true but leaving out details, like when you don't want to lie but really don't want to share everything. I waited to see if Helen would push him for more clarity. She didn't. She let the silence hang in the air and didn't let up eye contact. Winthrop finally gave in, like we all do under Helen's stare.

"As I said downstairs, it is understandable that you would come to the conclusion that you did," Winthrop continued. "I, too, am worried about the missing adoptee and do not judge you for investigating to the fullest extent needed. My family has assured me that they have conducted a thorough search in our own territory and have found no trace of the adoptee."

Winthrop sounded both sincere and patronizing at the same time. According to the documents Annie and Jordan had given to me to read, he was over five hundred years old and one of the oldest vampires in his family. I suppose if I were that old, I might feel parental to anyone less than a hundred years old as well. Helen didn't seem to take any offense to his tone, so I told myself not to either.

"However, while there is a small deception in what I was doing, it is not related to the missing adoptee, nor is it technically contrary to the rules of the families." He paused, definitely for dramatic effect. He looked deeply at Helen and then luckily not as deeply at me for a quick second before he continued, "I will tell you my story so that you may ascertain both the true intent and the facts of the situation.

"A vampire's life is long. Novel experiences become few and far between. It is not uncommon for vampires to engage in very brief love affairs with humans. You are fleeting and your vulnerability can provide an excitement that isn't found in a vampire mate. As long as discretion is maintained about our nature and they do not act as a donor, it is unspoken that any such affair is just that. An affair.

"Any deviation from the rules will be dealt with severely. No one has needed to be dealt with in several centuries. I myself have engaged in many appropriate affairs over the centuries."

Helen nodded her understanding and I made a few notes, trying very hard not to be obvious even though Helen had been clear that I was here to take notes. It seemed awkward, but I didn't want to miss anything that may have been important later on. I also wondered what a five-hundred-year-old's definition of *many* would be.

"The norms and customs are clear. Human partners are not to be informed, they are not to be donors, they are not to be adopted, and they are not considered mates."

That was the second time he had mentioned mates. I tried to remember what I had read about vampires and mates. If I was remembering correctly, not all vampires mated, and when they did it was considered binding for the rest of their existence. Until the second death, you could say. It was a very serious undertaking. I was pretty sure I remembered correctly that Winthrop, although five hundred years old, had never been mated.

"Also, no vampire would even think to ask the family for a human partner to be adopted or considered for a mate." He paused again, longer and more dramatic this time. I held my breath. "At least that's how I felt until three years ago."

Winthrop had been telling his story with a poem-like cadence. I found myself leaning forward. Helen looked similarly interested. This reveal had us hooked. We both nodded our heads slightly to urge him to continue.

He smiled a bit slyly at our obvious interest and picked up the cadence of his story, "Three years ago I met Angela.

Angela has the type of beauty and grace that I am often drawn to. I sought her out with the intention of having the typical brief and respectable affair. After several months I knew that what we have is not typical."

"What?" I whispered under my breath. At least I thought I had whispered it, but Winthrop's head snapped my direction. I quickly shut my mouth, but my wide eyes gave away my terror and embarrassment. Helen saved me with a subtle clearing of her throat. Winthrop turned back toward her and resettled into his statue-like posture.

"Not wanting to end the relationship but feeling the need to keep it discreet," he emphasized, "I have moved Angela into a new location every six months. We have continued our relationship and we will continue our relationship as we see fit."

He had made the proclamation firmly, but the clenching of his jaw came back after he said it. Helen and Winthrop both let the statement hang in the air longer than I was comfortable with. I was intent on keeping my mouth firmly shut. We could wait until dinnertime for all I cared; I was not saying another word.

Finally, Helen broke the silence. "I appreciate your candor with us and I understand the reason behind you wanting to keep it discreet. However, this puts me in a precarious position."

Winthrop growled softly behind closed lips. The room darkened, the light shrinking away from him, now pulling into the edges of the room. Helen didn't seem intimidated. I was lucky I didn't need to change my pants and that I wasn't alone in the room with him. Up to this point I'd been fascinated with this vampire, but now I saw the side of him that was a predator. I really hoped that Helen knew what she was doing.

"As I said, I understand the sensitive nature of what you have disclosed," Helen reassured him and tilted her head slightly in empathy.

Everyone really loves the word discreet *around here.* I amused and distracted myself from the scary creature sitting next to me with that thought. *Maybe I should start a tally.* But it was hard to ignore my heart beating loud enough that someone with an ear pressed against the door could probably hear.

"Here is my recommendation," Helen proceeded calmly and with a measured pace. "We will record this conversation officially. However, we will not submit it to shared records. I do believe that you are not involved with the missing adoptee. I also believe that you understand the magnitude of the situation you are currently in."

Winthrop relaxed a bit and the lighting in the room went back to normal, slowly returning to surround him. I made a mental note to find out if shared records were the same as Council records. Helen wasn't done with her recommendation, and I refocused on what she was saying.

"We are designated reporters to the Council. But I have dispensation to act within reasonable bounds and at my own discretion. Should your situation escalate—and we will know if it escalates—" Her tone was more promise than threat. "—then we will release this record, any additional records, and the appropriate recommendations to the family. And to the Council."

Helen was a badass boss, and had this been anyone other than a five-hundred-year-old vampire, I bet they would have been in tears. I was proud to work for her and only a little more terrified of the supernatural being sitting within arm's reach of me than getting on her bad side.

"I understand," Winthrop replied.

"Thank you. And thank you again for coming to speak with us," Helen said to close out the meeting. "We'll be in touch as needed."

"You're most welcome," he said as he unfolded from the chair, clearly done with this conversation as well. He bowed slightly to Helen, then turned to me and inclined his head. "Welcome to the community, Linda, it was a pleasure to meet you. Even though the circumstances were not ideal."

It may have been my imagination, but I think he winked at me as he said that. I was glued to my seat. Helen followed Winthrop out the door. A few deep breaths and some calming words to my head and my lady parts set me back to mostly normal.

I finished up my notes so that I wouldn't miss anything when I typed them up, and stayed put in Helen's office in the hopes that she'd fill me in on what had just happened. There were clearly things unsaid that both Helen and Winthrop understood. I wanted to understand as well.

WHEN HELEN RETURNED after several minutes, I was still sitting in the chair in front of her desk. She didn't seem surprised to find me still there. Feeling more fully in control of myself, I asked her what came next.

"We record the notes you took in our files only. I'll show you the correct files to access and add them to." Helen didn't expand on why we had files with limited access and who normally had access to our files other than us. I assumed the Council did, but was there anyone else? I didn't press for answers, but I did wait a moment to see if she'd continue explaining what had just gone down.

Helen spoke firmly, driving home what I already felt from the lingering chills of Winthrop's growl. "You might not fully understand the seriousness of this information yet, but I need to impress on you the need to keep this confidential. Of course, members of this team will be privy to the information as it might be applicable to future cases," she confirmed. Good news for Annie; I did have a story to tell and this felt like permission to share, with some color commentary of course. I wasn't sure who else Helen thought I'd be telling work stories to.

"If you don't mind me asking," I ventured, and Helen nodded her head for me to continue. "Why does Mr. Winthrop and Angela's relationship need to be a secret? It seems like the families don't mind relationships between vampires and humans."

"The length of their relationship is outside of normal bounds. More importantly, in this case there is a key fact that was left unspoken during the meeting: I'm quite sure that Mr. Winthrop would like to formally mate Angela," she said, ending with a slight sigh. "As he mentioned, there is no history of affairs with mortals leading to adoption and subsequent mating. I'd need to review the historical rules and guidelines to know if this is just a norm or actual family law."

Helen seemed almost sad about the doomed nature of their relationship. I added another mental line to my growing list of questions to see if I could dig up anything on vampire mating.

Helen shook off the sadness quickly and asked me, "Any thoughts or feelings that came to your mind during the conversation with Mr. Winthrop?"

Caught off guard, I couldn't imagine she wanted to know about the unprofessional feelings that I had fought to tamp down. "Nope," I squeaked out, a bit too teenage-like.

"Okay, well if anything comes up, please let me know."

NOTES WERE QUICKLY TYPED and filed how Helen had instructed. With only a short window before lunch, I tried hard to concentrate on the task with only moderate daydreaming about a certain voice. Soon enough it was lunchtime and I found myself in the kitchen with Annie.

As we huddled over the lunch of cheesy, layered lasagna, garlic bread, and a green salad provided by Mrs. Clark, Winthrop's visit was the obvious topic of conversation. It didn't take too much prompting for me to fill Annie in on what I felt was appropriate with a bit of color added in. Maybe too much color thanks to Annie's prompting and lighthearted teasing.

A throat clearing silenced both of us mid sentence.

Looking over my shoulder toward the fridge, I saw the worst possible person it could be. Hank was lurking in the open fridge door. Annie must have seen my face shift as Hank left the kitchen with a soda in hand.

"Don't worry about it, we all talk about cases together. Just don't do it outside of the office," Annie reassured and warned me. "Also, I'm sure you read that vampire's voices have an almost hypnotic effect of lust on everyone. I'm not surprised you responded that way, especially for your first encounter."

"Annabel Joanna Anderson," I said in my most exasperated but playful mom voice. "I did not know that! And you didn't think to give me any warning before I was in a closed room with a vampire?"

Annie struggled to respond through her laughter, "First, that is not my full name."

"I know," I acknowledged. "I don't know your full name yet but this behavior called for a full-name reprimand."

"Second," she continued, choosing not to give me her correct full name, "I had no idea that you would end up talking with him. We weren't supposed to be in the interview."

"Okay. You are right about that," I conceded. "I forgive you. But next time you need to warn me about stuff like this."

"I promise to give you more appropriate warnings," she said, holding up her hand to pledge it. "To make penance I'll tell you about my first time meeting a vampire."

"Deal. But first let's grab dessert and a tea refill," I suggested. Brownies and tea secured, we settled back into our corner of the kitchen table. Luckily we were still the only ones in the kitchen, unless Hank was lurking right out of sight to listen in.

"So spill," I urged her and then took a big bite of the gooey, caramel-and-chocolate brownie. It was still slightly warm and I wasn't embarrassed at all that some of the caramel clearly dribbled on my chin.

"It was several years ago," she started off. "We were out at the family's estate to serve them a notice from the local coven. I can't remember exactly what it was about, but I don't remember it being a big deal in the end. Some small squabble probably. They let me come along because I hadn't been around vampires much and Helen wanted me to have some exposure."

I nodded and ate another bite, only slightly feeling bad that her brownie was getting cold. She owed me a story.

"Steve and I were waiting in the sitting room as Helen talked with one of the family members. One of them, a woman, came into the room and just stood off to the side not saying a word."

"What? That seems strange," I interjected.

Annie nodded and I patiently waited as she chewed and swallowed a bite of her brownie. Chasing it with a drink of tea, she continued, "I thought so too, but Steve just sat still and didn't say anything. He looked a little flustered but didn't even acknowledge her, so neither did I." Another bite and sip of tea. "The woman circled the room and then came and stood right in front of us. She looked at both of us for probably only a minute at most, but it felt like ten minutes. Then she turned to leave and said, 'Be good, darlings.' And then she walked out of the room." Annie paused and I could almost hear the words echoing in the room with us as if she were there. "If Steve hadn't been there, I would have followed her out of the room. I actually got up to do just that, but Steve grabbed my arm and held it down," she concluded. Her eyes peeked up over her mug of tea, watching for my reaction to her story.

"Wow. That's intense," I said, thinking about what I would have done. If it had been like Winthrop, I would have followed her too.

"Yep," Annie said, taking the last bite of her brownie. "Steve has never said anything about it. I'm not even sure he told Helen."

The knowledge about this phenomenon and Annie's story helped me feel a bit better about my reaction—and worse at the same time because I still wanted to just sit and listen to him all day. I also wouldn't mind meeting the woman vampire either, just maybe not by myself.

12

———

Everyone gathered around the table for the one o'clock all-eyes meeting that Helen had scheduled, including Mrs. Clark. Apparently all-eyes meant all-eyes. It was the first meeting I had seen Mrs. Clark in. She sat at the end of the table in a chair that matched but wasn't normally there. We were in the same row, so it was hard to glance at her without being obvious.

Mrs. Clark was still a bit of a mystery to me. She consistently kept the kitchen stocked with delicious foods. Breakfast and lunch were always perfect. After my second day, I'd started skipping breakfast at home and coming a bit earlier so that I could eat what she'd prepared.

But it seemed no matter what time I came in to get food, she wasn't there or was just on her way out. I'd had two interactions with her: one brief and the other a bit uncomfortable. If I was more sensitive, I'd think that she was purposefully ignoring me. Just me; I know I'd seen her talk more with other team members in passing.

I wasn't able to linger on the problem. Helen was at the head of the table now. Annie had already done her rounds of ensuring everyone had what they needed to be comfortable. Laptops and drinks filled the table and everyone seemed ready to get started.

"As you've all heard by now, Mr. Winthrop has been cleared of involvement in Jane's disappearance," Helen kicked things off, and everyone nodded understandingly if not a bit grimly. We all knew that the clock was ticking and the outcomes were looking less and less likely to be good the longer Jane was missing. "At this point, we need to bring everything back to the table and reexamine all possibilities." Helen turned to me, and I hoped she didn't think I had the answers. "Linda, this is your first all-eyes meeting."

I nodded, as if she needed me to confirm the obvious. She smiled back at me and kept going.

"In an all-eyes meeting, we take it in three parts. First, we'll roundtable on any information that seems pertinent; just share what is top of mind for you. Next, we'll select the top three theories and then split into groups to dive deeper. Linda, we'll have you go with Cam and Steve. After the small-group brainstorm, we'll come back together and present to the broader group. We'll repeat this as needed and mix up the groups to get fresh eyes on a theory."

Everyone looked excited to get started. I was excited to get started too and to help find an answer.

"It's one o'clock. Let's time the first round to end by three and then we'll see how we are feeling about another round," Helen concluded and we were off.

The roundtable portion went about how I thought it

would. A few new ideas were shared and it was interesting to hear what came top of mind to everyone. Some theories were more interesting than others, including Jordan's and Cam's.

"Even though we weren't able to get a sample of Mrs. Wadsworth's blood for analysis," Jordan started off with a disappointed tone, "I do think that the blood properties needed would last in the stolen blood for a while. But they would be deteriorating and wouldn't have the same impact. If Jane is using that blood, she is probably getting sicker every day. She may have longer than the few weeks we first expected, but not much."

"The travel pattern models that we've been keeping updated indicate that Jane and her abductor could be just about anywhere by now," Cam shared with a similar disappointment.

Jordan added, "If Winthrop is right about the Southeast family's search, and her abductor is smart, she's likely in a borderland between vampire territories."

"You're right," Cam replied. "She could be on the other coast, or even in a different country by now. Especially if her abductor has access to Jane's personal financial accounts."

Helen turned to ask Hank, "Have we been able to get access to those yet?"

"No," Hank said with a frown. "The accounts are all international and they are being difficult."

My ears perked up a bit about the mention of the possibility of her being anywhere at this point. It made sense to me that someone who would kidnap a vampire from a family estate would need to be well financed and well connected to even attempt such a thing. I also thought that if I ever abducted someone, I'd want to get them as far away from the people who would be looking for them as possible.

Mrs. Clark's turn was the most interesting. I didn't realize she was up to date on the case, but Helen had stressed multiple times that everyone on the team had access and should be kept in the loop. Mrs. Clark was on the team.

"For centuries vampires have been the most influential group within the community," Mrs. Clark shared. She spoke like she was telling a story. "However, vampires have been on shaky footing as the group with top social standing for the last few decades."

All eyes around the table were focused on her, waiting for her to continue. No one interrupted or typed on their laptops.

"In their weakened state, another group may have a motive to sow distrust among the families as a way to further destabilize them," she continued, and as I glanced around, I saw some lightbulbs start to switch on in other people's eyes. "We should consider other groups and what they have to gain."

At her conclusion, Hank and Annie looked surprised, but Steve, Jordan, and Cam nodded in understanding and agreement. We'd been mostly focused on the conflict between the vampire families up to this point. Helen did not look surprised at the news or the idea. She looked impressed and gave Mrs. Clark one of her approving half smiles.

I was last in the group to go. Everything I had been thinking had already been brought up by another team member. The expectations I needed to meet to pass my probation were top of mind for me. But that's not what Helen was looking for. I needed to speak up and be free with information, but I didn't have anything to add.

"Everything I was thinking about has already been shared," I said as calmly as I could even though my heart was pounding. I felt dumb for not having anything to add. This for sure would be a count against me for my probation evaluation.

"That's okay," Helen said sincerely. "If you do think of anything you'd like to add, feel free to share at any time."

I nodded and tried to calm myself down. I told myself that I didn't need to be perfect and I did go last. Maybe it was common for the last person in these types of exercises to have nothing new to add.

"Alright, let's narrow it down to our top three theories," Helen said, continuing on to the next phase of the exercise. "Remember, we aren't discounting any theories. We are just picking the first three to explore."

The whiteboards had filled with more circles and spiderwebs connecting the ideas and information. The most interesting and compelling was Mrs. Clark's. At the end of the roundtable, we had three main theories highlighted. One, another rival family jockeying for position and using Jane as a pawn. Two, Jane was dead and a family member was hiding that fact. And three, Mrs. Clark's suggestion of another supernatural group trying to sow distrust.

We split into the three groups and had topics assigned by Helen to each group. Cam, Steve, and I were taking Mrs. Clark's new rival group theory; Jordan, Hank, and Annie had the *Jane was dead* theory; and just Helen and Mrs. Clark were going to continue on the rival family theory. It seemed like they did this a lot, but the group's sizes felt off. I wondered if I was the extra throwing off the groups or rather if there was a missing ninth person.

Cam, Steve, and I relocated to the kitchen so we could talk through ideas more easily. We didn't have many notes and files as this wasn't something that had been dug into yet. Cam grabbed some sticky notes, paper, and pens for us to use to brainstorm. They wanted to keep it in hard-copy format to brainstorm, then we'd transcribe and take pictures to add to the case file. Steve wanted to start with listing out the larger supernatural subgroups so that we could think through what motives each may have.

It was fascinating to hear them list and then talk through each of the groups. I took notes as I hadn't made it past the vampire and werewolf sections in the briefing documents that Annie had shared with me.

We started off with witches. They were the most common with populations much higher than vampires or werewolves. But unlike vampires and werewolves, witches were less organized. It was typical for them to form groups or covens. The covens had territories similar to vampires, but unlike vampires with their families or werewolves and their packs, witches were not required to join a group.

Also, witches' gifts of magic were hereditary. New witches were born, not recruited and made.

Like human genetics, witches mostly followed family lines, but powers could skip generations or pop up unexpectedly. Witches were required to register with the Council and would be easy for us to get more information on. There was an established coven in the area and there were also other known witches living around here. We made a note to research any witches residing within the family's territory and who had a history of run-ins with them.

The fey folk, on the other hand, did not have to register with the Council. The fey folk was a general group designation that included a lot of different species and types. Little was known about them and we quickly moved past them. There was absolutely no history of them interfering with or even interacting with other supernaturals or humans. In fact, it seemed like it was only happenstance that we even knew they existed.

Sirens were added to the list for consideration. Like Annie had already informed me, they were known to cause mischief with humans and supernaturals alike. Although they were most commonly found in the sea and around islands, Seattle was close enough to the coast and they also lived around the Sound and Lake Washington. I wondered where the woman at the door with the delivery yesterday lived.

We didn't have a theory on what a siren's motive could be other than just mischief, which seemed unlikely. We made a note to dig more into the motive for that group and to check the Council records to see if they'd generally had any run-ins with the vampire families in the last century.

Werewolves were the next group we talked about. I was excited about this group because it was the only one I knew anything helpful about. To better ensure that my research project was useful, I had brushed up on were-wolves a bit from the briefing documents.

Werewolves, like vampires, had family-type groupings called packs. Where vampire families mirrored the hier-archy of English royalty, werewolves mirrored the hier-archy of a military: alphas instead of generals, betas instead of lieutenants, and so on. The packs were very strict about how and who they recruited to join their ranks.

They tended to be a very disciplined group and were often used by the Council as enforcers when dealing with cross-group conflicts. Individual werewolves could live as long as vampires, the oldest on record being about thirteen hundred years old. However, due to their history of fighting on the Council's behalf, there weren't as many old werewolves as there were older vampires. The population of werewolves overall was in the tens of thousands, less than witches but much more than vampires. They had smaller territories compared to vampires, like the smaller Boston territory of the Northeast pack, but they had many more territories officially designated.

The additional insights into werewolves was interest-ing. Cam and Steve both added some color and connected dots that weren't apparent in the briefing documents, like their inclination toward concepts of justice. And though they were considered enforcers and could be very violent in the right circumstances, they were normally very friendly individuals. Cam mentioned that they were top of her list to ask if she ever needed a supernatural's help. Both Steve and Cam were quick to point out that it was really unlikely for werewolves to be the ones creating conflict with another group.

Steve was moving us along to the next group, demons, when I stopped him. In hindsight, learning about demons may have been a good idea. But something was itching my brain so bad that I couldn't let it go.

"Wait," I blurted out so strongly that Steve stopped midsentence and they both just stared at me, not saying a word. A thought slammed into my head so quickly that I didn't have time to think about it before saying anything. "Sorry," I started to backpedal. "I just, I think, well, are we sure werewolves wouldn't start something with vampires?"

Steve looked interested. I was half expecting him to be annoyed, but he wasn't. "Why do you ask?" he prompted.

My mind was spinning, and the anxiety of speaking up so boldly on a topic I clearly was not the expert in was starting to create tunnel vision. The tunnel vision flashed briefly to a daydream of a group of what felt like werewolves sitting in a meeting. It wasn't like they were actively in wolf shape. It looked like a normal group of people, but my brain said it was werewolves.

A large man was standing at the front, talking as if giving a lecture. It was like they were planning a battle or something. He talked about needing to do surveillance. He mentioned vampires, and Helen. He was making assignments to different people in the group. One of the people in the crowd asked about the possibility of banishment for the offender. I snapped myself out of my daydream and caught Steve and Cam both looking at me with concern and interest.

"Sorry," I apologized again. I wasn't sure what to say. Just because I had a daydream about something didn't mean the werewolves were responsible for Jane's disappearance. "It just feels like there may be something more there," I said dejectedly.

"Anything specific?" Cam asked gently. Both Steve and Cam paused and waited patiently.

"No," I admitted, but then I remembered Helen encouraging me to consider hunches. "Just a hunch, I guess."

Steve nodded approvingly and added a star onto the werewolf sticky note. We talked a bit more about possible motives of the groups, but all of them seemed rather tenuous compared to a rogue witch or a siren. After assigning tasks out for some additional research points, Steve declared that it was almost three o'clock. He suggested that we grab an afternoon snack and head back upstairs to rejoin the group.

CHIPS and seven layer dip for everyone in hand, we joined the rest of the team, who had also finished up. Cam had gathered our sticky notes and added them to a new whiteboard that we could use when it was our group's turn to share. Helen started off the meeting and asked Jordan's group to give their update first.

It was interesting and no one was rambling, but I was having trouble concentrating. The nagging in my brain I had downstairs with Cam and Steve had never really gone away. It was just getting worse. I scanned through my thoughts to try to get them to make sense, startling myself with a full-body jerk when I finally made the connection. I scared Annie, who had been watching me.

My daydreaming to create a story of what could be happening had led from the meeting of the werewolf pack to individuals in small rooms talking to people, like an interview. I couldn't see the interviewers, but the people I did picture were the six potential recruits I had been digging into for the Northeast pack. This felt right as a way to find out where Jane was; it felt like the interviews would be able to tell us something to get us on the right path.

Normally my daydreams just helped me make sense of what was going on and provided a fun diversion for me to fill the empty spaces. This time, there was something that felt more real. Something inside me was pushing me toward sharing my theory, as unfounded as it was, with the team. Helen's words to speak up about my hunches rang in my ears. She'd said that several times now and it was one of my three main job expectations. Did this count as a hunch? Also, what if this was the thing that could help us rescue Jane?

What was the worst that could happen? I'd look stupid. Everyone would give me bad marks on my thirty-day evaluation. I'd be fired. I'd have to start looking for a job again. It would take forever. I'd end up having to sell the house.

I was starting to spiral.

Taking a deep breath to stop the spiral, I was about to chicken out, but then I looked up and made eye contact with Annie. She smiled and nodded her head as if she could read my thoughts and was urging me to be brave.

"Helen," I half whispered as the conversation came to a natural pause.

She turned to me with interest and nodded her head for me to continue.

"Sorry to interrupt, and I wasn't sure if you were moving on to our group yet." I was hedging, giving her a way to move on if she wanted to.

"No, that's alright, please go ahead," she said sincerely.

"I have a theory that I want to add. It just came to me, so we didn't have a chance to talk about it in our group downstairs." I didn't want to make Cam and Steve feel like I was stepping on their toes. I glanced their way and they both seemed fine with me throwing a curveball to the group. "We were talking about rival groups that may have a reason to interfere. I don't know what the motive would be, but what if we looked into humans who were connected to a supernatural group but not supernatural themselves."

I needed to get to the point, but I wasn't sure how to connect the dots for them so that it wouldn't seem like I was pulling this out of thin air or from daydreams. Everyone just continued to make space for me, so I kept going.

"I've been vetting the new pack recruits. They would know about supernaturals but they aren't supernaturals themselves yet. They may not understand the seriousness of getting involved with vampires, and maybe one of them did something stupid, like kidnap a vulnerable vampire." I sped through the last part and then clamped my mouth shut. It was probably only a few seconds, but waiting for a response felt much longer. My heart was beating so loud and fast I'd be surprised if the whole table couldn't hear it.

"That is an interesting theory," Helen finally said, breaking the silence. I was ready for her to give a polite reason to dismiss it, but she didn't. She templed her fingers together and leaned back in her chair. We all gave her a minute to think. "Jordan," she said almost excitedly, "Are there any other packs that have a recruitment class right now?"

"No," Jordan responded quickly. "I can double-check the Council records, but I'm ninety percent sure there isn't."

"Linda, was there anything in the recruits' reviews that linked to any of the vampire families or Jane?" Helen asked me gently.

"No," I said, backing down a bit. "Not anything I can think of. But I wasn't specifically looking for that."

"That makes sense. There would have been no reason to look for that connection." Helen queried the group, "Does anyone have anything to add to this theory?"

"The Boston area was one of the likely points of travel in the models," Cam said as she clicked away on her laptop. "It's within the radius of how far they could have traveled, and it's a borderland between vampire territories."

"The pack vets the recruits pretty thoroughly," Hank added.

I knew if anyone would throw water on my idea it would be him. I was proud of myself that I didn't glare and kept my face neutral.

"But," Hank continued, "a recruit could be placed in that position by someone to cause problems for both the family and the pack. They could be acting as a spy or agent for a third group."

The theory sounded a bit more convoluted than my theory of someone just being dumb, but he could be onto something. It didn't make sense to me why someone on the verge of getting to join a highly influential pack, have access to almost unlimited funds, and live for a significantly longer time would give that up to kidnap a vampire. There had to be a motive for them, we just couldn't see it yet.

Everyone looked thoughtful, but no one added anything else. I tried not to throw up, reminded myself to breathe normally, and worked to make my heart beat slower. They were actually going to take this seriously. I hoped I wasn't leading us down the wrong path and wasting our time.

13

"That's a really interesting theory," Helen said again, thinking a bit to herself.

I saw several nodding heads around the table. I was just glad that it made sense at all. The pieces barely fit together to me, and I couldn't tell them that the idea came to me because I was daydreaming during Jordan's update.

"The motive is still unclear, but it's an interesting lead. Hank, would we be able to get to the Boston area tonight?" Helen asked, turning to him. Helen was going to run with this idea, literally.

"Yes. The plane is in the hangar and I know the pilots aren't off this week," Hank confirmed.

This was also when I learned that this agency had a plane and pilots on standby. Fancy. I made a note in my quickly growing file subtly named *Office Stuff*. I also wondered what other things this agency had access to.

They were more equipped and connected than the much larger firms I'd worked for before them.

"Before we start full on down this path, are there any other leads or theories that we should talk about first?" Helen asked the group one more time.

Everyone shook their heads. Annie hid a grin badly and looked at me with pride in her eyes. This group made quick decisions and ran with them. They really took the cliché saying from the early 2000s to *fail fast* literally. Hopefully they didn't hate me if this idea failed fast and the trip to Boston was a waste of time for all of them.

"Okay," Helen said and clapped her hands. I'd learned that she did that exact thing right before she was going to start to rattle off a plan and assignments. Her mind moved fast and everyone tried to keep up. Hands on the keyboard, I was ready to record everything so I could help.

"Hank, contact the pilots and see what the soonest takeoff would be for a flight plan to Boston," she said, motioning to him.

Hank nodded and made a note.

"Annie, I'll reach out to the pack to give them a heads-up, and then I want to pass them off to you to help coordinate accommodations and the interviews," she said, now pointing to Annie. "They should be able to do all the heavy lifting of getting the recruits to come in, just tell them what we need. I want the six recruits ready to interview with us by ten o'clock tomorrow morning."

Annie nodded.

"Also, make sure they know not to talk to any of the

recruits about this yet," Helen said sternly. "If one of them is involved with Jane's disappearance, we need to be the ones to uncover that so that the pack doesn't implicate themselves accidentally and start up a whole thing with the family."

Annie typed some notes on her laptop. I typed notes as well, thinking that I could help Annie if needed.

It was just after three o'clock our time in Seattle. I had no idea how long it would take to get to Boston, probably at least five hours. If they left this evening, they'd get there in time to sleep and do the interviews. At first it seemed too fast, but I supposed the math checked out.

A red dot appeared in the message tool on my screen telling me that I had a message from someone. I opened the chat and saw that Annie had sent: "Remind me to tell you about werewolves." After reading that, I raised my head over my screen to give her a questioning look. She just gave me a straight smile and raised her eyebrows. It took a lot of control not to laugh at the face she was making.

Helen was still going, and this distracting silent conversation almost made me miss her asking Mrs. Clark if she could help Annie prepare the go bags for the team and anything else she thought they might need.

"Do you want to include..." Mrs. Clark started and looked toward my end of the table without finishing the question.

"Yes," Helen responded, clearly knowing what she was asking. Knowing that this wasn't the first time they'd done this, I didn't give it a second thought. "Steve and Jordan, please work together on compiling a line of questions that we can use. We don't want to arouse suspicion, but we need to try to get an understanding of what these people know and if anything is going on." Helen was making her way quickly through the group. "I'll also want to talk directly with Michael," she said a bit offhandedly. "If something is going on in his territory, he'd know or at least have ideas.

"Cam, coordinate with Hank on any other equipment you want to bring from the home office. The plane should be fully stocked from our last trip, but reach out to the hangar to double-check. After I give the pack a heads-up, reach out to their tactical team to see what equipment they have readily on hand."

Cam seemed excited with Helen's instructions. I had no clue what would be on the list of equipment that would make Cam so excited. We were just going to interview some people.

Turning to me, Helen finally gave me my instructions. "Linda, do a quick once-over to see if there is anything more you'd like to add to the report and notes on the recruits. Don't worry about it being perfect. Compile the files into a new shared folder within this case's folder. Everyone can access it from there." Having made her way through all the assignments, Helen took a deep breath and then asked the group, "Are we missing anything?"

"Do you want to update the family before we head out?" Steve asked flatly.

"No," Helen responded with only a bit of hesitation. "Let's see how things are looking after the first round of interviews, and then we can call them if we need to."

"Are you sure? It would be better not to surprise them if we do find something," Jordan chimed in. I was impressed that Jordan felt comfortable pressing back openly.

I can't count the number of times that I'd heard an executive or leader make a decision that people clearly disagreed with. It was usually followed by side looks from the people who were in the know. Then after-meeting conversations, text messages, and gossip eventually made its way around the whole company if the decision was bad enough. So many bad decisions could have been prevented with someone being brave enough to speak up and leaders being willing to hear them.

Helen paused and tilted her head, thinking through the decision. She took a deep breath and looked gratefully toward Jordan and Steve.

"You're right," Helen conceded without sounding put out by it. "If something does happen while we're out there, it would be better if the family wasn't surprised by it. I'll make the call on the way to the airport. Thank you. Anything else?" she asked the team one last time.

Everyone shook their heads in response.

"Alright. Reach out if you run into any problems getting ready or if you need help with anything. I'll let everyone know our wheels-up time as soon as we get a flight plan."

With that dismissal, everyone gathered up their things and got up to move on to their tasks. I started to do the same when Helen stopped me. "Linda, can you come to my office before you start on the files?"

I nodded, finished gathering up my things, and then followed Helen to her office.

I SAT in my normal chair in front of Helen's desk, waiting for her to put down her things and get settled. She cleared away some papers on the front of her desk across from me and leaned forward on her elbows. She smiled softly at me for a moment, which had the intended effect of calming me down, before she started into why she asked me here.

"Linda, I realize that this is only your fourth day with us and it's been a busy week already," she started things off, and I held my breath for what might be coming next.

I wasn't really ready to hold down things at the home office while the team was away. It was one of the responsibilities I was most excited about, but not on day four. What if a new client showed up on our door, rain-soaked and crying because their partner had gone missing along with a million dollars from their shared account? The client would be so certain that they had been taken, there is no way they would have abandoned and deceived them. They weren't just partners. They were in love.

But then again, that probably wouldn't happen. And I wouldn't be alone. Annie and Mrs. Clark would be here, so I probably wouldn't really need to do anything. Helen must have sensed how distracted I was and cleared her throat to bring me back to the present.

"I'd like you to come to Boston with us," she dove right in, shocking me with the request. "Not only was this your theory, but you know the most about these individuals. You may be able to catch things we couldn't."

I probably looked at her like she was making a horrible decision. My face wasn't behaving and was clearly displaying the results of my internal monologue. Helen waited patiently for me to think it through and respond. She was a good negotiator, not giving away more than she needed to, letting silence and my own internal back-and-forth do most of the heavy lifting.

I didn't really want to go to Boston. I was sure I wouldn't be that big of a help to the team. I could answer questions over the phone if needed, even do a video call if the situation required it. It would have been different if it wasn't my first week. I needed time to better learn more about the team, how things worked, and what exactly away missions were before going on one. Likely I'd just be in the way, but maybe I could help carry stuff. What if I did something poorly and the team rated me low on my thirty-day evaluation because of it? And what about the unlucky-in-love client who could show up? All of that raced through my head.

"I'd need someone to feed my cat," I blurted out. How was that the first thing I came up with in response?

Helen smiled at my reply and said, "If you are okay with it, we can ask Annie to feed your cat while we are away. We should only be gone for two nights at the most."

"Okay." I'm still not sure if I didn't put up a fight because it was day four and my new boss was asking me to do something, or because these last four days had been more fulfilling and exciting than the last two years combined at my old job. I was prepared to do anything to make this work. Going on the trip would demonstrate an example of working with the team. I'd just need to be careful and be as helpful as possible. Also, maybe this new Linda at this new job was spontaneous. We were about to find out.

Looking at her watch, Helen moved things along quickly. "We need to be heading out soon if we are going to get in at a decent time. I'll fill you in during the flight with more information. If you have any questions, Annie or Hank should be able to answer them. You'll just need your laptop for this trip. We'll get you everything else that you need."

Helen finished up and I stood to head back to my desk. We were clearly done with the conversation now that I had agreed to come and Ilka's food was taken care of. She had said that they would have anything else I'd need, but I didn't have time to process what that meant before Annie came walking toward the office. I passed by Hank coming in at a quick pace as I went out. He nodded to me with a straight face as we passed in the doorway. I wondered for a moment if he'd be okay with me joining the away mission, but then I decided I didn't care.

Annie and I met at my desk. She rattled off what we would need to do to make sure the team was ready for the trip. I was given one task. Annie and Mrs. Clark would handle the rest. I needed to reserve the hotel rooms in Boston for the six of us. Annie gave me a phone number and a ten-digit reservation code on a sticky note to use when I called.

The phone rang only twice before a very polite man picked up. I told him that I would need six rooms tonight to be billed under the specific reservation code that I read off. He put me on hold to see what he could do. Gearing up to haggle to secure six rooms on such short notice, I was surprised when he returned and confirmed that all six rooms were reserved and asked what time we would be arriving. I searched my brain to give him a time based on some quick mental math, but he beat me to it.

"It's almost four o'clock in Seattle," he said as if working out the math problem for an exam. "If you take off around five, you'll be here around midnight."

He didn't wait for me to confirm. I was impressed that he knew the area code I was calling from was in Seattle and that he could do such fast math, including accounting for time zone changes.

"I'll ensure that we have adequate staff on hand tonight to accommodate any needs you and your team may have," he concluded. I thanked him for his assistance and hung up. It wasn't until after I messaged Annie that the hotel was confirmed that I bothered to look up where we would be staying. It was very swanky, and I was shocked that they had six available rooms on such short notice. But I didn't have time to dwell on that or how weird that phone call was.

Remembering my other task and how riddled with notes to myself the file was, I got to work fast. Helen came out with Hank on her heels, letting me know that the cars would be at the office at four o'clock to take the team to the private airport, and then they headed out to find the others and let them know.

Looking at the time on my laptop screen, I sighed—that was only twenty minutes away. This group moved fast. I supposed I'd have time on the plane to work on the files more if I needed to. I cleaned up the most embarrassing notes I had left for myself and then moved all of the documents over to the shared case file. I tried hard not to wince, knowing that this would be some of the first work that my new colleagues would see. Hopefully with these circumstances they wouldn't judge the half-finished work too harshly.

The cars arrived promptly at four o'clock. Helen, Hank, and Jordan loaded into one car after placing several large cases in the back. Steve, Cam, and I loaded into the other car. The trunk of our car was similarly packed with cases and bags. It wasn't until we were in the cars and heading to the airport that I realized I hadn't packed anything for the trip.

I had my laptop bag and whatever I could shove in there. Luckily I always kept some deodorant and a travel toothbrush with toothpaste in my work bag. A few too many late nights had taught me that lesson. But I'd still need to pick up some stuff around the hotel when we got in. I pulled up the hotel name on my phone. I saw that there was a store within walking distance; if I got up early enough, I'd be fine.

. . .

WE MADE it to the private airport in record time, our two black SUVs zipping in and out of traffic. I didn't get the name of our driver and he was silent the whole way. Steve seemed to be familiar with him but didn't offer an explanation or an introduction to me.

The driver and Steve chatted too quietly in the front seat for me to overhear what they were saying. Cam was texting on her phone the whole way, likely finishing up any plans with the pack that needed to be done. Not having anything to do, I put in my earbuds, turned on some music, and watched the city go by. Instead of heading to the main airport, we had made our way to a side terminal that was clearly used for private planes. It was smaller but way fancier. We didn't have time to linger in the lobby. Helen marched the group, including our drivers helping to haul the cases, right out onto the tarmac to a plane waiting for us. I only carried my laptop bag.

The team quickly loaded the plane and then boarded. I stood out of the way and followed them aboard. Everyone made quick work of stowing their individual bags and then found seats, looking comfortable in the private jet that the agency apparently owned. The private jet had not been included on the interview tour.

I sat uncomfortably by the window of the four-seat table section. Helen was across from me, already engrossed in reading a pile of files that she'd pulled from her large work bag. Hank and Steve were up in seats behind the pilot. Cam and Jordan were playing cards on the sofa behind us. Annie and Mrs. Clark were back at the home office, making arrangements and holding things together from their end. I probably should have been there with them.

Before we took off, I sent Annie several text messages about where to find Ilka's food and how much to give her. I had given her my house key to let herself in before we left for the airport. I reminded her not to let Ilka out and not to be surprised if Ilka hid from her when she got there. The cat tolerated me but didn't seem to like other people much. Annie texted back that she understood and would send me pictures if she did get Ilka to play with her. After sending her a good-luck gif, I switched my phone to airplane mode and focused on what was ahead of us.

We were heading to the East Coast to follow my hunch that Helen insisted we explore. I was brought along because I knew the files for the six individuals inside and out. Everyone seemed excited for me to come. Even Hank hadn't scowled at or side-eyed me once during the trip so far. I wasn't brave enough to decline the request on day four with my new employer. But I was somewhat glad I was here. New beginnings, like a new job, are a good time to reevaluate, and it felt good to be a bit braver and bolder.

However, I also wasn't smart enough to mention that I wasn't good at flying, and I wasn't sure I could talk myself into changing that. It had more to do with my stomach than my brain. Maybe a smaller plane would be better. I prayed internally to the universe as we took off down the runway that that would be true.

14

S mall planes are not better. Don't let anyone tell you how cool they are. Yes, I didn't have to go through airport security or make my way through crowds of people to get to the gate. And yes, it did feel smoother and quieter than a larger plane. But it didn't seem as safe to me and my stomach started to churn. I realized that I didn't take my pre-flight motion-sickness pill. I also didn't get my pre-flight chai latte and pumpkin bread. My whole routine was off.

Jordan must have had a sixth sense for these things. She plopped down next to me as soon as the pilot came on and said that we were leveled off enough for folks to walk around the cabin. With her came a bottle of water and a little white pill.

"I thought you might need this, you seem a little pale," Jordan said, offering up the water and drugs.

"Thank you. I usually don't forget to take something,

but this isn't my normal flying routine," I responded as I gulped back the pill with a swig of water.

"You should also probably try to eat something as soon as your stomach settles a bit. There's food in the cupboard and fridge, but let me know if I can help you get anything."

Jordan had always been nice, but her kindness seemed to kick up a notch with me not feeling well. She was the medical expert on the team, and that clearly included providing medical assistance whenever we needed. I'd have to find a way to figure out if she was a doctor or something.

An hour into the flight after everything had settled, including my stomach, Helen called a quick meeting. We all huddled close together on the two couches facing each other toward the back of the plane so that we could more easily hear one another.

"The pilot tells me that we'll be arriving in Boston a bit after midnight local time. Everyone should get dinner after we're done here. Mrs. Clark sent along a heatable dinner for each of us. Your name is on it along with the heating instructions. Then if you'd like to sleep, we've got these two sofas here, and the two chairs in the front lay out flat. You all know where to find blankets and pillows. Linda, if you need help, just ask any of us," Helen instructed us all. Based on the ease that everyone had found their spots, they had all clearly been on this plane before.

"Drivers will meet us at the airport and we'll get checked

into our hotel," Helen continued. "Because it's a late night for us, we'll meet in the lobby at nine in the morning. The drive to the pack's town is about thirty minutes. Breakfast and coffee will be in the car on the way to the town, unless you want to grab something on your own before nine."

Nine felt a bit early for me, but I should still get my eight hours. I might be able to get some sleep on the flight too. I still felt like I should have known all these details and had a hand in planning them, but I reminded myself for like the hundredth time that it was only day four and everything had been a whirlwind up to this point. I needed to give myself some grace, and I didn't mind that someone else, probably Annie and Mrs. Clark, had made all the arrangements.

"The pack has set up a house in town for us to conduct the interviews. We'll also have accommodations in town if we need to stay longer," Helen was continuing to fill in the team. "Annie and the pack leadership have arranged for interviews to start at 10:00 a.m. Hank, what did I miss?" She turned to Hank and gestured for him to take over.

"The recruits will come in two waves." Hank spoke evenly in the monotone voice that I'd come to expect from him. He sounded like a professor reteaching an intro class to a bunch of freshmen for the fiftieth time. "We'll double up in the interviews: one person to ask questions and one to take notes. The recruits are used to being asked to come in to talk with pack members, so they shouldn't be suspicious of anything. The pack will inform them that we are an external consultant group that they are bringing in."

Everyone nodded their heads, following along with the

explanation. I was busy watching the faces of anyone I could without looking too creepy. Still suspicious of Hank, I wanted to see if anyone else had any tells in their reactions toward him. So far, no luck. Maybe I was being too harsh.

"The interviews will be at ten o'clock and eleven o'clock. We will be done by lunch. We can do follow-up interviews in the afternoon if needed," Hank concluded dryly and turned to Helen.

"Thank you, Hank. Any questions or anything else to add?" Helen queried the group.

"The pack has recording equipment and each room will be set up," Cam shared, "but I'm not sure how much time we'll have to test it, so the notetakers shouldn't rely on that."

"Steve and I will finish up the interview questions on the flight and have those for everyone in the morning," Jordan added.

"We'll also have a member of the pack outside each interview room," Steve informed us. "If anyone needs anything during the interview, just knock on the table and then they'll come into the room."

"Alright, sounds like we are ready as we can be. Please make sure to get some dinner. Good work, everyone," Helen said, clapping her hands once like she was dismissing the team from the halftime huddle.

The meeting now concluded, I made my way to the little fridge in the sideboard to take Jordan and Helen's advice to get some food. Opening it, I found eight labeled and yummy-looking dinners in glass containers as well as drinks and snacks. The two names I didn't recognize must have belonged to the pilot and copilot.

I found my container and almost sighed out loud when I saw that Mrs. Clark had packed me some of the lasagna, garlic bread, and green salad that we had for lunch yesterday. I had gushed to Annie and Cam about how it was one of my favorite comfort meals. Either this was a coincidence or word had gotten back to a very thoughtful Mrs. Clark. I took a peek at the other containers, and they were all different meals, probably specially selected for the individual.

I followed the thorough instructions to reheat the lasagna and garlic bread, adding them next to the salad on the plate Cam had produced from a cupboard for me. Taking my plate and drink to the table, I settled in to enjoy the meal. Shortly after, Hank, Cam, and Jordan joined me with their unique and similarly delicious-looking meals. Helen and Steve were huddled in whispers up by the pilots.

We all dug into our dinner in silence for a few moments. I was happy to see that everyone had a similar satisfied grin as they started eating their food. After a few bites, Cam broke the silence: "Mrs. Clark always picks just what I need for flights."

"Does she always pack meals like this for the team?" I asked.

"Yes," Hank answered wistfully. "Anytime we are out of the office but close by or heading out on a flight, we get her cooking. But we won't have anything near this good while out of town or on the flight back. So enjoy it."

"Typically, we have clients who help supply what we need on away missions," Jordan expanded on Hank's answer. "Sometimes, though rarely, we'll eat out. But Mrs. Clark and Helen have strong feelings that we all eat healthy. And as the medical support for the team, I agree, although I do love a fast-food cheeseburger when I can get one."

Healthy food according to Mrs. Clark and Helen was something I could get on board with. All the meals I'd had at the office–and now on the plane–had been great. There were always fruits and vegetables, but Mrs. Clark didn't shy away from carbs or meat, and there were always treats in the office. I bet the other cupboard I hadn't explored yet on the plane was also full of treats. Maybe healthy food to them was more correlated with fresh and low preserva-tives. Thinking about it now, everything did seem to be made by Mrs. Clark. There wasn't a packaged snack cake or bag of chips in sight. Either way, I wasn't going to complain.

The four of us ate and chatted, mostly talking about the case, but then shifting to lighter topics. I learned that Hank had a wiener dog named Juniper but no partner. Jordan also lived alone and, like Cam and Annie, didn't have pets. I was starting to see a trend. No one seemed to have partners or children.

Not so strange for a group that seemed very career oriented and were able to drop everything to hop a plane to Boston at a moment's notice. It made me wonder about work-life balance. I probably should have asked more about that in the interview, although I didn't have much life to balance with work.

Cam asked if I wanted to stay up or take a nap. As a highly skilled and natural napper, I took her up on the offer to spread out on one of the back couches. She helped me find the blankets and pillows in an overhead bin. The overhead lights had been dimmed after the four of us had stowed our dirty dishes and cleared the table. I drifted easily asleep, lulled by the now not as loud rumble of the plane. The motion-sickness pill and tummy full of lasagna probably helped too.

Low voices and soft plane noises woke me from an easy sleep. Not sure how long I had been out, I slowly sat up just enough to look around. Cam was softly snoring on the couch across from me. Helen and Jordan were at the table with task lighting acting like a spotlight on them. The voices I heard must have been theirs. Steve and Hank had claimed the chairs up front and both seemed to be sleeping.

I laid back down and listened to Helen and Jordan. They hadn't noticed I was awake, and I technically wasn't eavesdropping. I just needed a few minutes to wake up fully and then I'd go join them like a normal person. My ears perked up as I heard my name.

"Do you think Linda has any idea?" Jordan half whispered to Helen, still talking loud enough to be heard over the engine noise and also, it turned out, loud enough for me to hear.

"I haven't seen anything that would make me think that. And she doesn't seem to be a secretive person," Helen replied. Jordan chuckled softly at Helen's description of me as not secretive. I was pretty free with my thoughts, often my mouth getting ahead of my brain, and my face usually gave away what I didn't say out loud.

"Has anyone else noticed anything?" Jordan asked, and I wondered who the *anyone else* was. I scrunched my face at the thought that she could be referring to the rest of the team.

"Nothing conclusive but a few signs that could point to it," Helen answered, still cryptic enough that I had no idea what they were talking about. My heart started racing as I made up stories in my mind of what it could be.

Were they already evaluating my performance? I raced through how the last week had gone. Every task had been completed. I was engaged and participated as best as I could. They didn't sound upset or disappointed, more curious and maybe anxious. If it was concerns about my job performance, I'd find out soon enough with my thirty-day evaluation.

At least I'd get a paycheck or two if they were going to let me go so soon. A sadness was taking over the anxiousness. I really didn't want to leave this job.

They had kept talking while my overactive mind had gone to the worst possible scenario.

"How are we going to find out?" Jordan asked Helen, leaning in closer.

"I'm not sure at this point. But I'm also not sure it matters yet," Helen responded and sounded resigned to the situation. "We'll keep a close eye on her, and if anything happens, we'll go from there."

The words sounded a bit ominous, but her tone was more like a worried parent wondering if their child was okay. Feeling guilty about overhearing, I made a loud enough waking-up noise so that they would know I was up. They both looked over at me, a bit startled. I smiled back at the both of them, trying to look innocent and like I hadn't heard them talking about me. Then I made my way to the biggest airplane bathroom I had ever seen. For real, there was a shower in there.

As it turned out, we only had about an hour left in the flight. A water and snack helped wake me up a bit more. I joined Helen and Jordan at the table.

"How did you sleep?" Jordan asked, and she popped a grape into her mouth from the shared bowl I'd brought over.

"Good," I answered. "It's the first time I've been able to lie down flat on an airplane."

They both laughed. "Yeah, this will spoil you for normal flights," Jordan replied.

"Do you always use this plane for work travel?" I asked, trying to keep to safe subjects and wanting to seem like I wasn't bothered by what I had overheard.

"Mostly," Helen answered. "As long as it is available. We only have the one plane, so if we need to split up, then some folks may have to take commercial."

"Oh, shame," I replied with a hint of sarcasm, like I had

already been spoiled by this new way of traveling and could never imagine myself going back to a big plane sitting next to strangers. Probably truer than I'd care to admit.

The pilot came on just then, the casualness of his announcement punctuating the difference of flying in the agency's plane. They told us that we'd be landing in twenty minutes. Everyone scurried a bit around the cabin to secure belongings and then settled in where there were seat belts. I was able to stay where I was, snapping my seat belt securely for landing.

Two very fancy black SUVs met us right outside the airplane. We deplaned down some metal steps, and people with the airport logo on their uniforms loaded bags and cases from the plane to the waiting cars. This still felt like a movie to me, but I just reminded myself to go with the flow and not act weird about it. I thanked the pilots as we left the plane. Helen did too, which was a good sign to me on many levels.

Steve gently took my elbow and guided me into one of the cars, Cam piling in after us. Helen, Jordan, and Hank went in the second car. Each car had a driver and another person in the front passenger seat. Hank had mentioned that the pack would be helping with logistics and accommodations. I tried not to stare at the back of the heads of the woman driving the car and the man sitting next to her.

Wracking my brain, I tried to remember if I had read about any physical traits of werewolves that would help me know if these were official pack members or not. No one had bothered with introductions, just some quick head nods and gestures, so I couldn't even try to match them to names I had read.

We drove about ten minutes and ended up at a very fancy hotel. I exited the car and stayed close to Cam. Hank hustled to the front desk as the four drivers unloaded the bags and cases from the cars onto hotel carts and handed them off to hotel employees. Hank returned shortly after handing a paper to the hotel staff before they whisked away the bags. He passed out key cards with room numbers to each of us and let us know that our go bags would be sent ahead of us to our rooms. He handed a card and a sheet of paper to Helen.

I hadn't packed a go bag, so I was prepared to sleep in the T-shirt that I was wearing. This hotel seemed fancy enough for amenities and I could probably call down for some things. Still, I hoped there would be time in the morning for me to pick up some clothes around the hotel or in the town that we'd be in. I was too tired at this point to venture out in search of a store. Also, not being an overly smelly person generally, I'd probably be okay for a day if need be.

OPENING the door and flipping on the light revealed a lovely room with a view of city buildings from the full wall of windows. Sitting on the bed was a black leather duffle bag. They must have delivered this to the wrong room. I wondered if I'd be able to tell who it belonged to from some light snooping.

Unzipping the main compartment, I saw a note with

Helen's handwriting sitting on top of some clothes. The note explained that they had put together a go bag for me as soon as they had realized I'd be joining them. She expressed hope that it would include everything I would need and that I'd be able to request specific items for future away missions. She also apologized for not being more thorough in her explanation on how this mission would go for me and promised to answer any questions if needed. She concluded the note with her cell phone number, even though Cam had already programmed it into my phone.

Pulling out the items from the bag, I quickly forgave her for any inconvenience and also thanked whoever had put this together. There were comfy pajamas, workout clothes, a pair of dark jeans that looked exactly like a pair I had been wearing yesterday, and three plain T-shirts in black, gray, and white. The pair of dress trousers and nicer blouse looked similar in style to what I had worn to my interview. There was also a stylish and warm-looking long gray coat, tennis shoes, and nicer dress shoes that would go well with the dress clothes. Socks, underwear, and bras rounded out the clothes.

It made sense now why Jordan had asked for my clothing sizes. I tried hard not to think about who had gone shopping. I really hoped it was Annie and not Hank who had prepared all of this. Two containers were below the clothes. The first revealed travel toiletries, a hairbrush, hair clip, and ties. The other held makeup of a much higher quality than I normally used but that clearly matched my skin tone.

In the excitement I hadn't noticed my laptop bag sitting next to the new away bag. I knew what was in that bag as I had shoved whatever supplies from my office I thought I might need into it, including some cookies from the kitchen.

It took me no time to get my phone plugged in on the nightstand and three alarms set so I'd be up on time. Snuggling into the cozy bed in my new, even cozier pajamas, I was asleep within minutes.

15

I woke up before my phone alarm Friday morning. My restless mind kept the dreams going all night and would not let me sleep any longer. Sighing, I pulled myself from the nest of pillows I had constructed around myself during the night. Waking up early did mean I had time for a longer shower. I stood under the hot stream of water longer than my water heater at home allowed me to and reflected on the past few days.

A few specifics stood out to me. One, everyone on this team seemed nice. For-real nice, not fake nice like you often found in office culture. I'd even gotten over most of my distrust of Hank. He was just bland, and maybe a little standoffish, but nothing sinister. Having a dog named Juniper—that I had seen pictures of as proof—did wonders for my impression of him.

Two, I wanted to be Helen when I grew up. Not that she was that much older than me, maybe in her forties at the oldest. She just had things together. Everyone respected her, and it was likely because she clearly cared about everyone on the team. She was firm and kind. Tough and empathetic. Decisive and collaborative. That collection of attributes in a boss was not something I'd seen in action before.

And three, I was in way over my head but honestly excited for the adventure. The past two years had been rough, and I don't think I realized how stuck I'd been. Learning about this new otherworld and being engrossed in this case had shaken me out of my stupor. Not that I wanted Jane to be missing, most likely kidnapped, maybe dead, but it was invigorating to be involved in something so important with a group of people so good at what they did.

Fourth and last, if Helen was already concerned about my job performance, then I would step it up. Next week, I'd get proactive and ask her for feedback. That normally worked to get on the right foot or at least get a manager to tell you if they had concerns. It was hard to fix problems you didn't know about.

The water never ran cold, but it was still time to get out and get on with the day. I decided on dressing in the trousers and blouse because that seemed most appropriate for conducting interviews. Repacking the duffle and my laptop bag quickly, I double-checked the room to make sure I didn't leave anything. Then I headed downstairs to wait the final ten minutes to nine o'clock. I did not want to be the last one to the meeting location. I wasn't.

. . .

THE DRIVE to the small town outside of Boston took about thirty minutes, as Helen had said. Sitting between the window and Cam, I was enjoying my donut and coffee when I got a text from Annie. I remembered that she had messaged something about werewolves during the meeting. I hoped that was what she was texting about now.

Annie: how's the trip going

Me: good so far, I didn't throw up on the plane so that's good

Annie: that's a good sign, lol

Me: hey, what did you need to tell me about werewolves

Annie: well only because I promised, but it probably won't matter for this trip

I watched as it said she was typing. Then stopped. Then typing again. If it was taking this long to figure out how to tell me, then I really needed to know what I was getting into.

Me: just tell me, I can handle it :)

Annie: they are scarier than vampires when they are in their wolf form, you'll want to run or freeze, I recommend freeze

Me: what?! why would they be in their wolf form for interviews

Annie: they probably won't be and even if they do go into their wolf form just remember they are on our side and don't run

Me: what if they aren't on our side

The typing and then not typing started again. I waited this time, picturing Annie sitting at the kitchen counter at the office typing and then erasing her message, thinking about what she should say. Finally a message popped up.

Annie: they are :)

Me: let's hope so, looks like we're here, I'll text you updates when I get a chance

Annie: thanks, have fun!

WE ARRIVED in front of a large old house. There were already a couple black SUVs similar to ours in the half-circle drive. People hurried in between the house and the cars carrying boxes and cases. A large, rugged-looking man in jeans and a flannel shirt stood on the steps to the front door.

"Welcome," he bellowed toward us with a volume that didn't match the gentle tone. "I hope your travels were uneventful."

"No troubles at all," Helen said with a smile. She walked up to him and they shook hands.

"We've got everything mostly setup," he said and turned to guide her into the house.

"Thank you," Helen responded, "and no one has spoken to them about Jane or the family yet, right?"

"Yes," he replied. "We understand that we are just here to assist you and your team."

"Perfect. I appreciate your understanding of the situation," she said. They had gotten ahead of us and were speaking in quiet voices now, so I couldn't hear what the rest of the conversation was. Soon enough, Helen turned back toward us, and the man went upstairs.

Helen huddled us all into the front room, leaving the unloading of the cars to the many capable hands already at the house. She explained that we'd have three rooms set up upstairs for the interviews that would start at ten, in about thirty minutes. The pack would be providing extra security but would try to be discreet. All the interviewees thought they were coming in for an interview regarding pack membership. Apparently that wasn't an uncommon practice, so it gave us just the right cover to not scare off any of the suspects.

The interview questions had been pre-decided and were passed around on paper to each of us. Luckily I would be the notetaker in our pair and I didn't need to worry about asking the questions the right way. Helen finished up and no one had questions, so we were excused to wander the house and check out the interview rooms.

I ENDED up in the kitchen with Jordan, both of us staying out of the way as the pack members, Steve, Cam, and Hank set up the remainder of the rooms with the recording equipment. I wasn't sure where Helen had gotten off to. Now seemed like as good a time as any to ask Jordan some questions that had been running around my head all morning.

"So are all supernaturals incredibly good looking?" I asked as casually as I could.

Jordan looked quite amused by my question. I felt like it was a fair question to ask. Winthrop had been shockingly good looking. It seemed like that might just have been the nature of vampires more than an anomaly with this particular one. The siren who delivered something for Mrs. Clark was breathtaking. And now I had seen almost a dozen different pack members, and they could have all been models or movie stars.

"Not all supernaturals. But there are many groups that tend to be appealing to our human sensibility of aesthetic appearance," Jordan responded a bit clinically. "Vampires and werewolves, the two that you've knowingly seen so far, fall into the appealing group. Their appearance helps with their individual survival."

"Do they only select adoptees if they are attractive, or does becoming a supernatural make someone attractive?" I continued my line of questioning. Again this felt like a legitimate question.

Jordan chuckled but was a good sport about answering. "They don't only adopt traditionally attractive humans. But the process tends to smooth out the less attractive parts and accentuate already appealing features. You'd still recognize someone after their change," she explained. "There are also some chemical aspects to the attraction. You may not think a vampire or werewolf are as attractive from a photo, but being in the presence of one would heighten your response to them.

"I'm not sure if this is where your train of thought was heading." Jordan seemed to get serious and offered a warning: "But it's strongly encouraged that you do not date or have relations with any supernaturals. And it's completely against Helen's rules to have a relationship with a client."

My ears reddened and I felt my cheeks grow hot. Had

that been where my train of thought was headed? I hadn't thought about that exactly, but I'm also not a nun, although my dating history of late may have suggested otherwise. No words would come out, so I just nodded my understanding. Luckily I was saved further embarrassment by Helen coming into the kitchen.

"Grab some water if you need and head to your interview room," Helen instructed. "The first group of interviews will be here in about five minutes. A member of the pack will escort them to the room and then will wait outside the door if you need anything."

Jordan and I both grabbed water from the fridge and headed to our respective rooms. I met Steve at the top of the stairs, and we settled into our interview room together. He would be the interviewer and had apparently memorized the questions, as he sat stoically without any paper in front of him. I slipped the paper with the questions under my laptop and prepared to take notes.

LUCKILY OUR INTERVIEWEE arrived soon after. I liked Steve, but I wasn't sure how long I would last listening to his too calm and even breathing. It took me only a few of his breaths to realize he had an even four seconds in and four seconds out cadence. It was like he was in the middle of a yoga class. And winning the yoga class, at that.

On the other hand, my breath was coming out a bit ragged, and I tried not to forget how to breathe altogether. Why did I feel so nervous? Oh, that's right, I was an EA, not a private investigator with experience interviewing suspects. It was a good thing that Steve would do all the heavy lifting for this.

Our first interview was with a kind-looking woman named Judy. Steve raced through the prepared questions and didn't ask follow-ups to get more information. Steve seemed to keep checking in with me, glancing my way after each question. I started giving him encouraging nods to move forward. I was a fast notetaker, so he didn't need to slow down or wait on my behalf.

Judy's answers didn't raise any concerns and she didn't really have any information on any of the other recruits either. She didn't hang out socially with any of them outside of recruit meetings. I gave her a friendly smile and nod as she left the room.

Michael, the pack leader, checked in with us after Judy had been escorted out. He let us know that the next interviewee was already here. We told him we were okay without a break and to bring them right in.

A TALLISH, average-looking man settled into the chair across the table from us. His body posture and face looked relaxed, but something behind his eyes was off. Steve dove straight into the questions. No introductions or pleasantries like there had been with Judy. I was startled a bit and started typing.

"Name?" Steve asked firmly.

"Brad O'Malley," he answered.

"Occupation?"

"Accountant."

I already knew the demographic information for Brad. Seeing him and hearing his name confirmed that he was my research individual number five. I typed ahead, filling in the questions and answers, confirming that I had remembered correctly as Steve made quick work of the first set of questions.

"Please recount your primary daily activities starting from last Friday to this morning."

"I was at work on Friday and then out with friends for dinner. On Saturday I was mostly at home, cleaned out my garage and ran errands," Brad started out. "Sunday I went to the recruit meeting and then I was at home. Monday was work. Tuesday was work. Wednesday, work. Thursday, work. And this morning I had to miss work to be here."

His answers were short and clipped, walking a line of disrespect but keeping his tone from outrightly being so. I thought Steve would dig into more details as those answers did not seem satisfactory, but instead he moved right on to the next question despite my side-eyed glances.

"Have you noticed any of the other recruits in activities that would be considered outside of pack regulation or acting strangely?" Steve asked.

"No. Everyone is continuing their normal activities around town and attending recruit meetings as required," Brad answered.

Again Steve didn't dig in with follow-up questions but continued to the next one: "What general knowledge do you have about other magic and otherworldly beings?"

With a small huff, Brad answered, "I've taken the

general course on otherworldly supernaturals and passed the required exams."

What? They had a course? I'd gotten a lot from reading the documents at the office, but I wondered if that was a course I could sign up for. I made a little side note so I wouldn't forget to ask. Looking up from my note-taking, I caught Brad's eyes.

Something flashed in my mind. I didn't get a picture or daydream of anything. Just an overwhelming feeling of anger. I must have been startled a bit because Steve stiffened in the chair next to me. Brad leaned back in his chair with folded arms and narrowed eyes. Only a short pause in the cadence from Steve's questions and then he continued, "Do you know Jane?"

I barely stopped myself from gasping out loud. That was not on the list of questions that we were supposed to be asking.

"No," Brad answered. His tone came out overly confused, almost like a forced confusion. But again something was off with his eyes as I dared a quick glance over at him. His eyes didn't match the tone or the words.

Something took over my mind and hit me like a flash. This wasn't a normal daydream—it was as if I was there. Brad was with a woman who looked like Jane. But unlike the picture I'd been seeing on the whiteboard in the office for the past four days, she was dirty and pale and looked terrified. We were in a cabin with rough walls and old seventies-style furniture. It was dusty and a too-small fire glowed in the fireplace against the far wall, barely providing warmth. I could hear the wind and maybe water outside. Jane was on a chair and Brad was pacing in front of her. They both looked up suddenly and seemed to make eye contact with me.

I snapped back to the interview room. Working hard to control my breathing, I kept my head down, letting my hair fall down and hide my face. I could feel Steve's and Brad's eyes on me. Steve stood up suddenly and knocked twice on the table.

Our door security, Michael, entered and asked Brad to follow him. His chair made a loud scratching sound as he stood, followed by angry footsteps and a closing door. Steve sat back down and waited. Before long I was back to counting his four-second breath sequence. My heart rate returned to normal and I looked up.

Steve looked concerned as I glanced his way. "Are you okay?"

"Yes, I think so," I managed to squeak out.

"Did you see something?" he asked, as if he already knew what the answer would be.

"Yes."

"I'm going to get Helen. Do you need anything?" he asked gently.

"No, I think I'm okay," I said, trying to convince myself more than him. It didn't register to me at that moment that he had asked me if I had seen anything and we both clearly knew he was referring to what I was now sure was a vision.

.   .   .

Jordan came in before Steve had returned with Helen. She also looked concerned, as if I was going to break at any moment. She set a cup of tea and a banana in front of me. Pulling the chair away from the table and closer to me, she sat down and faced me.

"I'm going to ask you a few questions. You can just nod or shake your head if that's easier," she said. I wasn't sure why everyone was treating me with such kid gloves. I must have looked like I'd seen a ghost. "Also, try to take some sips and eat a bit of that banana."

I obliged, almost choking on the over-sugared tea.

"Sorry it's a bit sweet, but the sugar will help," Jordan offered after my reaction. "Are you feeling dizzy?"

I shook my head.

"Are you feeling lightheaded at all?" she continued to press.

I shook my head again.

"Do you feel like you are fully present in this room?"

I nodded and then looked up quickly, finally making eye contact with her. That was a weird question. But then I thought back to how I had felt several minutes ago. It had totally felt like I wasn't in this room but rather in a cold and dusty cabin with a kidnapper and a terrified vampire.

The pieces were clicking in, and I realized that these people I had been working with for the past week may have known more than I realized. And even scarier, they might have known more about what had just happened to me than I knew myself.

· · ·

JORDAN SAT with me as I drank the tea and finished the banana. Helen came quietly into the room, giving Jordan a knowing look. They traded spots and Jordan took up the chair on the other side of the table.

"Linda, can you tell me what you saw?" Helen prodded gently.

It was clear that everyone but me had some kind of idea of what was going on. There wasn't any hiding this or dismissing this as a daydream. I was beginning to come to terms with it myself. If supernaturals were real, then why couldn't I be seeing visions? I always felt like I was hyper-intuitive and even joked with my mom sometimes that I was psychic; she had not thought it was funny. Everything was possible now that my eyes had been opened to what could be.

"I think I had a vision," I said quietly, giving a name out loud to what had happened.

Jordan and Helen exchanged glances again, and I could see that's what they thought as well. Helen gestured for me to continue.

"I saw Brad, the guy from our last interview, and Jane." I spoke quietly, as if it was still a secret to keep. "They were in a cabin. Looked like one room and was rough. Old and dusty like it doesn't get used much. Jane looked scared. She was dirty, her hair was greasy, and she looked really pale."

"Was there anything else you can remember? Did you hear anything? Smell anything?" Jordan nudged me gently to remember.

"I heard the wind and I think I heard moving water. But

that might not be right." I second-guessed myself. "All I could smell was the fire and smoke from the fireplace. They had a small fire going but it was still cold in the room."

"Anything else?"

"No." I didn't want to remember how they had both made eye contact with me. One set of eyes angry, and the other set pleading.

16

Helen patted me on the shoulder comfortingly as she stood up and then exited the room. Jordan remained in the chair, a strained smile on her face, trying to comfort us both. It wasn't working. We sat in silence for a few more minutes. Jordan kept checking her phone. I just sat staring into the distance, turning over what just happened in my head. Steve finally popped his head in the door and asked us to come down to the living room to talk with the rest of the team.

Everyone gathered on the comfortable couch and chairs around the coffee table. The pack members could be heard in the other rooms, but none of them joined us. Helen cleared her throat and the uneasy chatter stopped, all eyes drawn to her.

"We have a lead," Helen said and then quickly followed with, "It is promising, and I want us to move on this immediately."

Everyone nodded and looked eager to get moving. She

didn't expand on where that lead had come from, but based on the faces around the room and how they kept sneaking glances at me, I thought they all knew.

"Our lead is Brad O'Malley," Helen continued and then her face flashed with a hint of anger. "Unfortunately, Mr. O'Malley slipped away before we were able to detain him."

Uneasy glances around the room let me know that everyone was unhappy about this. Helen didn't dwell on how he had left or who had let Brad leave the house and no one asked her.

She kept the team focused on the task at hand with her quick, no-nonsense pace. "Hank and Steve, please work with the pack to get the information on Mr. O'Malley's common locations and then divide them up into teams to do an inconspicuous sweep. The primary goal is to find and tail Mr. O'Malley. It's preferred that he doesn't know we are tailing him, but priority is eyes on him over discretion."

Hank and Steve nodded in understanding, and Helen continued, "Cam and Jordan, I need the two of you to work with the pack's tech expert, Sarah. She is also familiar with the area. We need to narrow down areas that include one-room cabins. Prioritize remote locations near running water that are not commonly used. Start with a radius of thirty miles and then check back in and we'll see if we want to expand the search area. Sarah is already setting up the computers in the dining room.

"Linda," she continued, looking over at me, "you're with me. We are going to review the interview notes from the other groups and look through your research again. We'll all meet back here in one hour to decide on next steps. If you find anything urgent, call in immediately, channel eight."

Cam passed around walkie-talkie-looking devices to Helen, Hank, and Steve. Seemed overkill—we all had phones. Everyone dispersed to their assigned tasks. Helen and I spread out the interview notes and research on the coffee table, making a pile for each of the six.

"Let's focus on Brad's connections, who he knows and how that may connect to Jane," Helen said as she opened her laptop.

"I can dig through social media," I offered up. That was always my specialty. I had already reviewed all the recruits' socials, but I hadn't dug as deep. There hadn't really been a reason to do that until now.

Brad's socials, like most of the recruits, were really boring. He didn't post much of anything. Some likes and birthday posts were about all that was there, except for one memorial post for a friend.

It was a generic post on an anniversary date of the death and didn't have much information. But what was there was sad. It looked like it was a childhood friend who had died about fifteen years ago in a hunting accident around the age of twenty. Brad wasn't the only one to have given the message a heart. I clicked on the eight other profiles, opening new tabs in the window for each one.

The first few profiles were private and I could only see generic information. Nothing useful on the surface. I'd come back and dig more if needed. The fourth profile was public and this guy was more prolific. He was a similar age to Brad, which could mean that they grew up together.

A wall of posts and memes filled his profile. I scanned through to see if anything jumped out, specifically paying attention to faces in photos that were shared. I was back several years in the profile, making sure not to accidentally click *Like* on any photos as I expanded them. Nothing was jumping out and I was just about to move on to the next profile when I saw a grainy photo.

The image on the screen looked like someone had taken a picture of a hard-copy photo with their phone and had posted that. The clothes and hair were older styles. Clicking to open it up bigger, I could see that it was a group of seven people. They were all smiling and standing in front of a brick building.

Despite the poor quality, I found the guy in the profile and next to him a younger version of Brad. There were no tags with names, so I couldn't be sure. I looked carefully at the other faces. The friend who had died in the accident was in the photo for sure—the dimples and wavy blond hair were obvious in this and the memorial picture.

Looking at the other faces carefully, I gasped and caught Helen's attention. I pulled the laptop closer to my face to be sure. The friend that had died had his arm wrapped around the shoulders of a girl. The girl was Jane. I was almost positive it was her. The hair, eyes, and smile all matched.

"Look," I said and turned the laptop toward Helen. "I found this old picture."

Helen leaned forward and I pointed to the two faces that mattered.

"I think Brad knew Jane growing up."

Helen pulled the laptop closer to her and looked at the screen. I held my breath. This could be the final piece needed and some real evidence that connected Brad and Jane. We wouldn't have to just count on my so-called vision to help save Jane.

"I think you're right," Helen finally said, and I let my breath go. "Do you know where Brad went to high school?"

"Yes, he went to Dover High School," I answered and held up the paper where that was marked.

"Jane went to St. Mark's," Helen said.

I typed in *St. Mark's High School*. There were several. But one was in Delaware.

"Is it the St. Mark's in Delaware?" I asked.

"Yes."

"Dover High School is also in Delaware," I said with excitement. "They didn't go to the same high school but they probably grew up close to each other."

"This is a solid connection," Helen said with a smile. "Good work."

A squawk over the radio interrupted our conversation. "Cam to Helen," the radio emitted. "We have a location we'd like Linda to come review."

I could hear the double speak from the radio and the voices in the dining room. I was a bit puzzled that we were using walkie-talkies within shouting distance of each other, but then I remembered that Hank and Steve were outside. I guessed they needed to know as well.

Helen and I both made our way into the dining room, abandoning the files on the coffee table. Computer monitors lined two sides of a square, bar-height dining table. The three women were huddled around one screen and beckoned us over as we entered the room.

"Sarah found a link between a cabin near here that matches the criteria and one of Brad's friends," Cam explained. "It's actually a friend of a friend, so the connection is a bit tenuous. We wanted Linda to have a look and see if it feels familiar at all."

Add Cam to the list of people who now think I have visions that are going to help solve this case. Not wanting to disappoint or make anyone feel silly, I figured I'd at least have a look. Leaning over the computer screen, I saw an aerial map of a wooded area. There was a small stream to one side of the rectangle roof of the cabin. A single chimney stood out at one end of the roof. No tingles of familiarity. Logically it met all the criteria of our search, but Cam, Jordan, and Sarah already knew that. That's not why I was here to help.

"I'm not sure," I said, disappointed that I couldn't offer more. "I really only saw the inside of the cabin."

"Is there any chance it was bought and sold in the last twenty years or so?" Helen asked. "If yes, there might be real estate photos of the inside online."

Cam did some quick typing and checked a couple of websites, one looking very official. "No, it looks like it has been with that owner since the late 1960s."

"That time period would match with the vibe of the furniture I saw in the cabin," I blurted out. Everyone looked up at me, impressed. Cam nodded and smiled approvingly.

"Any other locations that looked as promising?" Helen asked the group.

All of the heads shook no.

"Do you think we should move on this one?" she asked the group again, and I watched her as she gauged reactions. Jordan looked skeptical. Cam and Sarah both nodded their heads. Helen looked at me, and I just shrugged my shoulders, not sure what it would mean if I agreed or not.

"Okay, let's call everyone back together and talk about the next steps," she decided after a slight pause.

EVERYONE GATHERED in the living room again, this time with a few extra members. I recognized Michael and Sarah as pack members. The other two faces were familiar but I didn't have names to put with them. Helen kicked things off as usual, asking for an update on the surveillance teams.

"We deployed three groups to Mr. O'Malley's home, office, and the local bar he frequents," Hank said. "All groups have made it to their assigned locations, but there is no sign of Mr. O'Malley. We've posted teams outside the three locations and are expanding the search around town."

"Any chance he's already left town?" Helen asked.

"Not likely," Steve responded. "We did locate his truck

parked on the street near his home. But no sign of him yet. It's unclear if he has access to other vehicles."

"Michael, does your pack have enough people to help us set up checks on the roads leading out of town?" Helen turned her attention to the pack member who had been assigned to my interview room. She always had a tone of respect when talking with people, but this was turned up a notch.

"Yes," Michael said. "We can call in the other recruits to pair up with pack members to help extend our reach."

"Great, I really appreciate your pack's support," Helen said with a slight incline of her head as thanks. "Okay. Let's set up those checkpoints. Hank, I'd like you to oversee the operations in town. Steve and Jordan, you are going to come with me. We are going to check out that cabin. Michael, I'd like you to join us if you can. Please bring anyone else you'd like."

"Of course," he responded quickly.

"Also, Linda found a connection between Jane and Brad," Helen shared with the group, giving me all the credit. "It looks like they knew each other as teenagers. We aren't sure of the extent of their relationship, but it confirms that Brad is likely our suspect."

Everyone looked toward me and smiled encouragingly. This actually felt way better than a vision. I was able to use my awesome research skills to help the team. *Add a gold star to my employee evaluation, please.*

However, I realized now everyone had a job but me. Maybe I could tag along with one of the checkpoints.

Before I started to feel too out of place, Helen continued, "Linda, I need you to stay here with Sarah and continue looking for possible cabins."

I nodded and smiled, grateful to have a useful role in things and one that would keep me inside. The wind was picking up speed as we rolled into lunchtime.

"Everyone grab some food to take with you from the kitchen for lunch. Surveillance teams, check in every fifteen minutes with Hank. The cabin team will check in when we are in sight of the cabin and before we enter. Plan on about twenty-five minutes for us to reach the cabin. Base team, check in if you get any promising leads." Helen divvied out instructions like a seasoned general. "Remember, no one goes alone, follow the check-in schedule, and stay safe."

JUST OVER TWENTY-FIVE minutes after the teams dispersed, we heard a squawk and static over the radio. Sarah and I had been huddled around computer screens talking back and forth about potential properties. We both went silent at the sounds for the radio.

Helen's voice cut through the static. "Cabin team checking in."

I held my breath. She had said they would check in before they went into the cabin. The image of the cabin and Jane's eyes came back to me. I hoped they were there and this would end with Jane back safe with the family by tomorrow.

"No sign of anyone. Will check inside."

My eyes closed in disappointment. We were wrong. This wasn't the cabin. The crackle of the radio came back in less than three minutes.

"Confirmed. No sign of suspects or other inhabitants. Returning to base."

Sarah looked at me with sympathy. "It's alright, it was a bit of a long shot but worth checking out. Let's keep looking."

I sighed and turned back to the computer I'd been using to search the map for cabins that fit. We had looked at a lot of locations and even expanded the search radius. There were a lot of little cabins. But most were either not remote enough, no running water nearby, or no chimney. The few that we did find luckily had been sold since the late 1990s and we could check out pictures of them online. They all got quickly disqualified, although there was one that I would have loved to buy had I the money. And if it wasn't over two thousand miles from where I currently lived.

We worked for another ten minutes, but both of us needed a mental break and reset. Not sure what to do in this situation other than keep working, I was happy to see that we were both clearly on the same wavelength. Sarah got up gracefully and stood behind her chair, stretching her arms overhead and cracking her knuckles. I took the opening to start up a non-cabin-hunting conversation.

"So are you a member of this pack?" I asked her with as much innocence as I could muster. I wasn't sure if this was an okay question to ask and I was pretty sure I already knew the answer.

She looked my way and smiled. "Yes," she replied, but didn't offer up more.

"Do you like it?" My ears reddened as I blurted that out.

She chuckled a bit. "Yes. I like it a lot. It's my family."

"I don't mean to be rude," I started off hesitantly, but decided to continue to see if I could learn more. Sarah had been so nice. All the pack members were really nice. Now was my chance to get some firsthand information from someone within the otherworldly community. Well, someone who wasn't a patronizing and terrifying vampire. "When did you join the pack?"

Sarah paused for a minute and looked up slightly as if she were trying to remember the date. "I've been with the pack since 1939."

My face must have revealed what was going through my head. Sarah looked to be in her early thirties at the oldest. Obviously mature and with a confidence that only comes with age and experience, but also young and fit with an ease that you see in people who haven't faced their mortality yet. I had known from the briefing docs that werewolves also had extended lifespans, but it was hard for my brain to connect Sarah's age with her appearance. Luckily, Sarah took some pity on me and shared more of her story without me needing to pry.

"I was orphaned during the Great Depression around the age of seven." Her eyes started to cloud with tears. "I don't know exactly what happened to my parents. Not sure if they died or just couldn't take care of me. I grew up in a girls' home until I was sixteen. It was right about when World War Two was starting. I was too young to join the war efforts, and I was a girl, so that didn't help," she said with a bit of humor in her voice. "The pack hired me as a housemaid when the girls' home kicked me out. I didn't know what the pack was at that time. I also learned later that the girls' home was one of many orphanages owned by the pack." Sarah's humor had shifted to be laced with a bit of anger, or maybe it was disappointment.

"The pack runs differently now," she said firmly, glancing at me, and I nodded to show that I understood. I wasn't sure I really understood. "Just after my eighteenth birthday, Isaac, the pack leader at the time, told me what the group I had been working for really was. And he offered me the option to join or be sent out west to make my own way."

"Wow, eighteen feels young to make such a big decision," I said before I could stop myself. At not quite thirty, I couldn't imagine making a life-changing decision like that.

"It is," Sarah said softly. "Luckily, all the packs came to an agreement over ten years ago to only recruit individuals over the age of thirty. It's really better that way. We had some unfortunate situations that I'm hoping the new age requirement will prevent.

"But for me and the circumstances at that time, I'm grateful for the chance. After the girls' home, those two years felt like I had a family." She looked at me with emotion welling up in her big brown eyes. "I wasn't going to be given up by a family again."

As a fellow orphan, I understood exactly what she was saying. I wasn't given up by choice, and my family had just been me and my mom, but I would give anything to feel like I had family again. We looked at each other and it felt like we had a shared understanding as well as matching tear-filled eyes. Any sense of professional decorum I had in the moment left me and I rose from my chair and opened my arms. Sarah smiled through tears in her eyes and walked into my offered hug.

We stood there for a few moments, rocking back and forth, and had a small but cathartic cry. Sarah patted me on the back and cleared her throat. I let her go and sheepishly sat back down.

"Thank you," Sarah said quickly, and any embarrassment about hugging a near stranger went away. "It's still an emotional story to tell, even though it was several decades ago. But the pack is great. I don't regret my decision at all and it's been an amazing life so far. So, that's my story. What's yours?" She leaned forward on the back of the chair with curiosity in her eyes.

"Um, well, my mom died two years ago and I never knew my dad. Orphan here as well," I said as awkwardly as I could and raised my hand as if I needed to be counted by a teacher. I felt the need to explain why I also had cried but didn't want to start the water works up again.

Sarah just laughed a bit at my awkwardness. She was really easy to talk with, and I thought for a minute that I might be forming a bit of a crush. But Jordan's warnings about dating otherworldly beings and remembering that we were on the hunt for a kidnapper quickly pushed any of those thoughts out of my head.

"You're new to the agency, right?" She changed the subject, helping the conversation move forward.

"Yes, I just started on Monday."

"Wow, that is new." She seemed both surprised and impressed. "What's your job with the firm?"

"I'm the executive admin. I'm supposed to help with schedules, travel, home-office stuff, and research. But, somehow I ended up here with the away team."

"Well, it sounds like you were already key in finding the Brad and Jane connection," Sarah said. "We've been looking for a connection with any of the recruits and Jane since Helen called about coming out and talking to them. We weren't able to find anything."

"Yeah, it was a bit of a lucky find," I said, not wanting to claim that I was better than a whole pack of werewolves.

"Not lucky," Sarah said. "Smart."

"Thanks," I said somewhat shyly, not fully comfortable with the compliment.

"How did you find the connection?" Sarah asked. "I'd love to learn."

"I used social media. The first thing I usually check is photos," I answered and then told her about how I had found the trail that led me to the photo of Brad and Jane.

"That's smart," Sarah said, encouraging me to continue.

"There was an older photo, one that wasn't taken with a phone," I said and pulled up the picture on my laptop so that I could show her what I meant.

I turned the laptop toward her so she could see.

"There's Brad," I said, pointing to him in the picture. "And we think that is Jane," I said, pointing to the girl in the photo.

Sarah gasped and leaned toward the laptop. "Can you send me this photo?"

"Yes. Sure."

I took a screenshot and then airdropped the photo to Sarah. She turned back to her own computer and zoomed into the boy who was standing next to Jane with his arm around her shoulders.

"That's the guy who died and who the memorial post was for," I offered.

"Was his name Paul?" Sarah asked in a whisper.

"Yes," I responded, confused. "How did you know that?"

"Paul was a member of the pack," she responded, still in a whisper.

I didn't know what to say, so I didn't say anything.

"He was killed on a mission very shortly after he was recruited," she said with pain in her voice. "He shouldn't have been there. He wasn't ready. He was so young." She was speaking out loud, but more talking to herself.

"Is Paul the reason for the age requirement for recruits?" I asked before I could stop myself.

"Yes," she said. "It took Michael years to convince the rest of the packs that we needed to stop recruiting so young. But he did. Michael was a new alpha and he never wanted another tragedy like Paul's."

"So Brad knows Jane and Paul," I said. "And it looks like Jane and Paul were friendly, or maybe even in a relationship. Now Jane is a vampire and missing. And Brad is on the verge of becoming a werewolf." I was saying my thoughts out loud now. "That seems like too much of a coincidence."

"We have to tell Michael and Helen," Sarah said as she reached for her radio.

Sarah radioed over to them to ask how close they were to getting back to the house. Helen responded that they were about fifteen minutes away.

"They can't do anything about it now," Sarah said to me. "We'll tell them as soon as they get back. Let's keep working through the maps for potential locations."

"Alright," I agreed.

My mind was racing too much about the conversation. I didn't think of myself as more than an EA at this job, but maybe I had a natural talent for investigations. It was clear now that Helen and the team had given more importance to my ideas, opinions, and feelings. They also seemed to immediately trust that I had visions and they believed them. It was getting easier to call them visions as I came to terms with what was going on.

The visions, or the potential of them, seemed like a key reason that they had brought me along. I didn't love that idea. But I supposed there was a level of trust that Helen and the other team members had given me— though I still felt like they were acting as babysitters at times.

Thinking about it more, I bet Jordan was just as caring toward Hank. Or Steve was just as protective of Cam. Maybe it was just how this team was with each other. I hadn't known them for long, but I needed to start giving them the benefit of the doubt instead of second-guessing their actions toward me.

My growling stomach was the signal for us to stop and see what was left in the kitchen for lunch before the team got back. I realized I'd only had a donut, a banana, a cup of coffee, and a cup of overly sugary tea all day. I needed to eat or I wasn't going to be much use to anyone soon.

"I'm going to get something to eat," I said as I stood up. "Do you want anything?"

"No," Sarah answered. "I'll grab something later. But if we are taking a break from cabin searching anyway, I'll go pull the recording equipment from upstairs. We can keep looking at cabins when you're ready."

"Sounds good," I answered and made my way toward that kitchen as Sarah headed up the stairs.

The kitchen was through a swinging door on the far side of the dining room. It looked a little rougher than it had this morning. Used plates and cups cluttered the sink, and various packaged foods littered the counters. It was understandable—everyone had been in a rush to get out the door, grabbing what they could without concern for being tidy.

I scanned the counter for anything that looked good. Only one week on Mrs. Clark's steady stream of home-cooked food and already prepackaged foods and snacks had lost a lot of their appeal. Deciding against any of that, I hoped that there would be some better options in the fridge.

My head was in the fridge evaluating the benefits of a premade turkey sandwich versus a premade salad. *Maybe I should just have both.* There seemed like plenty of food for me to have a combo lunch and still leave plenty for others.

The sound of a door opening made me pop my head up from behind the fridge door, ready to offer one of the options to Sarah. Instead of Sarah's kind face, I recognized the angry eyes that met mine. I barely had time for a moment of panic before the world went black.

17

My eyes fluttered open and I winced as a pain flared in my left temple. I gingerly probed the spot and my hand came back wet. In the dark I couldn't see what it was, but the smell of copper and the stickiness meant it was very likely blood. I took several deep breaths to calm down my rising panic and try to manage the pain. Have I mentioned I wasn't good with blood?

It took me a minute to realize I was in the trunk of a moving vehicle. The steady beat of tires against the road paired with my stomach reacting to the motion helped me draw this conclusion. Groping around, I could feel the lid of the trunk above me and a scratchy blanket under me.

I reached toward my back pocket, where I usually kept my phone. Before my hand even reached my pocket, I remembered that my phone was sitting next to the computer in the dining room back at the house. It would have been silly to bring my phone with me to the kitchen, and I didn't want to look silly in front of Sarah.

With no phone and no idea what was waiting for me when the car stopped, I almost started hyperventilating. The image of my self-defense teacher filled my head. I could hear the words almost like she was in the car with me: *Every car after 2002 has a trunk-release latch inside the trunk. Look for the latch, it will glow in the dark.*

Turning over in the car made my head spin, but I needed to find the latch. It was there, tucked off to the side. In my excitement I almost pulled it, but then I waited to think it through. I needed a plan of what to do once I pulled the latch.

I took a few more deep breaths and then felt around the trunk again, searching for anything that could be a weapon or a signal to other cars on the road once I got the trunk open. I found a backpack. Feeling around with my hands, I was able to find the zipper and open it. Carefully, I examined what was in the bag. It seemed like an emergency kit for a car, including water bottles, several things in plastic of various sizes, a foldable shovel, and jumper cables. And a flashlight.

I clicked on the flashlight and illuminated the space. A few blinks to get used to the light, and then I could see that the other items in the bag were food, a small pocketknife, a first aid kit, a plastic poncho, and gallon ziplock bags with clothes. All of these items would make a good trail of breadcrumbs for someone to follow. The team would be looking for me. The shovel I'd hold on to; it could make a good weapon if I had a chance to use it.

I separated out everything so that I could toss as many items as possible. I went to pull on the glowing trunk-release pull but luckily stopped. If I opened the trunk, it would fly up and whoever was driving would know I'd opened it. Shit. This wasn't going to work. I needed to keep the trunk from flying open.

Looking around at my collection of found items, I spotted a rope in one of the bags. I could use it to keep the trunk from flying open and alerting anyone in the car. I just needed it to open a crack so I could either signal a car or start tossing my breadcrumb trail.

Using the knife, I cut through the carpet on the trunk lid in two places so that I could thread the rope through. I didn't know how long we'd been driving at this point, but I startled when the steady thrum of asphalt was replaced with the crunch of gravel. I needed to get moving with my plan.

The rope was in place; I held it and my breath, then pulled the trunk-release tab. The lid popped open and yanked against the rope I was holding to keep it only slightly ajar. It worked and I almost started crying.

Peeking out the open slot, I could see a bit, but I couldn't see any cars. We were in the country on a gravel road. Just fields and trees and a winding road. I couldn't wait for a car that likely wouldn't show up, so I started phase two: Operation breadcrumbs.

Holding the rope taut with my left hand, I reached for the pile of items with my right and grabbed the first thing I felt, a water bottle. Only slightly feeling bad about littering, I let it go out the gap softly so that it would land in the road. It rolled slightly and then stopped. I kept an eye on it until it got small but was still within sight, and then I let the next item go. This went on for several minutes, dropping one thing after another. Before too long my pile was gone. I only had the shovel and the pocketknife left. I had even shoved the bag out through the gap.

I wouldn't be able to lead anyone to my exact location, but it was probably for the best that my abductor didn't know that I'd left even a partial trail. I tucked the shovel under the blanket and put the knife in my pocket. Not wanting to give up the light and fresh air, I decided to take a chance and keep the lid open a crack for now.

After a few more minutes, the car took a sharp left and then slowed down. It seemed like we had arrived at our destination. I quickly pulled the trunk closed and unthreaded the rope from the top. The rope got tucked under the blanket alongside the shovel.

THE CAR HAD STOPPED. My heart was in my throat and my mind was racing. I'd have given anything to be back on the winding road, even if that meant I threw up in the back of this car. The trunk opened slowly, letting in the full blast of wind, rain, and soft, stormy-afternoon light. I blinked in the gray light, letting my eyes adjust from the dark. A canopy of trees was overhead—we were in a forest. Brad stood at the open trunk and looked exasperated by the sight of me lying bloody and sweaty in the trunk of his car.

"Well, we're in a pickle now," he said, as if a joint decision we had made over coffee had gotten us here. I just stared at him, not able to make any sense of what to do or how to handle a clearly delusional individual. I tried to remember how to attack from those long-ago self-defense classes.

"Might as well come inside." He leaned over to offer me a hand out of the trunk.

I hesitated and reached back for the shovel. If I struck fast and hard, maybe I could get a chance to run. He grabbed my arm faster than I could move to get to the shovel. I was disappointed in myself that I hadn't been fast enough or brave enough to attack. I let him help me out and even steady me as the pain in my head flared again and my knees almost gave out.

We walked up toward a cabin, his hand still firmly locked above my elbow to guide me along and probably to prevent me from running. It was starting to rain hard and there were no signs it would stop anytime soon. I tried to look around inconspicuously, searching for any sign of Helen and the team. I didn't see them. Even worse, I didn't see the small stream that should be just on the other side of the cabin.

My heart sank even further as I realized I had been wrong about the running water. I couldn't see or hear any running water around the cabin. There was no way that they would think to look at this one in the search. I had led them in the wrong direction. Tears started to fill my eyes; I was truly scared now. The team would be looking for the wrong cabin. They might not ever find the trail I left for them.

. . .

WE ENTERED the familiar interior of the cabin. At least I had gotten that right, as much use as that would be. Jane wasn't here, but I did hear running water from behind a closed door and she might be in there. Brad guided me over to the brown couch facing the rock fireplace and sat me down. He then walked into the kitchen area and grabbed a washcloth out of a drawer. Handing it over to me, he gestured for me to press it against my temple. It had mostly stopped bleeding, but I was grateful to put pressure on it to stop it completely.

Brad slumped down in a chair to the side of me and just sighed. We sat in silence for a few minutes until the closed door opened. Jane stepped out of the bathroom wrapped in a robe and with her hair up in a towel. She looked quite a bit better than she had when I'd seen her in the vision, although she was still deathly pale.

It took her a moment to notice me trying to be invisible on the couch. She gasped in surprise and then looked angrily at Brad, letting a small growl slip between her pale, pursed lips.

"Brad," she whisper-screamed like a very angry parent to a toddler at a restaurant. "What were you thinking, bringing a human here?"

"I can explain," he almost pleaded. His tone had shifted drastically in the presence of Jane. Where he had been angry and disrespectful during the interview, now he seemed more like a sniveling sidekick to a villain. "Remember how I told you I was worried the pack was getting suspicious about me? Well, they brought in a group of humans this morning and I had to go in and get questioned.

"This one was in the interview," Brad continued, gesturing to me as I tried harder to sink into the ugly orange and brown plaid couch. "She had some kind of fit toward the end. Her eyes rolled back and she froze in place for like two minutes. When she came to, everyone freaked out and ended the interview immediately."

It was eerie to hear him describe what it had been like watching me during that vision. It made me wonder if I always looked like that when I daydreamed or if this had been the first time. This time had felt different than the normal daydreaming and everyone had reacted strangely to it. I think I had been too scared to really think about what had happened in that interview room.

"Do you think she could be one of *those*?" Jane asked with a little hand wave. She looked a little less angry and more intrigued.

"Yes, babe," Brad said, nodding with a hungry look now in his eyes, wanting Jane's approval.

I was too terrified to ask them to explain what they were talking about. My eyes kept darting between the two. Brad seemed less in control of the situation. Jane's eyes were pleading but also darting around the room in a frenzied panic. She looked completely on edge and ready to tip over it at any minute.

The more I looked at Jane, the more my mind started to pop up facts, pieces clicking into place. Jordan had said that an adoptee this young would need a constant supply of fresh blood to remain healthy. If they didn't get that, there was a risk of loss of control, psychosis, and death, something she had assured me hadn't happened in centuries. Families were so careful about adoptees. I didn't think Jane was totally out of control. At least not yet. But if it got to that point, neither Brad nor I would be safe.

"I stayed around the house and hid to see what was going on," Brad continued his explanation to Jane. "Most of them left after my interview. I had walked to the house for the interview, but I don't think they knew that. I'm pretty sure they were trying to find me."

Well, that explained why they found his truck parked near his house but not him. Jane had started to settle as he explained, and she moved to the chair across from him. Now placed between the two of them, I wasn't sure who to keep a closer eye on: the one who clearly didn't hesitate to hit a woman or the one who was clearly craving some fresh blood.

"They came back and I heard them talk about checking out my house and Ted's house." I assumed those were the other locations that Hank had wanted to check out. "Most of them went inside for a bit. Then almost everyone left the house and I overheard them talking about checkpoints on the roads out of town.

"They left her behind with only one female wolf. I thought we could use her as collateral if they found us. Or, if they don't, then maybe she can help us longer term with our plan." He looked expectantly at me as if waiting for me to spew out all the answers to their problems.

Jane looked like she was considering the idea as she

scratched her nails up and down her arm, leaving red marks but not drawing blood.

Brad had paused to watch how she would react, but when Jane didn't say anything, he continued, "Anyway, I stole a car. Some dummy had left the keys in the cup holder. And I barely made it out on the back road before a car rolled up to set up a block."

Jane continued to run her fingernails over her arm, the cross-hatching starting to look raised now. Her eyes narrowed in interest, but then she shook her head and growled under her breath. She didn't seem too happy with Brad.

"I'm not sure that was a good idea." She looked at me as she said it. Had I not been terrified, I may have reminded her that this idea had not been mine. "It's dark enough with the rain. Let's go outside and talk." Jane stood as she directed him toward the door. She must have decided that she didn't want me involved in the next part of their conversation.

STRAINING to listen in but not wanting to move, I couldn't hear much over the rain and wind outside. My head was hurting enough that I gave up trying to hear the conversation and instead took stock of where I was and what could be done.

It didn't seem like Jane was kidnapped. Either that or she had quickly developed Stockholm syndrome. She seemed more in control of the situation than Brad did.

Jane and Brad did know each other from high school, and they had a familiarity between the two of them.

It looked like Jane must have been surviving on stored blood that was taken from her adopter. The pack was likely to know if Brad had been acting as a donor for Jane. They must have been getting blood from somewhere. Neither seemed like hard-core killers, so I doubted they had been on a murder spree. Plus the pack would for sure know if there were missing people in their community. I bet if I looked in the fridge, it would be filled with blood packs.

But how did Jane get from the family estate in Seattle to this remote cabin in the northeast? My head started to hurt more as I searched my brain for answers. A phrase that I'd heard Annie say a few times came to mind: *You can buy anything in this world with money.* And Jane had money. Now, knowing that she wasn't kidnapped, I'd bet anything that she'd used her money and resources to run away and join Brad here.

That wasn't my main concern right now though. I needed to focus on what I could do to get out of this. It was clear that they weren't overly concerned with me running or they wouldn't have left me in here on my own.

Looking around more, there was a single entrance and only small windows. The only other door did in fact lead to a bathroom. A small fire was barely clinging to life in the fireplace. I wouldn't make it out a window, and the two of them were still standing just on the other side of the front door.

I looked around the room to see if there was anything I

could use as a weapon. There was a set of fireplace tools—the poker may do some damage but I could barely stand. I didn't think I could gather enough adrenaline to put up much of a fight. There didn't seem to be anywhere to hide, so I quickly dismissed that idea.

The best I could do was comply and use my charm and wit to buy time. Maybe Jane and Brad would get complacent and leave, giving me a chance to run. Or more likely, Helen and everyone on the team would find me. They'd find the trail. They were smart enough to figure this out, right? Plus they had the whole local pack to help them. Did werewolves have a supernatural sense of smell they could use to follow the trail?

Jane and Brad came back into the cabin before my mind could go too far down the winding and scary paths of what could happen. Jane looked determined and Brad looked chastised. She walked over to the fridge and took out a large pouch of dark red liquid. Her back to me, she made slurping sounds and then dumped the empty container into the sink. I had been right about the blood packs in the fridge.

"You aren't in danger," Jane tried to reassure me, now less anxious than she had been, likely thanks to the refreshment. Even so, I did not believe her. But her voice had started to take on some of the tone that I remembered from Winthrop's interview. The hypnotic quality almost got to me, but the pain in my head was keeping my other emotions in check.

She continued to explain the new plan: "We'll stay here

for a couple of days at most while we take care of some things, and then we'll let you go."

They must have decided that I wasn't worth the trouble of bringing along for their future plans. I was relieved at first but then started to worry. If I wasn't of use to them, what incentive did they have to keep me alive? Stories I'd heard too many times filled me with dread—maybe I shouldn't have listened to all those murder podcasts after all. I searched for a way to figure out what was going on and keep them talking. Maybe I could talk them into letting me go.

"I'm sure that this is just a mistake," I said in an effort to start a conversation to keep them talking. "Maybe I can help."

Jane just scoffed, and Brad avoided my eye contact but didn't say anything.

"I know the family is really worried about you," I said, focusing my attention on Jane. "We can help you get back to them."

"That family only cares about themselves," Jane said with a huff. "They just want more money and to 'keep the peace.'"

She actually used air quotes around "keep the peace." The money part I understood, but that I didn't. I decided to press my luck and see if she would keep talking.

I asked as gently and nonchalantly as I could, "What do you mean they just want to keep the peace?"

"Vampires are supposed to be enemies of werewolves, right?" she asked. I nodded my head to agree with her, even though I now knew that wasn't true. "But come to find out they are all buddy-buddy with them." Jane rolled her eyes like a teenager. This woman was over thirty, but I had to remind myself what Jordan had said. Newly adopted vampires are impulsive. Looks like they regress to being a bratty teenager as well.

"You don't like werewolves?" I asked. *Keep her talking.*

"No," she said.

Brad scoffed again but kept his head down and picked at imaginary lint on his shirt. I used Helen's technique and let the silence hang in the air, hoping that Jane would continue.

She did. "They use people. The pack convinces someone that they'll have a wonderful life if they join, but then the alphas just use them for dirty work and don't care who gets killed." Jane's voice went from bratty teenager to real sadness.

More pieces of the puzzle clicked into place. She was talking about Paul. And from the way she was talking about him, I would bet that they were high school sweethearts. So now I knew how they were all connected, but why was she here? And why was Brad here? And more importantly, how could I get out of this?

"That's terrible," I said, trying to sympathize.

"It is and they deserve to be punished." The teenage rage was back in her voice. "If the family won't help me, Brad will," Jane said and looked toward Brad.

He looked up and made eye contact with her. The look in his eyes conveyed that he would do anything for Jane. That, coupled with him calling her *babe* earlier, and I realized that they were now in a relationship. Or at least Brad liked Jane. Jane didn't have the same look for him in her eyes.

"Oh, so you and Brad are going after the pack," I blurted out and then clamped my hand over my mouth.

Jane laughed. "Well, not the whole pack. That'd be a death sentence," she said. Brad gave her a pleading look to stop talking, but Jane was clearly in charge. "We just need to get Michael," she continued. "He's the one responsible for Paul's death."

"That seems reasonable," I said slowly, just wanting to agree with the vampire on a vengeance mission. I didn't want to end up as a to-do item on her mission checklist.

"It is," she said, back to the teenage brattiness. "Brad was able to infiltrate the pack. Even if it's not likely he'll be recruited, we just needed to learn about what really happened to Paul. And now we know. It was Michael.

"It may take some time, but I'll gain my strength and then I can take him out," she said with a level of confidence that was delusional. I was not going to be the one to tell her that if she didn't get more of her adopter's blood, then she'd likely die. "But that doesn't matter right now. Brad shouldn't have brought you here." Jane practically growled with an angry glance toward Brad, who was now hunched down in the chair as if he was trying to make himself as small as possible. "After we leave in a couple of days, there is a road just to the west that you are likely to be able to flag down a car on."

I almost believed her, probably because I really wanted to believe her. Also, did she say a road? Could that have been the sound I thought was water? It was raining, and that was likely drowning out any car noises, but I hadn't heard rain in my vision. I was new to actually believing my daydreams were really visions. Maybe I had just misjudged the sound. Little good that did me now.

"We'll all just settle in here until the search dies down," she said.

"Okay," I said, wanting to reassure her that I wouldn't be a problem. I looked over to the fireplace and had an idea. "Could we add more logs to the fire? It's getting kind of cold in here."

"Yes," she said offhandedly. "Brad, make the fire bigger."

Brad quickly complied with Jane's demand. I kept my face blank as the fire grew and put more smoke out the chimney—hopefully a signal that this cabin was occupied to the people who were looking for me.

DESPITE JANE TRYING to reassure me that I'd be free in a couple of days, I was still worried about her need for blood and her self-control. She had the blood in the fridge, but Jordan was clear about new vampires needing fresh blood, and I couldn't imagine Brad was acting as a donor. I realized that not having fresh blood may have been why Jane was pale and listless looking, not the overly attractive vampire look that I would have expected. But I wasn't going to point that out to her.

Jane and Brad moved into the kitchen area to continue talking in hushed whispers. Tired, in pain, and still terrified, I couldn't make sense of any of the words I was able to catch as they talked. I willed my body to relax and tried breathing in the four-count cadence that Steve had during our interviews. Thinking of Steve turned into thinking about the whole team and that I might not see any of them again. That thinking led to tears welling up in my eyes.

Between the adrenaline crash and the head injury, I was exhausted. My alert state gave way to an uneasy sleep as I drifted off unwillingly on the ugly brown couch. I woke briefly when I felt the weight of a blanket being draped over me. I accepted it and kicked my feet up on the couch, lying down to give in fully to sleep.

18

———

I startled awake as Jane and Brad both rushed past the couch to the front windows. It felt like I had just closed my eyes, but I had no idea how long I'd been asleep. The sound of gravel crunching from several cars could be heard. From the looks on Jane's and Brad's faces as they glanced from each other to outside, these were not expected guests. My hopes rose that I had been found.

Jane growled at Brad and pushed him to the side, knocking him down. Brad clutched his arm and looked terrified in the split second I glanced his way. I looked up just as Jane made her way to my side, hovering way too close. Her hand wrapped painfully around my forearm. She leaned in more and I almost gagged on her rancid breath.

She hissed in a barely controlled rage, "I'm going to need you to come with me." Clearly she was spinning out of control, and it was not a good sign that Brad was backing his way into the corner.

I was given no choice as she dragged me to my feet and hauled me toward the front door. I glanced at Brad now crouched below the front window to the right of the door. He looked at the window and then looked at me with terror. I only had to wonder why for a moment before a howl rose high in the air and all the hairs on my body stood on end at once.

The warning from Annie came to mind: *Don't run.* The wolves were on our side. The single howl had been joined by a chorus that seemed to surround the cabin. The signal filling the air was a warning, letting every living thing know they had come for something. It was unnerving that that something was me. Relief and fear crowded for space in my head.

Jane pressed my face to the right of hers on the glass of the door's window, her right hand holding the back of my head and her left hand still gripping my forearm, forcing me to stand next to her with nowhere to go. Her face was contorted in rage and the growling from her was now accompanied with bloody spit spraying flecks on the window of the door. She was tipping over from rage to rampage and I was the closest one for her to take it out on.

Forced to look out the window, I saw three black SUVs. Doors were flung open and a few familiar figures were positioned behind them. Half a dozen unfamiliar and abnormally large wolves filled the space between the cars and the cabin's porch. Their raised heads were as tall as the SUVs parked behind them. Their teeth were bared, white fangs prominent. Their eyes were intense and serious with human intelligence and emotion shining through.

I didn't think I'd ever had this particular mixture of fear and relief at the same time. Instincts took over and I wasn't sure who I should be more terrified of: the single vampire who had me in a death grip or the several werewolves outside who could rip me apart in minutes.

Relief finally overcame the terror as I saw Helen step out from behind an open car door and walk to stand in the middle of the pack, three werewolves flanking each side. Black tactical gear replaced her usual immaculate outfit, and even from this distance I could see her face and her stance were set in determination. She raised a small bullhorn up to her face.

"Jane, and Brad I presume is there too. You know who I am and who I represent," Helen proclaimed firmly, projecting loudly through the bullhorn. "You need to release Linda to us. Then we will negotiate the terms of your surrender. If you comply quickly, we will take that into consideration."

With that last statement, all six werewolves seemed to get bigger. Jane's grip just tightened. Brad started sobbing, now backed into the corner of the room to the right of us and covering his ears to block out the growling coming from the larger-than-life werewolves outside the walls. Time moved slowly—what was probably sixty seconds seemed to last forever. Jane did not make any move to comply with Helen's demands, continuing to hold me in a death grip and spray spit on the window as she growled in reply.

I watched in an almost out-of-body fascination as Helen gave a subtle up-and-down nod and then all hell broke loose. A hole appeared in the wall to the left of us with a cloud of dust. Out of the dust, two werewolves leapt into the cabin. One charged straight for Jane and the other toward Brad.

Jane's grip loosened slightly in the chaos, and the instincts I'd learned in self-defense classes all those years ago took over. I took my chance to forcefully bring my unconstrained arm over the top of her forearm, breaking her hold. I dropped down, barely getting out of the way as the werewolf tackled Jane to the floor.

On my back, I glanced to my left where the hole was, just in time to see Steve in full black tactical gear looking more badass than he had any right to be.

Steve was at my side within seconds. He pulled me farther from the pinned Jane and the snarling werewolf. He did a quick sweep of my injuries and decided I wasn't at risk of dying right that minute. He hoisted me up into a cradle hold and made a swift exit with me out the new doorway that had been created in the wall.

Steve carried me all the way to the back of an SUV. The screaming from the cabin had died down by the time we got there, an eerie silence now filling the air. Jordan was waiting for me at the back of the SUV, where they had constructed a plastic tent hanging off the open trunk door to protect from the rain that was still beating down. Steve gently sat me down on the edge of the open trunk.

"Good job leaving us a trail," he said gruffly. "Glad you aren't dead."

Steve turned and walked back toward the cabin before I could offer a response. I was confused at his last words but smiled through the pain. My breadcrumbs had worked. They had found me.

"He doesn't handle injured team members well," Jordan explained. "He takes it as a personal failing if any of us so much as gets a scratch. So try not to take anything he says for the next couple of weeks personally."

"Okay." That was all my brain could come up with. I think I was in shock. Turned out Jordan agreed.

"You are probably in shock, so just let me do my job and know that you are safe now," she said as she got to work, prodding my head injury. Cam came into view and gave me a weak smile. Jordan handed her a wad of gauze and instructed her to start cleaning up the blood so that she could get a better view of my injuries.

With Cam wiping blood off my face, Jordan's gentle hands felt around to check for other injuries on my body. I winced in pain when she got to my left forearm where Jane had been holding on.

"Looks like this might be broken, or at least a deep bone bruise. We'll wrap it for now and then get an X-ray in town," Jordan explained. "Are there any other areas that are hurting?"

"My whole head, not just the temple," I said through clenched teeth, gesturing up weakly to the back of my head with my right hand.

Jordan turned me slightly so that she could see the back of my head, shining a light and moving my hair around to get a better view. I could feel the hair pulling at already drying blood.

"Ouch, looks like her nails punctured the skin on the back of your head. You probably have some bad bruising as well," she continued as she delicately probed my head. "It doesn't feel like there are any breaks, but we'll get a head scan. I'd want one for the blow to your temple anyway to rule out any fractures or bleeds. Anywhere else?"

"Nope, I think that's enough," I said in an awkward attempt to lighten the mood.

"Well, you still have your sense of humor, that's always a good sign." Jordan seemed relieved. "We'll get everything wrapped and stabilized. I'll give you some light painkillers, but I can't give you the good stuff until we get a few more things checked out at the hospital. It might be a bit of a rough ride down, sorry."

I'm not sure if it was the apology from Jordan or the second major adrenaline crash in one day, but any walls holding back my tears fully came down. Jordan and Cam looked startled for a moment, and then they both gently cradled me in a group hug. The three of us rocked slightly back and forth, and they continued holding me until the sobs subsided.

Helen found the three of us huddled together behind the SUV. I'd stopped crying and was concentrating on taking deep breaths as Jordan wrapped my arm tightly. She'd already bandaged my head, fully encasing it like a big white helmet.

"Linda, I'm so glad you are okay," Helen said softly. "We

found the items on the road. It helped us find the cabin. That was really smart."

I flushed a little at her compliment.

"I know you aren't feeling well," she continued as she looked at the bandages around my head and arm. "But I need you to tell me a little about what happened. Just the highlights so we can get a better picture of what we are dealing with. We'll get a more detailed debrief once you're feeling better."

"I was getting lunch in the kitchen, and then the next thing I know I was in the trunk of a car," I started from the beginning. "Brad must have hit me with something, I woke up with my head bleeding. I found a backpack full of things and the latch to open the trunk. I threw out the stuff from the backpack as breadcrumbs."

"That really was quick thinking," Cam added.

I took a deep breath. If everyone kept complimenting me, I'd probably start crying again.

The three women nodded along with my storytelling, Jordan grimacing slightly when I mentioned getting hit in the head. Cam looked like she would punch the next person who walked by. Helen kept it calm and collected on the outside, but behind her eyes I could see fury brewing.

"We got to the cabin and Jane was there. Jane wasn't kidnapped," I continued. "She was in it with Brad. They're after Michael."

"Interesting," Helen mused as I paused to take another deep breath.

"Brad said something about my vision during the interview and that maybe I could help them with their long-term plan," I continued. Helen and Jordan exchanged a quick glance, but I kept going, wanting to get the whole story out and not dwell on that fact. "They went outside to talk, and when they came back in I got Jane talking. She wants revenge for the death of Paul. She blames Michael." I was racing through the explanation, the adrenaline picking back up with my retelling of what happened. "Jane became a vampire because she thought the family would help her take down the werewolves." I gulped in some air.

Jordan looked at me nervously and then over to Helen. Helen just gave a slight shake of her head.

"But she found out that vampires and werewolves aren't actually enemies. So she had Brad become a recruit so that she could learn more about what happened to Paul and how they could get revenge." I wasn't sure if what I was saying was making any sense. It felt like I was just rambling. "Jane said that they weren't going to hurt me and that I could find my way to a road in a few days after they had left. I couldn't see a way out and I was exhausted. I fell asleep on the couch," I said sheepishly.

I felt a little silly admitting that I had fallen asleep in such a dangerous situation, but the words were already out. Glancing up at Helen, she gave me a comforting smile and nodded for me to keep going. At some point in the story, Jordan had reached over to hold my hand. She gave it a gentle squeeze.

"I woke up to Jane and Brad running to the front door and I heard cars outside. Then Jane was dragging me off the couch to the front door, where I saw all of you and the werewolves outside. After that you all probably saw what happened," I concluded.

"Thank you, Linda. That's all I need for now. You did great and that fills in a lot of information that we didn't have. Great job keeping calm and getting information from Jane. That will be really helpful for cleaning up this mess with the family and the pack," Helen said reassuringly, then turned to Jordan. "Let's give her some pain meds, then get her bundled up and into a car so you can head to the hospital before this storm gets worse."

Jordan nodded her head and started to reach for her bag, then almost as an afterthought she asked Helen, "Is anyone else injured that you need me to take a look at?"

"No," she responded firmly with a hint of anger and finality before she walked back to the action out of view from the back of the SUV.

THE RIDE down was about as bad as Jordan had warned me it would be. The drugs were barely taking the edge off, and my head continued to thrum with every heartbeat. The gravel road had more bumps than I remembered on the ride up; I counted them to help focus and to have something to be mad at. I was anchored on either side by Jordan and Cam, and they both huddled close, trying to hold me still as the car bounced along. Sarah drove as carefully as she could. Another pack member I didn't know rode in the front.

The four of them talked, catching each other up on what was going on. I caught some of the conversation but not all of it as I drifted in and out of sleep. Jordan updated them on my injuries, and I only startled slightly when they responded with low growls from the front seat. The image of six werewolves lined up growling toward me would be one I wouldn't soon forget.

"Brad ended up with some scrapes," Sarah shared as she navigated the turns. "One of our folks checked him out. He'll probably have some bruises, but nothing looks broken."

"His injuries aren't what he should be most worried about," the other werewolf, who I later learned was named Leo, snarled from the front passenger seat. Sarah made a noise of agreement.

"What are you all going to do with Brad?" Cam asked the two pack members.

"Michael's already called an emergency meeting for later this evening," Sarah replied. "And he is pissed, so it should be interesting."

My mind flashed an image of the meeting that I had seen in my head just yesterday. I was pretty sure I'd already seen some highlights of the meeting that they were going to be having.

"Everyone is throwing around theories about how things could have gotten to this point," Leo shared. "Michael will get to the bottom of it though. Things are likely to not be pretty."

"Nothing like this has happened as far as most of us can remember," Sarah added. It was clear that both of the pack members in the car were disturbed that one of their own had been involved with Jane's revenge scheme and my abduction.

"Did anyone hear anything about Jane?" Jordan asked the group.

"As far as we know she didn't have any real injuries," Leo answered.

"The werewolf who took her down was remarkably constrained," Sarah added. "I'm not sure I would have been, under the circumstances."

They didn't share who the pack member had been, and it seemed rude to ask. I had my suspicions though. The blue eyes that I made contact with as they barreled toward us looked shockingly similar to Michael's when he came into the room after my vision.

"Jane is really weak though," Sarah continued.

"I bet she hasn't had the proper nutrition since leaving the estate," Jordan chimed in. "A single tackle from a werewolf, even a full-grown one, wouldn't cause her that much damage."

"Well, sounds like she'll get what she needs back at the house," Sarah said a bit offhandedly. Leo growled under his breath.

"Helen would require that," Jordan responded firmly to the unhappy pair in the front of the car. They both shrank back like they had been reprimanded. Cam gave my arm a small squeeze as if to tell me that everything would be handled.

"So, what happens next?" I asked, trying to clear the tense vibe in the car and wanting to know what to expect.

"We are heading straight to the hospital," Sarah

answered. "The rest of the team will take Brad and Jane back to the house. That's where Helen wanted them."

"Helen will be questioning both of them," Jordan added. "Michael will be in the room with Brad, but I doubt he'll be in Jane's interview."

So much for clearing the tension. Sarah and Leo both bristled at that, but neither questioned what Jordan had shared. It was clear that even though Michael was alpha of the pack, Helen was still in charge of this case.

Cam leaned over and whispered to me, "Don't worry about them. Helen will handle it."

"Oh good," I replied, not entirely having my wits about me. I leaned into Cam and continued to count the bumps in the road to try to stay awake so I wouldn't miss any more of the conversation. It didn't work—I fell asleep and didn't wake up until we pulled up to the hospital.

AFTER WELL OVER an hour's drive due to some heavy rains, we made it to the hospital. I was whisked away to a private room as soon as we pulled up. Someone had clearly called ahead and let them know I was coming in. I was still in pain but not on death's door, despite how the gaggle of medical personnel made it seem.

Jordan directed the team, giving them the rundown of my known injuries, what medication she had already given me, and what my vitals had been. I realized that the hand on my wrist throughout the drive wasn't just for comfort—she'd been monitoring my heart rate the whole ride. She instructed them on what tests she wanted to run and what medications I should be started on. Everyone referred to her as a doctor, so at least one of my mysteries was solved.

After the head scan, everything must have looked okay because they let me have what Jordan called the good drugs. Jordan never left my side, and I quickly fell asleep even though people were still cleaning up my wounds and rewrapping my arm and head.

19

I woke up to the hum of monitors and low light breaking through some cracks in the blinds. Based on that, I figured I must have slept through the rest of the evening all the way to morning. Whatever drugs they had given me were wearing off slightly, and I winced as I tried to sit up. That must have woken Jordan, who had been sleeping in the chair to the side of my bed. She glanced up at me and smiled.

"Well, the right side of your face is going to be bruised for a bit, but the right color has come back to the other parts," Jordan said lightheartedly.

I tried to smile but ended up wincing again at that movement.

"You have a hairline fracture on your left radius, so your arm is going to be in a cast for a few weeks at least," she continued. "Surprisingly, you only have a mild concussion from the blow to your head and no fractures to your skull. I'll be discharging you from the hospital as soon as you eat some breakfast."

I was excited to hear that news. Grateful as I was to get the care I needed, I preferred not to be in a hospital at all.

"We can head over to the house in town and set you up on a couch until we're ready to return to Seattle," she said. "Helen is planning on having us back home before bedtime so that you can sleep in your own bed tonight. Annie and I will be having a little sleepover with you to keep you under observation for at least one more night. Or, if you prefer, you can use one of the rooms at the office."

"I'd rather sleep at home," I squeaked out.

Jordan smiled. "That's what Helen said you would say."

I ate my breakfast as fast as I could without choking on it. Luckily Jane had broken my nondominant arm, so I didn't have to try to eat oatmeal with my left hand. That would have ended up in a mess and possibly made them think my head injury was worse than they thought. At the best of times I was uncoordinated, and this was not the best of times.

Jordan spoke some more with the doctors outside my room. Things seemed to get a little heated as voices rose about something medical I couldn't make sense of. Jordan's voice got firm and I heard her mention Helen's name. Everyone got quiet again real fast after that—clearly Jordan had won whatever argument they had been having.

. . .

DRESSED in joggers and a T-shirt and bundled under cozy blankets, I sat on the couch with my legs up and facing the entrance hall so I could keep an eye on people coming and going. Everyone had scattered after I got settled in with a cup of tea and a plate of fruit. I sat patiently sipping my tea, trying not to fall asleep. Clearly there was still something happening in the house that had everyone a bit tense. No one had bothered to tell me what it was yet.

After about ten minutes, Helen came into the room and settled on the couch facing mine. She had changed out of her tactical gear and was back in one of her normal clean, modern outfits. However, her face was still just as grim. We talked quickly about my injuries and how I was feeling. I assured her that the team at the hospital, and especially Jordan, had taken great care of me. Also, that I was feeling okay and not in too much pain.

"That's good to hear," she said and then paused for a breath. "I'll update you on what we know so far. We were able to get some more information from both Jane and Brad."

I sat forward, eager to hear the update.

"As you already got from Jane, she and Brad were friends in high school. Along with a boy named Paul," Helen started out. "Paul was recruited for the pack right out of high school. He was killed during a mission."

"That's so sad," I blurted out. The pain meds were not helping me control my words.

"It is. I talked with Michael and it really does seem like it was an accident," Helen said. "But, as you learned from Jane, she blamed the pack and later specifically Michael."

"How did Jane even know about the pack?" I asked. "I thought all of that was kept really secret."

"It is," Helen confirmed. "But Jane had access to a lot of resources. She hired several private investigators. Human ones, not like us. One of them uncovered information about Paul and the pack." She was clearly frustrated. "We'll be helping the pack review how they were found out and see if there is anything we need to do to prevent it from happening again."

"Is that when she found out about vampires?" I asked.

"No, surprisingly that is a bit of a coincidence," Helen said. "The family recruits people like Jane. Wealthy, orphaned, few family connections. They reached out to her. But Jane jumped at the chance, thinking it would help her get the revenge she wanted. I will be talking to them about their vetting process," she added. "This vendetta should have been uncovered by the family."

All the pieces were clicking into place. But something was still bothering me.

"How did Jane get away from the estate and all the way to Boston?" I asked.

"Turns out we aren't the only ones with a private plane," Helen said with a small smile. "Jane still had access to most of her money. The family was not keeping close enough tabs on that.

"Jane wouldn't give details, but from what we can piece together, she had this plan in place before her adoption. She had hired someone to help her escape the estate, including a plane to get her to Boston," Helen explained.

"That's another loose end that we'll need to track down and speak to the family about."

"I'm glad you found us and that the trail I left helped," I said, but I still felt bad about a loose end from me. "I was wrong about the running water though. You wouldn't have known to look at this cabin."

"But you were right about so many other things," Helen said. "And you took action to help us find you."

"But I didn't run or fight," I said, tears starting to fall. "I should have been braver."

"You were brave, and better than that, you were smart," she said firmly. "Fighting or running probably wouldn't have gone well, and you could have been even more hurt. You knew we'd be looking for you and you did everything you could to help us with that."

"I did get them to restart the fire so there would be smoke coming from the chimney like I saw," I said through sniffles and wiped away the tears.

"See, smart," Helen said with a smile.

"So, what happens now?" I asked.

"I contacted the family as soon as we secured Jane last night. They are sending a delegation here. They should be arriving around lunchtime. We'll discuss with them about next steps for her.

"As for Brad," she continued, "Michael is weighing the choices. Obviously, he won't be selected for induction to the pack. But it sounds like Michael wants to talk to the family delegation before deciding anything more. If he and the family can agree on the outcomes for both Jane and Brad, then we agreed that they won't need to get the Council involved."

We wrapped up our conversation right before the rest of the team filed in and settled into the seats around the coffee table. Cam picked up my legs gingerly, settled on the couch, and then set them back on her lap. It was comforting to have the whole team in the room. Everyone smiled toward me and looked relieved at my condition. They all joked that they'd seen worse. A couple jokes were also made about my first mission scar, referring to the cut on my temple. Jordan playfully looked hurt and assured everyone that her stitches would never leave a scar.

Steve let Helen know that Jane and Brad were both secured away from each other and that the family delegation was on track to be here by lunch. Hank updated the team that the pilots were standing by and we could be headed home as soon as Helen gave the green light.

I let the updates drift in and out of my head. At this point, I would be little help and everything seemed to be handled. Surprisingly, I didn't feel guilt this time for not being helpful. It felt nice to be one of the things that was handled instead of doing the handling.

HELEN HAD GONE to talk with Michael again, but the rest of the group had stuck around. Everyone seemed to want to be near each other. A cold breeze and a flash of a vision that didn't make sense startled me out of the easy conversation that we were all having. Everyone looked toward me with concern and then turned as the front door flew open.

Standing in the doorway were three individuals who were clearly vampires. They had the same air about them as Winthrop had when he'd come to the office. The light in the front hall pulled toward them, darkening the corners of the room and creating a glow around the trio.

Helen appeared in the foyer and quickly ushered them into the dining room. Steve stood up and hustled to join them. The rest of us stayed where we were, frozen in place by the sudden change in atmosphere. We all looked at one another with questioning glances. Jordan was the one to finally make a face of determination and signal that we should stay and listen. So the four of us all leaned toward the dining room and strained to hear the conversation happening, like we were kids sent out of the room so that the grownups could talk.

Behind the closed doors, chairs scraped on the floor and it sounded like everyone was taking seats around the table. Voices spoke low and in an even cadence—they were probably making polite introductions at this point. Everything felt calm and orderly. Helen's voice took over the conversation. Based on some words I was able to pick up, she was recounting the events of yesterday. Everyone let her get through the telling without interruption. Surprising, based on what happened next.

She stopped talking and there was silence in the room. The group of us in the living room all looked around at each other with raised eyebrows, wondering what would happen next. Jordan mouthed *just wait* to all of us, as if she knew what would happen. We continued to comedically lean farther toward the room we weren't allowed in. We didn't have to wait long for things to go south.

"This is unacceptable," a loud and very angry voice echoed from the room. I didn't recognize it, so I was pretty sure it was one of the vampires.

Michael's gruff voice responded, "With what we currently know, the unacceptable behavior lies mostly with your kin."

Clearly this was not what the vampire delegation wanted to be told. Voices yelled and overlapped one another, and I was surprised that I didn't hear punches hitting flesh or things being thrown around the room. The living room group sank back a bit and continued to glance at each other with questions on our faces at overhearing the grownups fight. But we all stayed silent so we could try to hear what was going on.

"That is enough," Helen's commanding voice cut through the yelling, silencing the room. "This is all unprecedented," she continued, her voice slightly lowered but still commanding. "No one here did everything perfectly. But both parties were following the standard protocols that have been followed for centuries. Clearly those standards will need to be examined and updated.

"I recommend that we stop placing blame and instead focus on how both groups would like to move forward." Helen's tone was calmer now but still firm.

The tension that had been emitting from the room was noticeably lessened. I glanced over at Cam, and she smiled back at me and nodded. Everyone in the living room was clearly proud of our badass boss.

At this point, the volume of the conversation returned to a level that we weren't able to hear. I was okay that the yelling had stopped but disappointed that I couldn't follow along with the conversation. Even though we couldn't hear anything, the living room remained silent for the next half hour as the dining room conversation wrapped up.

WE ALL STAYED where we were and watched from the living room as Jane was brought down the stairs by a pair of pack members. The three vampires quickly took her, one flanking her on each side and holding an arm, the other close behind. Jane kept her head down, looking at the floor. The group of four hustled out the front door and into the waiting SUV. Then they drove off.

Michael stomped up the stairs, followed by a few pack members. From the sounds of chairs scraping, they were gathering for another pack meeting. Helen and Steve were the last to emerge from the dining room. They joined us back in the living room, and all eyes turned to Helen, eager to hear what had gone down.

"Well, I'm sure you all heard some of that," she said with a bit of a chuckle. "And I'm also sure that you all would like to know the outcome of the meeting."

Everyone nodded and remained silent so that she would continue.

"The family is going to take Jane back to the estate. I have agreed not to press for a tribunal."

Jordan, Cam, and Hank all seemed to bristle at that statement. Steve gave them a *follow orders* type of face, and then they all looked slightly chastised. I had no idea what she was talking about; I just tried not to look too confused.

"In response, the family will not ask for a tribunal of the pack for Brad's involvement in concealing Jane. Michael and the family both agreed to handle Brad and Jane within the pack and family respectively. And at their own discretion," Helen concluded.

"So they're just going to get away with it?" Hank blurted out angrily. This was the most emotion that I had ever seen from Hank. He looked from me to Helen, clearly upset with what had gone down. I was surprisingly touched by his reaction.

"No," Helen said calmly. "Both Jane and Brad will be punished as their leaders see fit. And we've avoided unnecessary involvement of the Council.

"I have been reassured that Jane will be under tighter security and that Brad will not be allowed any involvement with the otherworldly community. Additionally, the pack will take responsibility for Brad's whereabouts and behavior for the duration of his life, although he won't be a member of the pack," she stated firmly, and that was clearly the end of this conversation topic. "Linda, I do need to talk with you privately for a moment. Could the rest of you prepare to head home? We'll gather in the foyer in twenty minutes to head out."

Everyone dispersed quickly to gather their things and tie up any final loose ends.

. . .

"LINDA, there is the matter of human law enforcement," Helen started off. "It turns out a member of the hospital team reported your assault. They were not correctly informed about the situation and were just following protocol.

"However, because of this, the local police have asked to speak with you," Helen continued. "I will not ask you to lie, but I do want to caution you. We do not typically involve human law enforcement in our clients' business or affairs, even when they are troubling. For obvious reasons. We can, however, report Brad's assault, as he is technically still within their jurisdiction."

That made sense—this was human-on-human crime. He had assaulted me and kidnapped me. It seemed like the right thing to do was to report him and let him spend some time behind bars.

"Or we can leave without talking to them and have Michael smooth things over," Helen suggested and then explained, "My concern is that talking to them about what we could share would not fully explain your injuries and will draw unwanted attention to the local pack."

I nodded at what she said, realizing just how far outside of normal law I was now working. A small panic welled up in my stomach as my mind raced around the ramifications. Helen reached out and touched my hand. I looked up at her and she smiled calmly.

"I know this is a lot to take in," she said gently. "And you've been through a lot in a very short amount of time. I will support you however you want this handled."

I believed her completely. I also knew that this new

otherworld was one that I wanted to be a part of, despite a couple of vengeful people. Even the human world had those types of people. And the pack had been so kind to me throughout this whole experience, I didn't want to cause them trouble. I pictured Sarah's face as she had told her story and laid claim to the new family she had joined all those years ago. Family mattered, and I didn't want to do anything that would jeopardize that for her or for the other kind werewolves who had worked with us this weekend.

"Let's go home," I finally said as my answer. Helen sighed with a bit of relief and patted my hand.

20

The back couch on the plane had been prepared for me. At least they had let me walk myself with only light assistance across the local airfield's tarmac and then onto the plane before fussing over me. Jordan had surrounded me with blankets and propped a pillow under my arm. They thankfully positioned me facing toward the front of the cabin so that I could see everyone and still be involved.

I was given strict instructions to not get up without Jordan's help. Joking that it was my head and arm they had broken and not my legs did not go over well with her. She handed me a collection of pills that included my motion-sickness pill, told me to be a good patient, and then we were up in the air.

Helen came over to talk with me after we leveled off, taking a seat next to Jordan on the opposite couch. Jordan got up to leave us to talk, but Helen gestured to her that she should stay and be part of the conversation.

"Jordan let me know that you'd like to go straight home." Helen half asked and half stated.

I nodded.

"Okay, I'll sign off on that as long as you let Annie and Jordan stay the night so that they can keep an eye on you. If you are still doing well after the weekend, then we can let you convalesce at home for a couple of weeks with only occasional check-ins."

"Two weeks?" I yelled in disagreement, drawing all eyes to me from throughout the plane. In my defense, I was on painkillers that were blunting my impulse control.

"That is standard practice for injuries," Jordan said, trying to calm me down.

"I can't sit around for two weeks," I pleaded as memories of the six months of unemployment and being alone in the house came flooding back. There wasn't enough to keep me busy and I didn't want to miss anything that may happen in the office while I was out. Plus Ilka had seemed less moody now that I wasn't in the house all the time. I didn't want to rock that boat. "Let me come into work," I practically begged, the first time in my life I had ever begged to work. "I'll come in late and go home early if I'm not feeling good. Please don't make me stay home for two weeks."

Helen and Jordan shared amused smiles but didn't seem surprised by my reaction. I had my suspicions that the standard practice of two weeks off for injuries wasn't followed by anyone on this team.

"I'll make you a deal," Helen said somewhat sternly. "You can come into work. You'll use one of the suites for rest if you start feeling pain or need to nap during the day. We'll have a driver take you to and from work. And Jordan will do checkups with you to assess your healing progress."

"That all sounds great to me," I replied quickly.

But Helen wasn't done with her deal. "In addition to that," she continued even more sternly, "you have to agree to talk with Jax, the team psychologist, twice a week until they clear you."

I had no idea we had a team psychologist. That was not covered in introductions. Neither of them expanded on that, even though I was sure confusion was all over my face. They both just looked at me and waited for my response. I was planning on starting up therapy again when I had health insurance, so it wasn't a big deal to me.

"Deal," I said quickly before they could backtrack or add to the terms.

That now settled, Jordan told me to get some sleep and let her know when I got hungry. I snuggled down into the pillows and blankets and let the medication I was on finally take over fully as I drifted off to sleep for the remainder of the flight home.

We ended up extending the sleepover—or medical observation, if you want to be technical about it—through the whole weekend. Annie made a run to the grocery store to fill my mostly empty fridge and pantry. She also turned out to be a surprisingly good cook and spoiled us all with some amazing brownies. She was not as good as Mrs.

Clark on the healthier stuff, but that didn't need to be said out loud.

Cam showed up Sunday morning when she found out that Jordan and Annie were sticking around. I was happy for the company and realized how much I had missed having friends around. They all made themselves at home, and surprisingly it didn't feel weird having them rummage through cabinets and closets to set up beds for everyone. I directed from the couch that they barely let me leave to help.

The four of us watched the almost six-hour-long *Pride and Prejudice* movie and whatever childhood animated movies we could find streaming. Jordan convinced us to take short walks around the neighborhood in between the movies. She said it was mandatory for her to sign off on my coming back to the office. I didn't have the heart to argue. We talked more about our personal lives and how we grew up. That weekend together seemed to solidify our friendship.

Ilka took immediately to Annie and would not leave her side. She hadn't purred that much in the last two years she lived with me. I tried really hard not to be offended and came to terms with their friendship. Annie had been the one to feed her for two nights while I was gone.

At first we avoided talking about work. I didn't know if they were the type to gossip about work and the other team members. Everyone seemed to avoid the topic. Side comments made me think they were worried about me and the ordeal that our work had just put me through. It didn't bother me, but I was feeling pretty unfazed by all of it, or maybe it just hadn't sunk in yet.

We finally started to talk about work and the team members that weren't with us when I brought up some behaviors of people that I had noticed. The conversation wasn't bad or mean; we stuck to funny quirks.

"So does Steve always hover like he's a dad watching over the kids?" I asked playfully.

All three of the women laughed.

"What do you mean?" Annie said as she stood up, leaned slightly back, and crossed her arms, her mouth in a straight line. "Like this?"

I couldn't help laughing. "Yes. Exactly."

"Yeah, he does that all the time," Cam confirmed.

"And does Mrs. Clark always seem to leave the room when you enter, or is that just me?" I asked, being a bit more vulnerable.

"It's not just you," Annie said. Jordan and Cam nodded in agreement.

"She's just not that talkative," Jordan said. "I wouldn't read anything into it."

"Oh, I have one," Annie offered. "Have you noticed the way Helen says 'okay' with a single clap?"

"I have," I said with a laugh. "I've taken it as a signal to get ready to take a lot of notes."

"You catch on fast," Jordan said with a smile.

It was fun to have the other women confirm that these weren't one-offs but things I could look forward to on a regular basis. This had broken the floodgates for us to talk about work, and we continued to do so all weekend. However, it was late on Sunday before I finally felt brave enough to ask specifically about Hank. It had been bugging me all week and now seemed like a safe time to bring it up over a second batch of Annie's brownies.

"So, what's Hank's deal?" I asked, trying to sound nonchalant.

"What do you mean?" Annie asked innocently and then took a big bite of brownie.

I sighed. *In for a penny, in for a pound, I guess.* If things went off the rails and I sounded delusional, maybe I could blame it on the pain meds.

"I get a weird vibe from him and I feel like I've seen him somewhere before." I looked around the group after I said it and caught Cam and Jordan exchanging a knowing glance. No one spoke up, but I took a page from Helen and just waited for someone to say something.

Annie broke first. "He's a bit shier than the rest of us."

Not super helpful, so I pushed more. "One of the first mornings I was in the office, I saw him go into your office," I said, gesturing to Jordan. "You weren't in the office yet and he snuck out after you got in. It seemed weird, like he was snooping or spying on something."

Jordan started laughing, then Cam and Annie both joined in. I did not like this. It wasn't strange to think that was a weird thing for him to do. Jordan quickly picked up on my discomfort with the laughter.

"Sorry, we aren't laughing at you. I promise," she said. "It's the idea of Hank snooping around. That's not like him at all—you'll understand after spending more time with him. He takes a while to warm up."

"That still doesn't explain why he was in your office," I pressed.

"Hank thinks that I kill plants and he takes it very personally," Jordan said. Cam and Annie both nodded at Jordan's statement. "He goes into my office once or twice a week before I get in to check on the plants and make sure I'm caring for them properly," she explained. "I regularly get into the office and find sticky notes with instructions for watering or fertilizer left on my desk in his handwriting. I'm still not sure why he doesn't just talk to me about it," Jordan said exasperatedly. "But it's become a bit of a game between the two of us."

Cam and Annie were still giggling about this.

"I know how to take care of my plants," Jordan said sternly, defending herself. The giggling got worse. "It was only one time and I really think the plant came to me sick."

At that we all cracked up. Jordan sighed with exasperation and then joined the laughter.

EVERYONE HEADED HOME early Monday morning to get ready for work. Annie reminded me that the car would be there to pick me up for work at quarter to nine. That was the earliest that Helen would let me start work for the first week. It would get me to the office just in time for the morning meeting. I didn't mind.

I was able to take my time getting ready and then clean

up the house a bit more. There wasn't much cleaning to do. The women had left everything neatly folded and had washed dishes. I had to stop them from doing all the laundry. Annie had offered to wash all the bedding along with any dirty laundry I had needing to be cleaned.

House now clean and things put away, I wrapped my arm in plastic like Jordan had taught me and took a hot shower, reflecting on the last week as the water washed over me. It had felt like more than a week, but I'd never felt so close to coworkers so fast. That may have been due to trauma bonding. I was sure the psychologist I would start seeing this week would have some thoughts on that.

I had met several werewolves. They matched the description I had read in the briefing documents, though I'm not sure how much of that was confirmation bias. I did agree with Cam now—they would be one of the first groups I asked for help if I was ever in trouble. Although I could happily go the rest of my life without seeing them in their wolf form.

A lot of the questions that had been bothering me had been answered. I was feeling better about Hank, although I still couldn't place why he seemed familiar to me. The Jane and Brad mystery was solved and it did seem like my daydreams—sorry, *visions*—had been a major factor in that. The mystery of why I had visions was not solved, and I couldn't wait to get into the office so that I could access the files to see if visions were covered in any of the documents.

The shower ran cold before I wanted it to. Memories of

the hotel shower with the endless stream of hot water had me doing math in my head to see if I could look into getting a tankless water heater installed so I could have endless hot water at home. The new paychecks I would be getting soon would help with that.

21

———————

Aside from the cast on my arm, walking into the office Monday morning felt nothing like last week and the first-day-of-work nervousness. Although, last week now felt like a year ago. This was the most eventful first week of work I'd had in any job, including the first day at the coffee shop that fell on the first day of my sophomore year of college, but that's a story for another day.

Thinking about coffee, I smiled as I could smell good coffee brewing and some kind of pastry baking in the kitchen. There was a comforting low chatter of voices coming from upstairs that made me smile even more. The lower floor was empty as it usually was this time of day, so I swung through the kitchen to grab a well-deserved breakfast pastry and then headed upstairs.

Heads turned toward me as I entered the room. Surprisingly, it didn't make me feel self-conscious. Every one of these people had seen me in a much more vulnerable state at some point last week. Smiles and greetings were shared, and I walked into my office to set down my bag before the morning meeting started. Helen's office doors were closed. I could hear her voice but couldn't make out what she was saying. She must have been on the phone.

Everyone had gathered around the conference table with breakfast and laptops. The familiar and pleasant smells of coffee and pastries filled the space. We were all chatting in small groups as we waited for the meeting to start. I checked my laptop and was surprised to see that it was five minutes after nine. In my short time here, we'd never started a meeting late. Helen walked up to the table before I could point out the time to anyone.

"My apologies for being late," Helen said as she set her laptop on the table and sat down. Annie had already placed a cup of coffee and a scone at her seat for her. She saw it and smiled at Annie. "I was just on the phone getting an update from Michael," Helen said and we all looked toward her with interest. "They've decided to transfer Brad to a pack in Alaska. He'll be working for them for the time being."

"That's a good idea to get him away from his contacts in Boston," Steve added approvingly.

"Yes. That was the idea," Helen confirmed. "Also, the Alaska pack's territory is bordered on all sides by the Northwest family's territory. They will be keeping an eye on him as well."

"Any update on Jane?" Jordan asked.

"She is recovering. The family is still discussing rehabilitation paths for her. For now, she is confined to the estate and will be secured at all times."

"The same estate she managed to escape from," Hank said with some attitude.

"Yes," Helen said calmly. I was sure she picked up on the tone but must have decided to ignore it. "They've also located all of her independent accounts and will be establishing a trust to oversee all of her personal finances. I'll be following up with the family on their plan to ensure there is not another incident. Any other questions about that case?"

Everyone shook their heads.

"Alright. Please remember to finish writing up your debrief documents if you haven't already." She looked around the table.

I made a note for myself that I'd need to talk with someone about what was expected in a debrief document.

"For now, we don't have an active case," Helen said, moving the meeting along. "If you want some PTO, now would be a good time. Come talk to me about that if you'd like."

Smiles and head nods around the table indicated that there would likely be at least a couple people taking some days off. I didn't want to take any time off just yet.

"Let's move on to roundtable updates on new and long-term projects."

One by one, everyone gave updates on the projects

they had been working on before the case came in or new ones they would be starting. Some of them sounded interesting, like Jordan's project to map the gene sequence of an especially gifted lineage of witches. Others sounded boring, like Steve's project to review the vetting procedures of the families for adoption candidates. I only felt a little bad that he had to take on that project, but if it prevented another case like Jane's, we'd all benefit.

Annie brought up that she and I would be starting the redesign project for two of the suites on the third floor. She told the group that if anyone had requests, they should let us know by the end of the week. I was excited to work on this project with her. It would be a nice change of pace. Jordan reminded the both of us that I was on desk duty for at least another week, so no moving furniture.

We wrapped up the updates and everyone dispersed to their offices. Back at my desk, I started with a to-do list of items to get done for the day. The biggest one: talk to Helen about job performance. Through all the commotion of last week, the lingering thirty-day probation and peer evaluations kept creeping into my thoughts. But that conversation would probably wait until I'd worked up the bravery to talk with her this afternoon.

Typing with one hand slowed me down, but I made my way through some Monday morning tasks. Email, check. Calendar, check. Although both still seemed emptier than I would expect. To-do list for me, partial check. We hadn't really had time to go over normal duties and tasks last week. I made an item on my to-do list to do that. At a bit of a loss for what to do, I decided to clean up the recruit files for the pack. Obviously I'd skip over Brad. No reason to finish that; he wasn't getting in. But I figured the rest may still be needed for them to make a decision.

The files came together quickly and I sent the finished version to Helen's email for review. After meeting the pack and spending some time with a few members, I had new insights into the type of people they were and how they worked together as a team. The extra insight into how the pack functioned was helpful for me and I flagged a few concerning items that seemed contrary to that nature in some of the documents. I had my bets on who they would end up selecting and who they would probably not, but I kept those to myself.

It was almost lunchtime and I was already getting distracted thinking about what Mrs. Clark may have prepared for us. I was debating if it was too early to go down—I didn't want to distract her or make her uncomfortable by my presence. Luckily, Cam came to the open doors of my office and asked if I was ready to go to lunch. Closing my laptop in response, I joined her immediately.

As it turned out, almost everyone was ready for lunch. This was the first time I saw everyone gathered for lunch in the kitchen. Helen was the only one missing from the group. She hadn't left her office all morning, and no one had gone in to disturb her.

We filled our plates with fish tacos, rice, and beans and gathered around the table. Steve kept looking at my face and making a pinched face of his own in response. I knew from looking in the mirror this morning that the bruising had started to fade to a more greenish-yellow color. The bandage that Jordan had given me was smaller, just covering the stitches, and the swelling had gone down and I could open my eyes all the way without pain. I thought it looked better, but his face didn't seem to agree.

"Steve, stop staring," Jordan finally said what I had been thinking but didn't feel okay about saying.

"I wasn't staring," he said sheepishly.

"Yes, you were," she retorted. "You should know from past experiences that people don't like attention brought to injuries. And we all know you, for sure, don't like people to comment on your injuries."

Steve still looked sheepish, but the tension was broken quickly by laughter filling the table. Steve gave up and joined in with the laughter. There was clearly a story here that I didn't know. Annie took pity on my looks of confusion and filled me in about an away mission they had a few years ago where Steve had taken a wooden stake to the butt. He had had to waddle around the office for several weeks in what looked like a very large and very full adult diaper.

To keep the peace in the office and stop the onslaught of jokes about the situation, a truce had been brokered that injuries and the resulting healing process would be politely ignored by everyone on the team. From the details shared about the truce, it sounded like Helen was not in the know about this and that she probably shouldn't be told.

Although I was not here when that peace treaty was agreed upon, Jordan insisted that I be amended into the agreement. Steve only agreed as long as I also agreed to never bring up the butt injury story and that I, too, kept to the terms if there were any future injuries to be ignored. Of course, I agreed.

Steve stopped staring and the lunch continued in peace. The conversation around the table turned to how everyone's weekends went. Both Steve and Hank were disappointed that they hadn't gotten any of Annie's brownies. She promised to bring some into the office later that week.

AFTER LUNCH I took a walk with Jordan around the block; apparently that was still part of the agreement for my being in the office while I healed. Back from that, I settled behind my desk to dig into the general files to see if I could find anything on visions. I didn't get far before Helen walked in and asked me if I could join her in her office. I grabbed a notepad to take notes, which was proving easier than typing right now with one arm still in a cast.

"How are you feeling?" Helen started off after I got settled into the chair.

"Okay. I was able to sleep really well last night, and I'm off the heavy pain meds so I'm thinking more clearly," I reassured her.

"That's good," she said. "Jordan let me know that she's cleared you for light office work as long as you take breaks if you become fatigued."

"I will," I reassured her again. Annie had mentioned over the weekend that she'd make sure a room would be ready for me on the third floor. It would be set aside for me for at least two weeks and longer if needed. I hadn't checked it out yet but was excited to see what the rooms upstairs were like. Even if I didn't need a nap, I was planning on going up there later this afternoon.

"I'm glad to hear it," Helen said, and then her tone shifted more to her work mode. "Steve will find you later this afternoon to do a full debrief. It's nothing to stress about, just share what happened in your own words. He'll type it up and it will go into the case file. Everyone on the team will be doing something similar."

I nodded; that didn't sound so bad, especially with Steve doing the typing. It would be interesting to read everyone's statements to fill in some of the gaps of what happened.

"Tomorrow will be your first appointment with Jax, the team psychologist. They aren't technically part of the team, but they keep an office here to make it easier to schedule sessions. They've been out on vacation for the last month."

That filled in some of the questions I had about the mysterious team psychologist and why I hadn't seen them around the office. They must have had an office behind one of the closed doors on the second floor that I hadn't explored yet.

"I want to reassure you that anything shared with them will be confidential," Helen continued. "The only information I'll receive is if they recommend more sessions or when they clear you."

That was reassuring. I had assumed it would be private, but it was good to have her say it out loud.

"You also have the option to continue to talk to them even after you've been cleared," she added.

I nodded. I'd see if this therapist was a good fit and maybe continue with them if it wasn't weird. It had been about a year since I had stopped working with the psychologist I had seen after my mom's death, and I didn't necessarily want to start seeing them again.

There was a pause in the conversation and I was about to ask about when we could go over my normal tasks and responsibilities. Instead, Helen cleared her throat loudly and said something that would change my world forever, again. "Linda, I need to tell you something." For the first time that I could think of, she sounded and looked a bit nervous.

I smiled to try to reassure her. Whatever it was, it couldn't be that bad and couldn't be more shocking than revealing that otherworldly supernaturals existed.

"I knew your mother, Malinda, and I don't think her death was from a heart attack."

I was wrong. That was more shocking. That floored me. I hadn't talked with Helen about my mom or her death. I had barely talked with Annie, Cam, and Jordan during our extended sleepover about my mom. I had only told them that she had died and that Ilka had been hers. I hadn't shared anything about how she died.

The room went silent. I could only hear the thump of my heart in my ears. My vision started to tunnel and I worried that I would black out. Helen gave me a moment to recover but not long enough for me to fully grasp what she was saying and why she was telling me this.

"I knew your mother because she was one of our clients," Helen shared.

I sat there, dumbfounded, slouching into my seat in front of Helen's desk. The pieces started to click together fast and I knew what this must mean. But it couldn't be true. "But my mom was a human. I'd know if she was a vampire or werewolf or something," I said, mostly to convince myself.

My mom was my mom. She was kind and caring. She was open minded and active in the community. She was a bit quirky compared to the moms of my friends. I had always attributed that to her being older when she had me and that she raised me on her own. Knowing that Helen only worked with magical and supernatural clients, I should have been able to guess her response.

"Your mother was an oracle," Helen said gently but firmly. "There was a lot that you didn't know. She wanted it that way, at least until we knew more about you." She spoke clearly and calmly, probably knowing that this information was hard to take in. "She always planned on telling you, but she was gone before she could."

My face was probably showing all the emotions and confusion that I was experiencing. Helen kept explaining.

"She was unsure if you would inherit her gifts. Most oracles don't manifest any gifts until their mid twenties or later. And not all oracles pass down their gifts to their children. Often their offspring live their lives out as normal human beings. She didn't want to burden you or make you feel any shame if you didn't inherit her gifts. Likely you had only just started showing signs of visions before she died."

The tunnel vision was clearing and the words she was saying were settling in, but my brain and heart weren't connecting to make sense of what I was hearing. A mix of emotions competed for space: anger and aching that my mom hadn't told me this, but also a growing feeling of relief that maybe this could explain what had been happening with me. Unable to speak just yet, I nodded for Helen to continue.

"We helped your mom relocate to Seattle and get settled when she was pregnant with you. After we got her settled, we handed off her security to the Council, as is protocol." Helen took a breath and then set her face firmly as if bracing herself to keep going. "Oracles are rare. And there are some fringe groups within the supernatural community that feel like their gifts are too powerful and need to be controlled. Or eliminated."

She let that last part hang in the air for a moment and watched my face as it sank in.

"The Council put a ruling out over a century ago protecting oracles and imposing severe penalties for anyone going against those rules. This helped to quell a lot of the assaults against them, but it didn't stop them completely."

"The Oracle Accords," I whispered. That small paragraph in the Council's document had been percolating in the back of my head, and it now clicked into place.

"Yes," Helen said with a bit of disbelief. She paused for

a minute but didn't ask me how I knew that. "I've been investigating your mother's death," Helen said quietly.

"But she had a heart attack," I interjected, my brain still rejecting that part of her revelation.

"Yes," Helen agreed. "That's what the medical examiner determined. But we did our own investigation. She was poisoned."

22

I couldn't believe what I was hearing. For two years I had grieved my mom, my best friend, the only parent I had. Something had always felt off about her death. But I thought that was because she was so young, just over sixty. Now, hearing Helen say that it wasn't just crappy fate but that someone killed her burst the dam I had been carefully building around that idea. Surprisingly, I didn't cry. All I felt was rage.

"I think, based on your reaction, that you believe me," Helen pressed gently.

I looked up and saw that her eyes were also starting to fill with tears. She clearly had cared about my mom, and I decided to lean into trusting her.

"Yes. I do," I agreed, still somewhat hesitantly.

Helen sighed with relief and then paused to give me space and time to work through my memories and emotions. Tears started to fall silently from my eyes. I let them fall. The rage and sorrow continued to well up in me, and I didn't know where to start. My mom used to say to just start at the beginning and see where it takes you. So I began from that horrible beginning.

"Why did you even investigate? Who would poison her? How? Why?" I asked, fading into a whisper, trying not to devolve into sobs. I was starting to spiral.

Helen clasped her hands together. I concentrated on her knuckles turning white to stop my head spinning.

"Malinda was young, especially for an oracle," Helen said, only a step above my whisper in volume. "We'd been hearing about more unrest within the community. People were unhappy with how the intergroup conflicts were being handled. I know Malinda was involved with helping to quell the conflicts, but I don't know to what extent.

"When she died, it just felt off," she continued. "It was easy enough to get samples to run our own labs. Jordan tested for everything we could think of. Much more than what the normal medical examiner would have done.

"She discovered a combination of herbs that cause the symptoms and effects of a heart attack." Helen had started to speak clearly and factually, but the emotion could still be felt behind her words. She was doing a better job not letting the tears fall than I was. "Those herbs are not common. We worked with the local coven to try to track down who would have access to them," she said. "But we weren't able to find a lead. And we have no idea how Malinda would have ingested the herbs."

"Okay," I finally said, at a complete loss of how to react.

"And that's where we've hit a dead end," she said frustratedly. "We've been keeping the case open, but we haven't had any new leads in over a year." Helen hesitated for a minute. "We've also been keeping watch over you."

Flashes of memories clicked into place. Images of a forgettable man who had been around enough to not be so forgettable. I remembered the feeling of knowing Hank when I'd seen him in the office and my suspicion of him from day one. It made sense.

"You had Hank watching me," I stated more than questioned. I was struggling between feeling violated and protected. I felt strongly that Helen cared about me and that she had cared about my mom. But was this too far?

"Yes." She looked a bit chastised. "Hank has been periodically watching you and the people you interact with. He was also looking out for anyone else who may be watching you. If someone came after your mom, then there was a good chance they would come after you as well," Helen said with a hint of anger. "Especially if you started to demonstrate the powers of an oracle.

"We haven't seen any suspicious behavior from anyone, but it was getting harder to be discreet. When we had the option of offering you this job, it made sense to bring you into the team. We needed a new EA and we wanted to protect you." The soft tone of her voice was helping me overcome the initial aversion I felt about being watched.

All I could do was nod. It made logical sense but still felt violating. And I know it sounds small compared to everything else, but it hurt to think that this was why they hired me and not because I was best for the job. If I hadn't spent a week in such an intense situation with this group and felt like I had made real friends, I would be running out the door in frustration and anger. After a few moments, Helen took the plunge to change the subject. "I know this is important, and we'll come back to it. I promise," she said sincerely, catching my eyes to see my reaction. "But we need to talk about something more pressing."

I furrowed my brow, not sure what could be more pressing than the murder of my mother. The thoughts clearly danced over my face and Helen did what she did best, waiting for me to process it. And then something inside me just knew. It was obvious and I felt dumb that it took me as long as it did to realize it.

"You think I'm an oracle," I said softly. "Like my mom."

"Yes," she said, nodding with a small smile.

It made sense. Once I started to believe that my flashes of images and daydreams were actually visions, they felt more real. And looking back at other recent daydreams, I could easily connect them to things that had then played out in reality. I had always thought I was just good at finding patterns and had good intuition, but now I could see that maybe it was more than that.

"What does this mean?" I asked more to myself than to Helen.

"We don't know for sure yet that you are, and we don't need to get ahead of ourselves," Helen reassured me.

"Wait," I interjected. "Is that why you jumped at my idea that a pack recruit was involved with Jane's disappearance and rushed us all to Boston? You thought it was a vision?"

"Yes," she responded firmly but with empathy.

Well, that at least made more sense now. And then

another, more devastating thought hit me. I blurted it out before I could rethink the idea: "Did you hire me because you thought I may be an oracle like my mom?"

I was already feeling hurt that they may have hired me just to make it easier to babysit me. But now I was conflicted that I'd been hired so this potential ability could be used by the agency. This job had come out of nowhere, but between being desperate for work and the excitement of learning about this new otherworld, I hadn't stopped to question why I was here. That all came crashing down and any confidence I had in my skills vanished. Nobody wants to be used for something they have no control over.

"I'll admit having you work here and be aware of the situation will make it easier to keep an eye on you and protect you if needed." I deflated even more. "But," she quickly continued, "I would not have hired you into this position if I didn't sincerely believe that you could do the job well. And do the job well regardless of whether you have inherited your mother's gifts."

She sounded like she meant it, but I was still feeling wounded by the reveal that there were alternative reasons for my being here. Everyone, even Hank, seemed so good at their jobs and the team worked well together. I would not be the weak link on this team. So I did what I do best and compartmentalized that concern in a small box in the back of my head. I would prove that I could do this job and that I wasn't just here to be babysat. Or worse, to be the office fortune teller.

Another thought hit me like a brick: *Does everyone know about this already?* It was clear that most of the team knew something was going on. Now that I knew, I could see that they had dropped signs along the way. Was I the last to learn this secret about myself and my mom? I wasn't sure how to ask, so I just blurted it out.

"Does everyone know about this?"

"The rest of the team is aware of my suspicions about your gift," Helen admitted. "And the agency was involved with both your mother's relocation and the investigation of her death. Her voice turned somewhat stern. "Remember, we do not have secrets within the team. There may be things that are confidential, for good reasons. But if there is information that is needed to be a functional team, serve our clients, and keep us all safe, then we do not gatekeep that information.

"I know this is a lot to take in," she continued, the gentle tone back in her voice. "The plan was always to share this with you. But I didn't want to drop it in your lap all at once. You've clearly shown signs that you may be an oracle, and that is why I think it's important that you have all of this information now. But we don't know for sure if you are an oracle or if you just have minor psychic gifts."

This was a lot to take in. I had only come to terms with magic and supernatural people existing a week ago, and now I may be one of them. All the information was swimming around in my head, and then something that had bugged me all week pushed front and center.

"Does the Council know about me?" I asked before I could rethink the question.

Helen looked at me with a bit of surprise, raised one

eyebrow, and stayed silent, waiting for me to explain why I was asking.

"The Council keeps coming up. I've barely found any information about them in the briefing docs," I pressed. "But from the sounds of how people talk about them, they keep tabs on all magical and supernatural beings. If I'm one now, do they know that?"

"First," Helen said calmly but firmly, "we don't know for sure if you are supernatural yet. There are some humans who have supernatural ancestors far enough back that they aren't considered to fit within that classification. Or they have smaller gifts that aren't necessary to track. That may be the case for you.

"Second," Helen continued, lowering her volume so that I needed to lean in a bit, "if we do not need to put you on the Council's radar, we won't."

This did not sit well with me. The Council seemed to be in charge. But Helen seemed to want to keep them out of things wherever she could. She had both used the Council as a warning for Winthrop while also deciding to keep his problematic relationship off their radar. Dealing with the vampire family and the werewolf pack, she had pushed hard to resolve the issue between the two groups and not involve the Council. I trusted Helen, so should I not trust this mysterious Council?

I asked the next question that popped into my head: "If I am an oracle or even if I have a small version of that, what does that mean for working with all of you?"

I didn't want to commit to using whatever this may be. It still seemed like something I wasn't ready to have the whole team count on. Who knew how it even worked or if it would work when needed most. I had been wrong about the water by the cabin, and that could have led to much bigger problems.

"If you are an oracle or you have smaller abilities, it is your choice how and when you want to use your gift," Helen responded firmly, locking eyes with me to ensure that I heard her clearly. "No one on this team will ever make you use your gift if you don't want to. But there is not a lot known about oracles and how their visions work. And there has never been an oracle on this team, so I'm not sure how it will work. If you decide to use your gift to help clients, we'd need to work out together how that would go."

I had sunk back into my chair and chewed on my fingernails, a habit I thought I had long since kicked. This felt like too much. I didn't want to give up this new world, this team, or this job. But all the insecurities and imposter syndrome I'd ever had were clouding out all the positive things that Helen was saying. Again Helen sensed my discomfort and offered me an out.

"You don't have to stay," she said softly.

I was startled at her statement. Did she want me to leave? Luckily, she continued quickly.

"I want you to stay. But you don't have to. Now that you know more about what it will be like to work here, and more about your situation, you deserve a choice. If you want to leave, I can get you into a new role with a traditional law firm similar to what you had before. Same compensation as we are providing," Helen said almost sadly and then waited.

This was a lot to think about. In the one week I'd been here so far, I'd learned that there was magic and supernaturals and I think Steve had even mentioned demons at some point. I'd been kidnapped and held hostage by a near-raging vampire and Brad. I'd learned that I may be an oracle, whatever that really means. I learned that my mom was an oracle. And I learned that my mom may have been murdered.

I was looking forward to talking to the psychologist soon.

Helen let her offer hang in the air, giving me the time to sort through my thoughts. Despite everything that had changed in my life over the last week, one thing stood out. I felt like I had a purpose and I felt like I was making real friends. And that was worth hanging on to.

"I want to stay," I said firmly in a half whisper.

"Great," Helen said, smiling, and then turned and picked up some papers. "Let's talk through your job tasks and responsibilities."

She was my boss after all. We had work to do, and I had a probationary period to pass.

23

———

The long second Monday at my new job was over —the car would be picking me up to take me home in five minutes. I packed up to leave and then walked over to Helen's open doors to say goodnight.

She was sitting at her desk, the low dusk light filtering in through the windows. No lamps had turned on yet and the golden-hour glow haloed around her. She looked up from the paper she had been reading and beckoned me in from the doorway where I had lingered.

"Linda, I want to thank you again for your help so far and for hearing me out on all the information I shared with you today." Helen smiled and gestured for me to have a seat. "It's been an eventful start to your time here with us. I can't promise that it will get easier. But I can promise that you will have the full support from this team and from me."

The tears started to well up in my eyes again and I was surprised to see teary eyes looking back at me from Helen.

The words didn't need to be spoken but I was still grateful for them. The actions of everyone recently had solidified for me the bonds of this team I had joined and that I was one of them. I uttered a thank-you, trying to hold back tears, the emotions finally catching up with me.

"I also wanted to let you know that Mr. Winthrop has reached out."

She paused after this, seemingly to see if I had a reaction. I sat still and kept my face blank, trying not to think about that voice.

"He would like to employ our services to help him figure out how to approach the family and the Council for a dispensation of adoption and then permission for him and Angela to mate."

LATER THAT NIGHT, Ilka sauntered into my bedroom and sprawled over my lap as I lay reading in bed. This was a complete anomaly, but one I welcomed. Trapped as I was, my mind wandered over how my life had changed in the last two weeks.

It was the first time I'd had a moment to really think about everything that I now knew. Who killed my mom? Could I be an oracle like my mom was? What would that mean for my life? And why did I picture Helen locked in fear every time I thought about it?

ACKNOWLEDGMENTS

This book is a dream I decided to no longer procrastinate. However, it could not have come true without significant help from many people who gave me constant support, encouragement, and advice.

Thank you to friends turned beta readers, specifically Allie Lee, Desiree Jones, Erin Spannan, Hannah Seegmiller, Hailey Dinkins, Jett Jones, and Kristin Young.

Thank you to Oren Ashkenazi, Ariel Anderson, and Erin Spannan for being patient editors that helped a new writer learn so much.

Thank you to my family: Alyssa for using your artistic talents and skills, and Nick, because without your unwavering support this would not have been possible.

ABOUT THE AUTHOR

JANELLE SEEGMILLER spent thirteen years in corporate jobs until she decided to take a break and chase a dream. Now without the hustle, Sunday scaries, and endless meetings, she is pursuing a journey of writing fiction that showcases what she wishes work could be like.